STONE OF THE ANGELS

THE FIRST ARKLE WRIGHT NOVEL

RAYMOND S FLEX

1: HORTENINE-6

I GOT INTO ALPHA PORT around ninth hour, just in time for the late-night customs shift. Just my luck. No matter what they tell you about the late shifts, that these are the guys who just don't care, let me tell you right now that that is complete and utter bullshit. These guys, the guys who get into these customs jobs, they're put on these shifts to prove themselves—to give them a shot at promotion. And let me tell you that when you have a chance at promotion on Hortenine-6 you seize it with both hands. Only way of getting off the planet if you're born here. Luckily I wasn't.

I shrugged out of my seatbelt straps and slipped my navigational computer out of its slot—whenever these customs clowns get to poking around your ship things always tend to go missing. Funny thing is that they always seem to be *expensive* things too. So I was taking no chances. The reason Hortenine gets picked to make drops is because customs have no scanners, no budget for stuff like that. Their planet's on the edge of everything, the middle of nowhere.

I looked over the troops, three of them, all staring me down —looking dapper in their dark-blue uniforms, space-blue even, the official colours of Hortenine-6. What Hortenine doesn't have in job opportunities it makes up for in colour scheme, let me tell you that right now. These three, Jesus, real classic types. There was the fat one, the short one, and the skinny, arch-backed one, as if their superiors had picked them out on the basis of physiological variety. They all had really shiny bronze badges which caught the bright lights of the spaceport. The way the other two joked while the skinny one didn't so much as flex a smile told me who would be serious about promotion in this bunch. I had to take care.

As they radioed up, asking me for the fifth time for permission to board, I checked over my hiding places a final time— taking special care that the slot beneath my pilot's chair was right down flush with the floor, the only place I had contraband —and then I accepted their request. Just as I'd pegged it, that skinny one slipped his crooked nose in first of all, his two goons following on his heels, hands to the blasters on their belts, as if they'd actually ever kill someone. They were so hopped up they didn't even bother to check me for weapons. If they'd done so they would've found a blaster here, there and everywhere. They'd have had a tougher time getting them off me. That would've been a bone of contention, I can tell you that for nothing.

The skinny one introduced himself as Officer Clive Wodd. He had that distinctive Hortenine accent, that twang eating through the otherwise smooth tone like battery acid. And damned if he didn't come close at least twice to actually finding one of my hiding places. The second time I truly had my hand ready to draw my blaster, and I was preparing for a quick launch. But he turned away without success. Perseverance equals success. No promotion for you, buddy.

As I escorted the officers off the ship, I caught Wodd's eye. I have no idea how he saw something there, but, next thing I knew, he was calling his companions back to stand at his shoulders. He looked me up and down then said, "I've seen your picture."

My heart told me to go for my blaster, but my brain told me to wait this out—to give the situation a chance to reveal itself before I did anything rash. So I crossed my arms over my chest and stared him out. "Yeah?" I said. "Then what's my name?"

"You're Arkle Wright."

Not too far off, at least that's one of the names I use. In fact, it's my birth name, so I got a little touchy about it—annoyed that he'd fluked across the real one. Or had it been a fluke? Maybe I'd misjudged Wodd.

"You're wanted all through the Fritten System."

"That so?" I said, fingering the grip of my blaster, ready to make that speedy lift off—someone this sharp, at this time of night, was either perceptive or somehow in the loop, perhaps someone higher-up had briefed him. And if it was the latter then he might well have a bunch of cadets waiting in the wings, ready to take me down. "Well, it's a good thing we're not in Fritten, ain't it? That is unless you've got a warrant?"

Wodd narrowed his eyes. "No, I haven't."

"That's a shame. So am I free to go now?"

"We've got no reason to hold you."

"Are you going to stamp my file, have my ship's contents cleared for entry?"

Wodd held my gaze. He failed to respond then led his men away.

I guessed that I'd just got my clearance.

I waited till the customs officers had returned to their station, which was fitted with a large, single-way window—the mirror portion looking out, of course—and I dipped down into the ship and removed the panel beneath my seat. I withdrew the small case—about the size of a cigar box—and slipped it into the inside pocket of my jacket.

My ship—the *Navaplastas*—has just about the tightest security you can get your hands on. Whenever I meet up with my smuggling chums they're always taking the piss out of me, joking that I've got a fetish about it. That whenever I get paid off for a job first thing I'll do's get the *Nava* down to a shop and rework the door protocols, have a master programmer whack another framework of code onto the security system. I guess, recently, I've been thinking that maybe my buddies are right. Then I had an iris, blood and fingerprint scanner, a skin sampler, a body size analyser along with a series of increasingly complex computer codes to solve—which only I had memorised the sequence to, and which would time themselves out within a mean frame if the right answers weren't spoken. Just for fun I added a little electric shocker, nothing more than a couple of volts, to administer punishment to anyone who even dared attempt unauthorised access into the *Nava*.

So I went through all that protocol, the actual locking up of the ship wasn't all that tricky, and I stepped away. I headed along the gangplank which led up to Alpha Port Terminal—not much more than a fried mushroom stand and a ramshackle ticketing desk—and then out into the darkened street, the almost silent night. Silent, that was, apart from the raucous singing and drunken shouting coming from *The Bitch's Leap* just about smack-opposite the terminal. I like making drops on Hortenine —*The Bitch's Leap* is my kind of place. Just about the best watering hole in the galaxy. Or, at least, the best one I had access to at that point, no chance of getting arrested and extradited from. The main cause for confidence is that it's a good bet that whenever I step in there there're at least ten other guys more wanted than me. I'm small fry compared to the regulars. That night, though, was a bit different. I could tell with pretty much utmost certainty that I would be the most-wanted man in there.

Whereas everywhere else in the galaxy—even most places on Hortenine—there're nice *swooshing* metal doors, *The Bitch's* has an old fashioned wooden one. You've actually got to *push* it open to get inside, you have to *feel* the weight of the wood. And that was what I did then. Just another night, killing time at *The Bitch's* till my rendezvous came up.

Overhead, just as you go in, there's a great big chunky sign with a greyhound—I guess the titular 'bitch'—jumping over a shrub. Her muscles are tight and her eyes black-dead. It always makes me think, looking at her, that she's running away from something. And then I try to put that thought to one side, because I'll be damned if I'm going to start empathising with a lick of paint and some deadwood.

The Bitch's was only half-full, not uncommon. If there's one thing you learn quick running slime around the galaxy, it's that it only takes a handful of guys to cause a hell of a lot of noise. I ordered from the service droid and then took up my place in a dark corner, where I could scope out my surroundings. Even in *The Bitch's*, even in a dirty little nook like Hortenine, I never felt totally safe. I slurped at my moiser—what we call the alcoholic moisture they hand out in places like these—and eyed the guys at the bar. All beards and guts, leather jackets—pretty much like me thinking about it. There is a certain 'look' among us smugglers. They were clearly drunk, almost falling off their stools as they sang and told jokes. One of them caught my eye.

Immediately, I looked into my moiser. Too late.

"Eh! You!"

I kept my eyes down, feeling the package against my ribcage.

"Oi, you deaf or what?"

Reluctantly, I tilted my head up to examine the lout.

He had white hair plaited into braids—it looked like the work of Lucy, one of the prostitutes who hangs out on Terminal Road on Pollax, it's part of the Fritten System so I was banned from landing there. He also wore tight trousers. Way too tight. I could see the lump at his crotch staring back at me. "Oi!" he said, as if he hadn't realised that he'd got my full and undivided attention.

"What?" I said.

"Wanna join us?"

I glanced around *The Bitch's*. Since these were the only guys in the place it followed that my connection hadn't arrived yet. Turning these guys down would only lead to trouble—bar fights had started over much less. So, keeping the package tucked beneath my jacket, I stepped up to the bar and took up a place beside the inviter.

He leant forward and slapped me on the thigh, making an almighty *thwock* sound. His grin consumed his entire face, laughter lines eating into his flesh. A stench of body odour mixed with leather seized the air in its meaty fist. "Wha ya drinking?"

I wondered how far gone he was. In places like *The Bitch's* you get moisers and not much else—maybe a *zap* in the nuts from the service droid for being funny. Even the droids in these places have attitude.

I looked over the other guys' faces and established that I didn't know any of them. But, like I said, this being *The Bitch's*, I had no intention of underestimating them. I knew the class of people who came here. "I'm fine for a drink," I said, indicating my moiser.

The man's gums flapped open in realisation.

I guess he was drunker than I'd thought.

I counted the other guys, four of them. They had all formed a conspiratorial circle behind me and my new buddy—the kind of circle that you know to keep well clear of unless you want to find yourself flushed out into space. I returned to my moiser, hoping that now this guy had got me here, to the bar, that he would realise I wasn't any fun at all.

The guy leant into me. "You're Arkle Wright."

My ears perked up and I shot the man a sidelong glance.

"You are, ain't ya?" the man said, closing one eye.

"Who wants to know?"

The man let out a spluttering laugh and pounded his knee with his fist. The conspiratorial group glanced over at us. I forced a smile, as if this guy had just told me the greatest joke known to man. When the guy got himself back under control, swaying slightly on his stool, he eyed me closely. "You really wanted in all the Fritten?"

I shrugged.

The man snorted a laugh. "Yeah, you must've done something to really piss them off."

I waited out the silence, with no intention of elaborating.

"Go on, you've gotta tell us something."

"I don't have to tell *you* anything."

"Come on, fella, I invite you here, order you a drink and all's you can think of is to be all standoffish, and that. Throw me a bone, will ya? We're all friends here or at the very least"—he licked a glob of spittle from his lower lip—"colleagues."

"The whole point of our occupation is not having a boss."

He chuckled. "Oh we've all got bosses, just more than one, ain't that right? Don't you tell me that the last person who paid you a job wasn't your boss."

Again, I stayed quiet.

The man shook his head and then sucked back the rest of his moiser. He glanced off to his friends who continued to speak among themselves. One of them, who had sleek, black hair and emerald green eyes was gesticulating wildly—obviously getting caught up in whatever was for discussion. I tried to look away at the right moment but it was too late. He'd seen me looking. I concentrated on my moiser, but I knew I'd already made a fatal mistake.

The guy with black hair rose from his stool and pranced up to me. I had thought him younger when I'd seen him further away, but now I made out all the leathery wrinkles on his face. Maybe he dyed his hair. He seized hold of my collar in his fist and got his halitosis stench crawling up my nostrils. "You like what you hear, eh?"

I stilled my muscles and resisted the urge to reach for my blaster. Nothing good can ever come from four—five if you included the drunken inviter—against one. Especially when all sides are smugglers. Here's a little hint: us smugglers, we never, *ever* fight fair. His grip was strong, so strong that I could hardly move my throat to form a reply. "So—sorry," I said. "Your friend here, he just—"

"Shut up!" the black-haired guy said. "My *friend* here is a piss-headed disaster zone."

"Right," I said, not having any inclination to argue.

However, just then, I started to doubt my judgement of the drunken inviter as being totally useless as he spoke up for me. "Rick, this here's Wright. Arkle Wright."

For a moment the grip tightened and then, all of a sudden, the black-haired guy let go. He glared at me then grimaced, showing off a row of crooked teeth. As he stepped away I caught sight of the laser blade at his belt. I'm sure that he would've loved to have a go using that.

I sat slumped on my stool, in a stupor, for several seconds, worrying what I should do next. My contact would be along shortly to pick up the package, but, at the same time, I was sure that my welcome at *The Bitch's* had well and truly worn out. As it turned out, though, the group of conspirators got to their feet, murmuring among themselves. One of them caught hold of the drunken inviter and yanked him to his feet, as if drawing a dog after him, at his heels. When they reached the door, the drunken inviter gave me a limp-wristed wave goodbye and promptly disappeared.

I let out a long, breathy sigh and ordered another moiser from the service droid. Goodness knows I needed it. As I slipped the glass toward me I noticed a wrapper one of the guys had dropped. It was bright yellow with bold, black writing on the front. I picked it up and inspected it further. It was one of those sweets I'd seen around more and more recently: Fonch. The inside of the wrapper still had pink goo clinging to it and I dropped the wrapper back on the bar.

When someone tapped me on the shoulder I just about leapt right off my stool and cracked my head against the bar. I turned and almost did so again. It was a woman: long honey-coloured hair, peachy eyes and crimson-dabbed cheeks. They certainly don't make them like that on Hortenine-6. I muttered something incomprehensible that apparently sounded a little like an invitation since she sat down beside me. She was wearing a flowing, vermillion dress. And, my goodness, the girls on Hortenine sure as hell don't wear anything like that either.

"I'm Foy," she said.

"You most certainly are," I said, glad that my smutty smuggler-talk hadn't quite deserted me.

She flinched at my remark then said, "There's a problem."

My gut dropped. I knew it, just knew it. They'd sent a pretty girl out here to soften the blow—to tell me that something was wrong that, most importantly, I wasn't going to get paid. "What?" I said, already dreading having asked the question.

"I can't take the package off you."

"Why not?"

"I was followed here."

"Were you now?"

"Radley's men. I scanned the ship's imprint."

Radley, I thought to myself, *damn*. He operated just about the largest racket in the whole universe, seemed to have a finger in just about every pie. Hell, I'd probably worked a dozen or so jobs for him without even knowing it. Then another thought struck me, one of those instincts which have a habit of stopping you getting killed.

"How did you know for sure it was one of Radley's ships?"

She winced and her eyes darted about. I was sure that this was her first job—her whole getup, the dress, the nervous manner, letting slip with this information.

"Who are you?" I said.

All at once she jerked forward, her hand making for her thigh.

I caught her wrist before she got within even a forearm's length of the blaster strapped there. Now, I never like to lay hands on a lady without being given permission . . . as long as they're not intending to kill me. My fingers dug into her supple wrist and, with a lurch, I spun her around and tore the blaster—holster and all—from her thigh. Still keeping hold of her, I said,

"Now, my dear, is there anything else you've got there that I should know about?"

Her throat bobbed and she stood there, wide-eyed.

"Well?" I said. "Who're you working for?"

She remained silence, seemingly more terrified than anything else. Maybe I'd been a little too rough on her.

I examined the blaster, holding it up to the dim light. "Nice piece, this. Must've cost a packet." I checked out the grip then smiled. I glanced at her. "You know, if you're planning on pulling a gun on a fella, it helps to flick the safety off first." I pulled back my jacket to show her my blaster—one of them. "See?" I said. "Way I see it, if you're already packing something, it's better to leave the safety off. If you get busted by the authorities they're taking you down with or without the safety on. And on places like Hortenine most of the cops are off dealing with escaped pigs and sheep, so there's not much need to worry."

She pressed her lips together and shut her eyes. "If you're going to kill me, will you do it quickly?"

I almost fell over laughing. "Kill ya?" I said. "A little old thing like you?" I shook my head. "Nah, you're my contact, more importantly you're the one who's supposed to make sure I get paid. In fact, why don't we get back to that now?"

"It's better that you kill me, or they will."

"Who's 'they?'"

She nodded toward the door of *The Bitch's*.

"What? You mean those the guys who were just in—"

Before I got the chance to finish my inane observation, a blaster beam shot through the door to *The Bitch's*, leaving a large, burning hole. The service droid at the bar wound itself down below the counter. I tugged Foy down beside me, beneath a thick table. That's another great thing about *The Bitch's*, the tables are built to last every type of fight you might imagine.

Another beam *fizzled* through the air.

I kept our heads low, clicking the safety off Foy's blaster. No way had I reached the point of trusting her. Not quite yet, anyway. The image of her reaching for her blaster at her thigh was still fresh in my mind—and not just because of that glimpse I got of her cleavage.

One of those guys just went berserk and stuck his blaster on rapid-fire. Beams lashed the air, turning the whole place into one great big smokescreen. I grabbed hold of Foy and together we crawled our way toward the back of the bar, toward the toilets—a place I knew well since I'd puked my guts out there many a merry time.

I tried not to think about the unscrubbed, unsterilized floors we were putting our meat hooks all over, in fact there wasn't much trying involved. When there're blaster beams flying all about it has a habit of concentrating your mind on more important things. Namely not getting shot.

I'd got us into one of the cubicles in the long-neglected women's toilets when I noticed the blasters had stopped firing. Not wanting to waste a moment, I hoicked Foy up to the small, letterbox-shaped window and primed my blaster, ready to shoot at whoever came in through the door. She got her slender frame through the opening quite nicely, for me, though, it was a bit more of a challenge.

One thing about smuggling is that you spend an awful amount of time in your ship—that is a lot of time sitting at the controls, taking on energy pills and the like. Now, maybe some of the more astute might suggest I invest in a small on-board gym—divert some of those funds for my security into a cycling machine or a treadmill—but, and I have to be honest, I find exercise nosebleed-inducing boring. The upshot of which is that I've got a gut. Quite a gut.

As I managed to snaffle myself up through the window, I heard the heavy boots sound over the barroom floor. That gave me just enough motivation, the prospect of getting one of my buttocks fried with a blaster beam, to suck in my gut and get through the window. Even so, I heard the shout and a blaster beam tore through my right shoulder. I landed without bending my knees on the hard asphalt outside in absolute agony.

Foy was still standing there, a little to my surprise, and, even more against the odds, she helped me to my feet. I clutched my fried shoulder and clasped her hand, dragging her up the road, headed for Alpha Port. Already I was getting my brain into gear, thinking through the take off procedure. Trying to work out how I might get us away from those guys—Radley's guys, apparently —and up into the relative safety of empty space. For all the stick I get over investing in the *Nava's* safety on the ground, I do make sure that the thrusters are up to snuff, at least able to outrun any respectable patrol ship. One of Radley's ships might be a different matter, though.

We burst through the terminal, sending an old lady and her packages flying. I glanced over my shoulder and muttered an apology. I dragged Foy through the turnstiles leading into the private docking area, scanning my fingerprints and hers quickly. We ran onward, for the *Nava*. When I got there I shot through the safety routine, managing to get it all right first time. Hey, I've had a lot of practice. You can never underestimate the importance of being able to make a hurried getaway.

And then I was up in the cockpit, doors locked, shields engaged, with Foy sitting there beside me. I can't deny that I felt a bit of a buzz there, with a pretty girl at my side, making a daring escape, that was kind of one of the reasons I got into this line of work—that and the money. And being able to use a blaster. And being able to fly through space unchecked as a privateer. This job rocks.

Just as I engaged the take off program, I caught sight of the men—all five of them, even my buddy the drunkard dawdling away at their heels—they all had blasters drawn and wasted no time whatsoever in firing them off at the *Nava*. I shifted all the power I wasn't using for take off into the front shields. I watched the beams flash bright yellows, blues and purples as they struck the invisible barrier. Tiny cracks appeared in the layer as the beams strobed against it. I grasped hold of the control stick and leant it back, lifting the *Nava* up and tilting her skyward. The beams continued to lick at the shields and then there was a hefty *jerk* and an unnerving mechanical *squeal*. Unfortunately I had good ideas of what those sounds meant—that the beams had got through the defences and were making headway into the ship's physical shell. Lucky for us we were all ready to go.

With a final look back at them, catching the glare of the black-haired guy, his body tensed as he fired away on his blaster, I shifted the thrusters back and then full forward. We launched upward, barrelling into the sky, through the artificial atmosphere bubble and out into space. Only when I'd levelled us off, got us flying at maximum speed in the opposite direction to Hortenine, and the Fritten System, did I dare to leave my seat. "You take charge," I said to Foy. "It's real easy, everything's on autopilot. If anything shows up on the navigator it'll make a nice *ping* noise. You won't miss it."

Foy seemed too scared to speak, but she sat there and watched on.

I did leave the system locked. You can never be too careful with someone who's recently tried to kill you—even if you've just saved their life.

I peeled off my shirt in the toilet and slid open the medical unit. Inside I found the tactical spray—an army supply which I bartered off a young kid at a trading post a while back, he probably got into big trouble when they did inventory, not that it's my problem. I sprayed over the afflicted area, going over it three or four times till the bleeding stopped. As I looked at myself in the mirror, examining my pallid complexion and vein-stained eyes, I checked out the scar just below my left pectoral—that rigid, knitted fucker, staring back at me like a black cat in headlights. Just as my mind was turning over memories I'd much rather forget, I caught sight of some motion in the corner of the mirror. I spun around, simultaneously slipping my blaster out and pointing it at the target.

It was Clive Wodd. The customs officer.

"What the hell are you doing here?"

He smiled at me, sheepishly.

2: STOWAWAY LEAVING HORTENINE

I KEPT THE BLASTER pointed at Wodd's chest. He was still dressed in his uniform, of course, although I noticed he'd donned some latex gloves—so he wouldn't leave finger-prints, evidence.

"What you're doing is trespassing," I said. Do you mind telling me how you got into my ship?"

"I . . . I," he started, staring at my blaster.

"Come on, out with it."

"Are . . . are we in space?"

"Yup, now how did you get around the security?"

Wodd gulped and backed up into the corner. "I thought you might be hiding something here. I wanted to come back and take a look."

"That's not the question I asked."

"Right, right," he said. "Uh, I don't know, I've always been good with computers, technology, and all that. I was able to bypass the security. Nothing fancy. I just did it."

"You don't 'just' get past the security on this ship."

He stared at the barrel of my blaster. "Are you going to shoot me now?"

"Is it just you aboard or did you bring Tweedledee and Tweedledum along for the ride?"

"Just me."

"I was thinking that letting you out into space might be a better prospect."

"No," he said, "wait, please. I can explain." He took a few moments to compose himself. "The reason I wanted to break in here, get aboard, I wanted to get off Hortenine-6, I had to, and when I recognised you, saw your ship here, I knew that you'd be doing your best to avoid all the checks, not going across any borders legally. I'd never be able to get the right chips to open doors."

"You could've just kept on working the customs job. I'm sure they would've promoted you eventually."

He shook his head. "No, that's not likely to happen at all. You really have no idea what's going on back on Hortenine, do you?"

"Probably some tilling of the soil, somewhere some guy will be milking a cow. Am I far off?"

"Radley."

"What about him?"

"He's taken over the whole place, the administration, made it some sort of hub, like a final jumping off point into the Fritten System. He has big plans, and he's keeping all the government authorities in their place. Not that that's difficult considering most of the council is just made up of a few old, crooked farmers. They're taking whatever Radley wafts their way and, in return, they don't ask questions about what he wants with Hortenine."

"And I suppose your idea was to get off the planet, go away somewhere, get training, only to return one day when you would overthrow them all?"

Wodd's lips open and shut.

"Don't think that you're the first stowaway I've had aboard." I scowled. "Just the first that's managed to get through the *Nava's* security systems and live to tell the tale." I paused. "So far."

His eyes bulged, almost out of their sockets and he clasped his hands before him in prayer. "Please," he said. "I know why you're in trouble, why you're being searched for in the Fritten System. Don't you want to know how you managed to get onto their most-wanted list?"

Actually, I have to admit, I had been racking my brains over it. The way the authorities are organised I always figured they just picked a name off a minor offences list, probably attached to a dartboard. "Is it because I'm a big scary smuggler who doesn't wash enough?"

"Because someone grassed you up, blamed you for something you didn't do."

"And what might that have been?"

"Have you checked inside that box, seen what's inside it?"

"Nope, part of the deal was I was to deliver it unopened."

"Don't you think you should take a look now?"

I stewed over that for all of two seconds and then I lifted Wodd by the scruff of the neck and shoved him off down the corridor, in the direction of the cockpit. Everything was just as I'd left it—Foy still at the controls, not having touched anything or, at least, not having seemed to. "Box," I said, looking at her— I'd given it to her for safe keeping during the frantic take off.

She obeyed and plucked the box up from the floor, then handed it over to me.

I took it, weighed it in one hand. Whatever was inside felt solid. I gave the box a shake.

Wodd lurched forward. "No!" he said.

"What? What is it?"

"I'd take care with that if I were you."

"Look, kid, if it was going to break I'm sure it already would've done sure during our daring escape from Radley's men. Now cool down a little, won't you?"

Wodd did cool down but his intense expression, his adamant concentration on the box didn't cease.

I have to admit I was getting a little nervous, what with Wodd looking like he might blow out a liver at any second, so I picked that moment to glance over at Foy, who was watching the opening, or the discussion of the opening, of the box with utmost interest. "What's inside?" I said.

She continued to stare at the box. "I don't know."

"What do you mean, 'you don't know?'"

"They just told me I had to get hold of it—that if I didn't manage to get it from you that they would burst in through the doors and kill us both."

"Amateurs," I said.

"Don't you want to hear how I got involved in this?"

I held up my hand, not ready—just yet—to hear another sob story about a pretty girl getting prised away from the her family by a group of mobsters. "Maybe some other time." I busied myself with the box, checking over the packaging. It was sealed with a standard plastic coating. I got my multi-tool on the job—if there's one bit of kit you can't do without in space, as a smuggler, it's a multi-tool: laser opener, screwdriver and a good old-fashioned metal blade, for when you're feeling nostalgic. Approximately ten seconds later I got the sealing clear of the box and blew off the residue.

Wodd continued to stare down at me as if I were doing nothing less than defusing a thermo nuke.

I slipped off the lid and examined the contents. Inside there was a single, brown-yellow stone nestled on a small felt cushion. The stone itself was maybe the size of my thumbnail. I crunched up my features and glanced up at Wodd. "This is it?"

Wodd, however, had gone all pale again. "Don't you know what that is?"

"Nope. Worth anything?"

"'Worth anything?'" Wodd said, flushing a touch. "*That* is nothing less than the Stone of the Angels."

I groaned. "Who the hell called it that?"

Wodd looked like I'd just stomped on his birthday puppy. "What does it matter what it's called when it holds the key to all of sub-space."

"'Sub-what-now?'"

"Sub-space. For hundreds of years, ever since man became acquainted with space we have been searching for the secret to pass into sub-space. With this, the Stone of the Angels, we believe that we might be able to harness sufficient energy to pass inside."

"Sounds like a bunch of new-age crap to me."

"Oh no," he said. "You're very wrong about that."

I kept my enthusiasm to myself. Whenever it comes to anything mildly spiritual I'm wont to switch off my brain, to give it some much-deserved rest. And, since I was more likely to believe a more sophisticated, better-travelled person, I decided to call on Foy for her opinion.

"Well," she said, "of course I've heard of it—but no one really understands its power. And as for all that business about it opening sub-space, if that even exists, I'm not sure anyone can say for certain. There are other uses it could be put to if the stories about its untapped energy are correct."

Wodd stuck to his backward Hortenine, believe-anything-if-it-sparkles mantra. "It definitely does. It's just that it needs further study." He reached out for the stone. "If I might be permitted to take a look I could—"

I slapped his hand away. "Oh no you don't. You're still in hot water, mister. Don't forget you got yourself on board my ship without asking." I looked over to Foy again. "There's just one thing that doesn't sit right with me. When they found out who I was—back in *The Bitch's*—why didn't they take the stone from me there and then?"

"They had no idea what you had," Foy said.

"Or," I said, "I think I have another theory."

"What?" she said.

I brought the navigational screen down and studied my

map. I analysed my previous journey, to the point where I had picked up the stone—from a tiny moon just inside the Fritten System. "I think we'd better take a visit back here, see if there's anything to find. I get the impression that the guy who handed this stone to me had a good idea of what was going on."

"What do you mean?"

"I think he was working for Radley."

———

We whizzed through space, eating up the pebble trail I'd left behind from my previous journey. I sucked in my gut as the navigational computer informed us that we were entering the Fritten System. This place was remote, right on the edge of the System, but that didn't mean I was anxious to push my luck with the authorities.

There wasn't so much as a terminal on the moon so I had to set the *Nava* down on, what looked to be, a fairly stable patch of ground. I always feel a little apprehensive about landing on anything other than terminal, spaceport, because it has a nasty habit of either being flimsy or being alive. Anyway, I got the ship down and had Foy stay behind. I decided, on balance, that I trusted Foy more than Wodd since she didn't seem to have an intimate knowledge of the *Nava's* security systems. And if Wodd knew how to get through the security systems there was no telling what he might do—unchecked—with the navigational computers, or he might even decide to commandeer the ship for himself. The upshot of all this dithering was that me and Wodd set out across the lunar landscape, dressed in spacesuits—owing to the lack of oxygen, or atmosphere, on this moon.

We reached the outer bubble a while later. It was one of those temporary ones—the ones that were used to set up colony outposts in the hope that *one day* a backup group would arrive to help form a more permanent atmosphere. But, like always, the budget ran out and, it turned out, people greatly preferred living some places than others. Granted, living on a pile of dusty rocks which go through several months, if not years, of darkness, doesn't sound greatly appealing. Not that the guy who had given me the package seemed to mind it.

Our first obstacle came in the form of the communicator. I announced our presence, and intention to speak with Kools, the pseudonym my contact had insisted I used, and were promptly denied entry. I looked to Wodd. "Gonna work your sweet magic?"

Wodd stood back. "Isn't . . . wouldn't this be illegal?"

"Breaking into my ship was illegal. You're a Hortenine on the run, without the documents required to be *in* the Fritten System. Don't you think it's time to cut loose a little with the well-worn moral convictions?"

He seemed to get my point—or at least he slipped off the casing for the communicator, fiddled around with the wires and then boosted us through the gate and into the bubble. If only I could get him over to the dark side Wodd might well be a valuable ally, as long as I could get him to shake off those ridiculous dreams of going back to 'liberate' Hortenine-6. The only liberation that place needed was from its plane of existence. I didn't say that out loud, though. If there's one thing I've learnt over the years with nationalist nutters, it's that they don't take too kindly to having their countries belittled or threatened with extinction. Maybe one day I'll be able to fill a book with all my space smuggler advice.

Once in the bubble we took off our helmets while Wodd gnawed my ear off talking in poetic terms about the strange glint that the bubble around us gave the fabric of space, and other such nonsense. I tuned him out and kept him walking toward our goal: the central building—the only building in fact—not much more than a tumbledown shack. This whole settlement made Hortenine look like a bustling metropolis.

We reached the building and, again, were denied access. Wodd worked his magic yet again and got us inside. The whole place stank. I thought Kools might've heated up an instant dinner and then left to rot. Then I saw that, in fact, it was Kools who was doing the rotting.

I pinched my nose and wandered closer. As I stooped over his dead body, a trickle of dried blood running from his mouth down onto his wrinkled chin. His old man's face was contorted in an everlasting scream, shock and surprise etched onto those empty eyes. I heard Wodd vomiting behind me. If he really wanted to save Hortenine he'd have to get some steel in that stomach.

I examined the wound in Kools's chest, gaping, burnt-out flesh. It was a blaster shot. Now I was convinced. It had to be Radley. Who else would bother coming out here with the sole mission of killing Kools? He couldn't have been anything to anyone out here. When I looked across the room I saw that the main communicator had been sabotaged. I tried to remember whether it had been like that when I'd met Kools, or whether his killers had bashed it in as a sort of reflex. That's not uncommon with thugs. Quite often they get themselves all hopped-up on adrenalin and can't help themselves.

As I left Kools's side, I noticed a squished sweet lying beside him—a gooey pink mess. Kools had never struck me as the kind of guy to go in for treats, but, then again, I guess no one really knew him. He was secretive, all alone out here. Still, I was curious, something about the wrapper struck me as familiar, and I turned the sweet over and examined it. The brand name, written out in chunky, pink bold letters: Fonch.

I tossed it away then said, "Let's go."

Wodd appeared wiping his mouth with a paper towel he'd plucked from some bathroom I had no intention of investigating. If this place looked as bad as it did from the outside, I had no intention of venturing in there. "What's this?" he said.

"What's what?"

Wodd stooped over a desk and picked up a handheld communicator. It was kidney-shaped and reams of static buzzed across its screen. However, looking over his shoulder, it was just possible to make out what was written through the interference. I snatched it off him and tried to make out the writing.

"Says that he's very sorry and that he's led a terrible, miserable life, . . . yadda yadda yadda . . . the recipient's someone called Susie, and that she'll understand how this happened, why it had to happen." I looked up at Wodd. "Do you suppose he means how he ended up all dead?"

Wodd, still looking visibly queasy, said, "I don't know. I thought you said that he was killed by Radley's gang."

"That seems the most likely thing, but that doesn't mean it's the only thing that could've happened. If you say that that stone's important, that it's got some sort of decent standing in the galaxy then why would Radley—once he'd got his hands on it—then give it to Kools, to give it to me? Why wouldn't Radley cut out all the legwork and unnecessary running about and just take it for whatever he wants it for?"

"And why would he want you to have it in the first place?"

"That's just what I said."

"Unless . . ."

"What?"

"Well, what if he wanted to frame you, or something?"

"'Frame me?'"

"Think about it, back on Hortenine. They made you come to Hortenine, ensuring that you'd have the stone, then—"

"Nah," I said. "I set up the meeting on Hortenine. Always do. *The Bitch's* is the perfect place to swap goods, get business done on the quiet."

"So you think it's just a coincidence that Radley's taking over the place politically, and that you just *happened* to set up a meeting there?"

"Yup."

"Okay, maybe you're right."

I sighed. "All right, kid, as long as there's nothing else pressing around here—anything kicking around the dead man's quarters we might've missed out on—then I suggest we bounce."

"You do understand that the authorities, everyone in the Fritten System wants to get their hands on the Stone of the

Angels, don't you? How long were you on the run with the stone, waiting to make the exchange at Hortenine?"

"Dunno, I had to lay low a couple of months, terms of the deal."

"Yes, so don't you see?"

"See what?"

"That was all the time that Radley needed to blame you for the theft of the stone, to get you onto their most-wanted lists, to have everyone scouring the Fritten System for any sign of your entrance, your reappearance with the stone. They wanted to make you a scapegoat. Getting you into *The Bitch's Leap* and having you killed there. It would've been perfect. Everyone would believe that you stole the stone *and* it would've fallen into hands unknown. They would have to give up the chase, be willing to admit defeat. And Radley would be home free with the stone."

"Just one problem with all that."

"What?"

"How does Foy fit in?"

"She was the gun. She was supposed to shoot you."

"Are you sure?"

"Yeah, I think so."

"It just doesn't make sense to me, why they'd send in someone as callow as her to get the job done and then, when things start getting hairy, I find Foy's gun, they decide to just blow the both of us away. What was the plan then? To fish for the stone from out smouldering corpses?"

Wodd shrugged. "It would fit. I mean, I could see them

managing something like that. It would make sense from a logistical—"

I held up my hand. "It's okay now, Clive, my boy, you don't have to be careful about what you say, you're under the command of the *Navaplastas* now, not Hortenine Customs."

"When you say 'under command' do you mean like as a real member of the ship?"

"Or maybe I mean that you're my prisoner. Stay on your best behaviour, keep opening doors for me and we'll see whether or not we can negotiate."

Wodd stepped out of the central building, leading the way to the airlock leading out of the bubble and back to the *Navaplastas*. I lingered back a moment, checked over the shack one last time, looked at Kools's cold, dead face and knew that I had to dig further. None of this made sense as it was. I had to get talking to Susie and see what was really up. She would know whether or not Kools really was just a crazy old man out here, willing to do whatever it was that Radley and his boys commanded. He certainly died for them. I slipped the handheld communicator into my jacket pocket.

When I came around from my deliberation, I noticed that Wodd was pointing excitedly at the sky, out into space. As I followed his finger I came to realise why. There were five ships —the authorities of the Fritten System, or Fritters as I affection- ately refer to them. Although I have to say, in that moment, they didn't look all that affectionate to me.

3: UNDER ATTACK ON UNKNOWN MOON

ONE THING WITH FRITTERS is that they don't always play fair. I mean, you'd expect all the dirty fighting tactics from a smuggler—it comes with the territory— but you'd expect a *law*man to actually have to follow some kind of rules, to play up to all that bullshit. Not so with Fritters.

I broke out into a sprint, marvelling at what my physical condition might be like after a few days of these chases, hurried returns to the *Nava*. The door was standing wide open, the entrance slope down. I thanked my lucky stars that Foy hadn't decided to play with any of the controls in the cockpit, and then considered my decision to bring Wodd with me—with all the bonding it had entailed—to have been a good choice. If the Fritters had arrived after the *Nava* had gone, there would've been nowhere to run to.

We clambered aboard just as they started firing. I got the shields up a few seconds after. We took fire all over the body, the damage gauge *wapped* away to itself with each new complaint. I glanced to Wodd. "Kid, are you as good with space-ships as you are with security systems?"

Wodd gave me a nervous grin. "I used to do a lot of tinker-ing, actually my dad—"

"Does this look like a good time for a delightful chinwag? I said get busy sorting out the damaged areas." I dug through the storage space beneath the control stick and withdrew the portable damage mapper, which I thrust into his hands. "That's got all the information you need. It's very simple. Look for the red and plug it up. Got it?"

He nodded vigorously and then sped off, his footfalls sending metallic echoes around the ship.

I turned to Foy. "Now, as for you, honey—"

"Don't call me that."

"Listen, missy, you're on my ship, I saved you from those *evil* men, now you're going to do exactly what your captain tells you."

She glowered.

"Now, I'm going to open the weapons systems for you and I want you to do your best to take out as many of those Fritters as you—"

Without needing any help from me, she got the weapons systems open, tapped away until she got the main blaster cali-brated and then took aim and fired at the first Fritter. She struck it on the hull and it blew into a thousand pieces. She sneered at me. "You never did give me the chance to tell my story earlier. I—"

"Yeah, yeah," I said. "I'm sure it's a real tearjerker. Now do that again!"

It turned out that the second time was more difficult, and the third and the forth, and so on. I guessed that the Fritters hadn't bargained for return fire after such a long wait and so we'd caught them off guard—they'd switched power from their shields to their primary weapons. I knew that as long as they wanted to get their hands on the stone they would stop short of blowing us to smithereens, but, still, we needed to get into space as quickly as possible. If they managed to get through the shields they could disable whatever they wanted on the ship. They could board us without my consent. And if that happened I'd be going to prison: Krykelseare-14, fifty degrees below zero on a summer's day.

I booted up the take off system and got us off the ground, into space. Foy provided us with enough covering fire to keep the Fritters occupied—occupied enough to not dare getting too close. We made inroads into space, leaving the Fritters behind in our wake, tailing us, waiting for their opportunity to strike. I knew they were monitoring the ship, calculating which shield generators they could take out first so that they could disable our forward motion. I was a little worried—okay, more than a little worried—because after our eventful exit from Hortenine-6 I'd had no chance of patching up the ship. Actually, I'd intended to get the *Nava* fixed up right after paying Kools a visit. I regretted not having taken a quick stop off to get things fixed up.

The ship jolted once, twice, three times, then over and over again, as they stuck us with their rapid-fire cannon. I hoped that whoever was operating that thing back on the Fritter knew what they were doing. If they kept up at this rate they might just 'accidently' blow us to smithereens.

The reverse thruster was the first to fail. I hardly batted an eyelid when it did, the prospect of landing so far off in my thoughts at that time. And then, more worryingly, the front thrusters went. That meant we were struggling to keep our distance from the Fritters and then they started gaining on us. I called out to Wodd, wanting him to hurry up and fix our thrusters, but they remained out of action. With nothing else to do, I watched the Fritters approaching us, drawing closer every second. Foy shot another few beams at them before the weapons systems went down too. She looked to me for what to do next and I just gave her a shrug. What could we do?

I called Wodd back to the cockpit, although he was reluctant.

"I can still do it," he said. "Just let me have another go. I can patch up the thrusters at least—maybe even the weapons systems if you give me some more time."

I eyed the navigational screen, watching the dots close in on us, those Fritters. I shook my head. "Nah, there's nothing to do now, they're going to catch us."

"But they'll put you in prison, send you to Krykelseare-14."

"I had a good run, I guess."

Both Foy and Wodd burnt holes in me with their stares. I wanted to tell them the truth, that, really, I just didn't care. If they were going to take me away—if the whole universe had somehow conspired against me to land me with the blame for this stone thing, then what choice did I have? I couldn't hide away forever. They'd have caught me sooner or later entering the Fritten System on some errand or other. In fact it was kind of a relief. For all the incompetence of the authorities, I'd much rather be in their hands, get dealt with by them, than by some of Radley's thugs. If Radley did want me dead then at least I'd be safe in custody.

The ships continued to close on us, getting within range to begin a manual approach. It would only take them a matter of minutes to pull alongside the *Nava*, shoot out a walkway and have one of their engineers hack through the security system and force the doors open. Well, as long as the engineers weren't of the same calibre as Wodd, then the security system might take them a little longer. But they would get it open given time, and without power or weapons there was little we could do to stop them.

So with the two of them looking to me, wanting me to tell them what to do, to introduce some previously unseen loophole, I sank back in my captain's chair, trying to remember all that was good about my job—the many contented hours I'd spent in this cockpit. I'd have some happy memories to take with me to Krykelseare-14. Warm memories.

———

The troops burst in through the door about an hour or two later. I did raise a slight smirk that it had taken them so long to actually bust through the security systems. Foy and Wodd just looked scared, and not without reason. Wodd would be in big trouble. And I hadn't yet had the time / inclination to listen to

Foy's past, so maybe she had something tucked up her sleeve she wasn't telling us about either.

They wore their ugly grey uniforms and held their blasters out straight in their hands. I saw the twitches in their eyes as they approached with the magnetic cuffs. Most of these guys were kids doing their three-year-long service, as all respectable kids in the universe must. In fact, doing mine was when I first got to hold a blaster—and I got to wondering what else I might be able to do with it other than run down criminals for the Fritters. Needless to say I didn't wonder all that much.

The kids yanked our arms behind our backs and cuffed us. I complained they were too tight, more because I'd seen it in movies and the like than actually being in any discomfort. The kids just looked all the more frightened and jumpy, and I decided, for the time being, to keep my mouth shut.

A leader appeared finally, obviously waiting to check there wouldn't be any resistance, that one of his underlings would get shot instead of him, before poking his nose into proceedings. He wore a slimy great grin across his chops as he strutted up to me. "Arkle Wright, I presume?"

"The same."

He cocked his head to one side and I noted that he wore his cap at an angle so that a tuft of white-blond hair sprouted out from beneath it. I suppose this was his 'look.' "My name is Captain Reynolds." He cleared his throat like he wanted to give me a little time to absorb it, then said, "I would've thought you'd have put up a bit more of a fight than that."

"Yeah, well, you disabled my ship. Congratulations."

His nostrils flared as he sniffed up the atmosphere of the *Nava*, as if considering the odour, storing it somewhere in his conformist brain for rapid access later on. I don't suppose he brought in many criminals—not the ones in my league, in any case. "Shall I give you a moment, Captain?" he said. "You know, to say goodbye to your ship for the last time? I know that it must be an emotional time for you, that all your ill-dealings have finally caught up." He inspected the cuff of his uniform sleeve. "Perhaps it's a bit of a relief. At least now you shan't need to worry about being caught any longer. You can do your time and leave a free man. Start all over again."

"What makes you so convinced that I'm guilty?"

He glowered at me, as if furious that I'd even had the nerve to float such a notion. "The council on Garton-1 has decided that you are the most-wanted man in the whole of the Fritten System. Do you think they would bother to go to such trouble to get hold of you if that weren't the case?"

"They don't encourage much out-of-the-box thinking in the authorities, do they?"

"I have no idea what you are talking about."

"No, I don't suppose you do."

Reynolds barked an order to one of his adolescent officers and I felt a tight grip on my wrists—an *enthusiastic* grip. Someone clearly was looking at promotion here.

I allowed the officer to lead me out through my ship and onto the walkway. Did I want to say goodbye to the *Nava?* Not a chance. I had every confidence in myself that I would be back here. Sooner or later.

———

We were all brought to the mother ship, its name being the catchy: *FSA-01061*. Myself I've always thought it a great insult to a ship to leave it without a name, no matter how big and ugly. As we approached it on the shuttle I examined the large cannons at either side of its hull. It had been a while since I'd got a look at a Fritter ship so I took the opportunity to fill my boots. I had to admit that they'd seen the frailties in their weaponry and equipped themselves accordingly.

I clocked Reynolds's first mistake soon after boarding the mother ship—he had us all led off along to the holding area, *together*. Now if I had been in his shoes, not that I was or would ever want to be, I would've had us put in separate *ships* let alone separate parts of the same ship, and lesser still in the same impound. But here we were. As a prisoner I might well have been able to get myself used to Reynolds's slack command.

As they shoved us down corridor after corridor, I managed to sneak a glance out of the window, back to the *Nava*. I watched a pair of ships approaching her, coming up alongside. They would be searching for that damn stone, and if they found it I supposed I would be finished. There was nothing to do about it now. If they found it, they found it. I would be going to Krykelseare-14.

They gave us each a little push into the cellblock before bringing up the laser shield—a sequence of several laser 'bars' each separated by a couple of centimetres. If you got to close to them they would burn through your skin without much hassle. If you attempted to run through them—as I've been assured by various accounts down at *The Bitch's*—you'll get yourself sliced into dog meat. I had no reason to prove or disprove that particular urban myth. But, then again, I suppose that not being curious might be a contributing factor as to why I've managed to live out so many years and, if I keep on the same track, I hope to live many more.

Around this time Wodd slumped to the floor and started sobbing, wailing about how he would get sent back to Hortenine and he'd get into all sorts of trouble at work, and that, if Radley or whichever crony was in power back there found out he'd been with me, that he'd kill him and his entire family. I did my best to calm his melodramatic outpourings, and probably half-succeeded.

Foy, on the other hand, remained quiet. She crouched in the corner, as if not quite daring to land her pretty bottom on the cell floor. To be fair, if there was any possibility of bacteria in a sterilised ship in the Fritters' fleet then it might well have been on the floor of the jail cell. She tilted her head back and examined me. "Are you ready to hear my end of things now?"

"Dunno," I said with a sigh. "It's not depressing, is it? It's just I think I've had my daily dose of depressing."

She scowled. "Of course it's depressing—it's the story of how I got mixed up with Radley and his lot."

"Could you at least, you know, put some sort of a positive spin on things? Give it a little bit of a positive twirl?"

"'A positive twirl?'"

"Yeah," I said. "Just to give us a bit of a lift."

"Well, how about this," she said. "I'll tell it in reverse. That way it'll start out all nasty, but you'll get the nice bits at the end. Would that work for you?"

I got myself comfy, as comfy as I was getting in this cramped cell without any walls to lean against—unless I wanted to end up in little bits leaning against the bars—then I shut my eyes.

"You're sleeping!" she said.

"Nah, I'm just getting ready for the story."

She simmered away for a while longer.

I noticed that Wodd had stopped his whimpering. I guess he'd come to the conclusion that we were all just as doomed as each other and so we might as well just take it quietly and with dignity—that way, when we had a chance to make a difference, angle for a daring escape, we would have the energy to do so.

"Right," she said. "Then I'll begin."

4: FOY'S STORY FROM TRIVUS-3

THE DAY I MET YOU in *The Bitch's Leap* I was travelling with Radley's men, those guys, you know the ones, that guy with the black hair, his name's Gus and he's in charge, although I guess you realised that. Anyway, we flew into Alpha Port and got ourselves checked out by Clive and friends. They didn't find anything, of course, Gus saw to it that we kept our weapons well-hidden, and he was always ready to sneak a shot—to take one of the customs officers out—if they so much as *looked* like they might be about to cause trouble. Luckily none of them did.

If there was one thing about my whole involvement with Radley, and his men, it was that I absolutely hated their willingness to shoot anything that got in their way. On our way to Hortenine we were approached by some hawkers, wanted to sell us some energy capsules and they were persistent. Well, I'd be first to admit they were kind of annoying, but that doesn't justify what Gus did. After they'd been bugging us for an hour or more, I guess we were in a quiet stretch of space, Gus asked them aboard, told them we'd buy whatever crap it was that they wanted to sell us. Well, he met them at the airlock and he whipped out his blaster and shot the guy right then and there. I remember standing at his shoulder—remonstrating with him not to do it, but he did, all the same. Just as Gus holstered his blaster I saw a kid—I guess it was the hawker's son—look around to see what all the noise had been about. Gus just slid the airlock shut and gave that ship a kick, back out into space. We left it behind. That kid all on his own drifting into nothingness.

For the rest of the trip to Hortenine I just broke down. It had been a hard toil, and I know I promised you that I'd end this all positively, but I can only tell the truth. The ending is a happy one, I can promise you that, which is to say that my past life was a happy one. Anyway, Gus didn't turn out to be so heartless after all and, away from the other guys, he confided in me that he felt pretty bad about what he'd done—and then he informed me of what Radley would've done to him were he to have left that hawker alive. The hawker might've clicked something about our mission, realised where we were headed. I thought that all a little farfetched, more than a bit paranoid, but I suppose that's the kind of world that hoods like Gus inhabit. They can't take chances. They live by the credo of 'shoot first, think later.'

Throughout our emotional mingling of minds—I guess it's not difficult to get to that zone if you're a woman, since these men find themselves floating out in space with only a ship full of men for company—I managed to garner something about our mission. He told me that there was a smuggler running the Stone of the Angels to Hortenine and that we had to take it from him, make it look like a real messy operation. Gus really had no idea what the stone meant. As far me, though, I knew it's significance. Well, I put that stone stuff to one side, my mind did, and I just broke into tears. I don't know, part of it was conscious, I wanted to show him that I just couldn't tolerate any more loss of life, that it wasn't fair to keep me along with them so I could witness all this without being able to intervene, and so I managed to convince him—don't ask me how—that I could go in there first, I could speak with the contact, make him feel good, get the stone from him, maybe even give him a parting kiss, before the other guys would move in to shoot him up. He even gave me a blaster, strapped it to my thigh, for my own protection, although just as you saw, I had no idea how to use it.

I don't know. I guess I just felt fatalistic at that point, like if there was nothing I could do to stop this group's almighty stomp through space, killing whoever got in their way, the least I could do was to make the victim feel more comfortable. That was it, I think. Give them comfort, something nice to think about as they died. Stupid, isn't it? And well, as it turned out, you were a little more than they'd bargained for, not content to take it lying down. I suppose I always had the intention of escaping them but you made it real. So, thank you for that. I mean, maybe it was just to get captured here. But, whatever, at least I'm with people who don't kill on sight.

So, yeah, the plan was for Gus and the guys to get the stone, and to make it look like some bandits, or other, had just plain robbed you of it—the idea, obviously, being that the Fritten

System Authorities would give up chasing around for the stone, give it up as lost, when it was with Radley the whole time. Anyway, I guess that it all went pretty wrong. From their perspective, anyway.

Okay, so I said that I'd get to the happy part of the story last, give everyone a bit of a lift, although, to tell the truth, despite being locked up here I feel about a million times better than I did with Gus and his psychopaths. I lived out in the Corfus System, right out on the edge of the Diwinian Parallel. I'm sure you've been there at some point. It's a pretty well-known gangster passageway into the Fritten System—not that I knew that until I met Gus, but I suppose all people of your occupation, or anyone around it, must know the truth. Anyway, though you might've passed it by a few times, you probably never stopped off on any of the planets. I used to live on Trivus-3. It's a small system and Three's on the outer rim, the last of the three planets there. It's a calm place, got lots in common with Hortenine I'm guessing, though I didn't get much of a chance to look at it when I landed with Gus. It's all farming too. I grew up on the pastures, milking cows, riding horses, it was pretty great. There's one thing about the Corfus System, though, and that's because of its unique position, surrounding the Fritten System, an obvious target for anyone trying to break through—we keep a pretty mean, well-oiled army between the three planets. I say army, maybe it's more of an air force. We learn to fly and shoot. That's why I'm not much good with blasters—fighting hand-to-hand.

Boys and girls, it's all the same, we all go through the same training. Our parents shove us into groups when we're about three or four, we're given our units early on in our lives. While all the normal stuff goes on: the education, school, the boy and girlfriends, so does the Corfus Protectors, just like any rite of passage. Oh we have gun turrets, fitted with all the latest blasters we engineer ourselves, and we have small, quick fighters —Turkeys, we call them—so that if there ever comes a day when a galactic war breaks out, heavens forbid, then we'll be ready, on the frontlines. Ready to protect the Fritten from invaders. We've always been proud of how we defend the Fritten and been proud of how we pay our taxes, do our service, as good, if not better than anyone else. And so, when Gus and his men showed up, no one much liked it.

Of course, us Corfians being polite and hospitably as we were, we took them in, and gave them the repairs they needed. But I'm sure that there wasn't one man, woman or child in my village who wouldn't have been glad to have them out of the place as quickly as they'd come. Anyway, even though we got the repairs done sharpish, Gus complained about the cost—claiming that he should get it free, and he started throwing around his associations with Radley, as if that were any way to get into our good books. All it did was make us resent them even more. About that time, Gus started hanging around our farm: Buckles Ranch, never actually coming in, but he'd sit on the edge of the gate and suck on some pipe, blowing blue smoke into the air. I told my daddy lots of times, told him that he should get him to leave, but my daddy, well, he's a mild, old soul, said there wasn't anything much wrong about Gus sitting up there on the fence, and he could smoke his pipe to his heart's content. That's when I should've put my foot down—told him that he had to get him to leave. But I didn't.

Gus and his boys came for me in the middle of the night. I guess sitting up there on that fence he'd spent all his time studying our habits, above all working out which of the rooms in our farm house was mine. He brought his ship—repairs bill still unpaid—to hover over Buckles and he broke into my bedroom and dragged me away with them. I recall the few blaster beams that accompanied us out of the atmosphere. I knew—the Corfus Protectors being as efficient as they are—that they would have had the information that I was on board. All they could do was flex their muscles, but Gus knew they'd never dare shoot one of their own out of the sky. And so they took me.

Anyway, I told you that I'd end on a positive note, so let me tell you a little about my life on Buckles Ranch. It was a wonderful place really. It's funny that when I think back about it I don't remember any of the boredom, the yearnings I had to get off the planet and go and actually see something. That was always there I suppose. And I guess that's what I'm doing now. But, at the same time, I want to settle down there, I want to meet my husband back on Trivus-3, have my own ranch, bring up my kids there. They'd do all the things I'd done, join the Corfus Protectors, and I could help them through it—I can't describe it, it just feels like it's my duty. I have to put something back.

But the days, they're what I really miss. It seems weird to you all to think that I'm in my mid-twenties now and I just mooched about on my father's ranch all that time. But that's how it's done back there. You don't leave home until you're married, and sometimes we move into one of the family homes with our spouse. Maybe you both think that I'm a loser, but whatever, I was happy, and I want to go back when all this is said and done. I'd get up in the mornings, the light from Corfus would flow in through the window, sending a glow through everything. It's difficult to describe that phosphorescence, other than to say once it's gone you notice—the sheen leaves everything, like the magic's been stripped off it. Then I'd swing out of bed and go off to milk the cows. There's this apple tree I've always loved. In fact, at the base, I know this sounds stupid, but I've always kept a box of things buried there—things that are in important to me. I have family photos, some of my baby teeth, sentimental stuff like that. It's my secret place, and I've never told anyone about it till now. And, to be honest, I really don't know why I'm telling you at all. I guess you deserve to hear me speak from the heart, maybe you'll trust me then.

Later in the day I'd go with Dad into market and we'd sell whatever we had that morning: the milk and eggs, the herbs and spices Mum had picked from the garden, I just remember those smells, sitting in the wagon beside all our produce and feeling the warmth of the day on me. Maybe I could've existed like that forever if Gus had never shown up. But he did. And so, here we all are, awaiting our fates.

5: ON BOARD THE FSA-01061

"SO WHAT DO YOU THINK OF ME NOW?" she said.

I was still reeling from the story, not quite sure how to handle it actually. I mean, she had pretty much saved my life. I thought about being back in *The Bitch's* how Gus had had me around the neck till someone had snapped him out of it—obviously reminding them of the plan, to let Foy in first. That was when I started wondering whether there was more to the story between Foy and Gus, whether there was another dimension she was leaving out altogether. She had seemed to skim over most of their relationship beforehand and, from the way she talked about them, I got the impression she'd been kidnapped a fair time ago. She'd probably been privy to quite a few conversations on how to deal with me, how to pin all this on me. But the important thing was that *she'd* saved my life. Just as I'd saved hers.

I opened my eyes and forced myself upright, into a sitting

position. I looked her right in the eye and said, "Sister, I have no reservations. Not about you. You're just fine."

Even despite everything, being locked up here in a Fritters mother ship, she gave me a nice, pearly-white smile.

Bootfalls echoed their way along the corridor, catching all of our attention, bringing us back to reality. My old friend Reynolds appeared before us, looking much sterner than he had before, maybe someone had just told him the amount of data he'd have to file on me. Nothing like a bit of bureaucracy to take the buzz off a coup. He looked between us all, looking to Wodd first, then Foy before finally resting on me. "Captain," he said. "I can't find the stone anywhere."

I got to my feet. "I don't know what you're looking at me for."

"We *know* you have it. We've got extremely reliable intelligence declaring that. So it'll save your time and mine if you simply hand it over."

I glanced over Foy and Wodd, then shrugged at Reynolds. All I could do was tell the truth. As far as I was concerned the stone was still in its hiding place underneath my pilot's chair. But, whereas Wodd and his squad of customs agents had overlooked it, there seemed little to no chance a group of well-trained, if slightly inexperienced, FSA officers wouldn't find it. That said, I wasn't about to give everything up that easily. I can't say that I enjoy being arrested.

"Really," I said. "I have no idea where it might be."

Reynolds flushed and pressed his lips together, so that he resembled an angry radish. "Captain, you do realise that whether or not we find the stone will have no impact on you being set free? You're to be kept in our custody. We have reasonable suspicion to keep you imprisoned until such a time as the stone's found."

"You got any witnesses?"

"That's none of your concern."

"Well, quite frankly, if it's a question of my balls getting frozen off in Krykelseare, I think it is my business, actually."

Reynolds kept schtum, no doubt calling up all his training back at FSA Officer 101—Lesson One: The Silent Treatment.

I scratched the back of my neck. "Look here, I'm no lawyer but if you can't find any witnesses that say I did something I didn't do, and you can't find any evidence of whatever it is that I haven't stolen, then I can't see that you really have much of a case."

Still, the pursed lips, the scarlet skin tone.

"And under Fritten System Laws you can't hold me for longer than ten hours without pressing charges."

"Would you like me to press charges?"

"I really couldn't care less."

More silence, only the light crackle of the laser bars breaking total quiet.

"You know," Reynolds said, "we might have found *other* things on your ship, things which would be reason enough to charge you."

Now, I might be a jobbing smuggler—a little less than a top pro—but I do have a sense of professional pride, an entry-level standard that almost all of us abide by. And one of the basics of that standard consists of keeping the ship clean other than the contraband. The last thing you want if you're being tailed by a

Fritter is to have to be dumping all your goods right into their flight path, leaving a little trail of Christmas presents—or laying out the rope for your noose, whichever you prefer.

I snorted a laugh. "Yeah, but you haven't *found* anything, have you?"

No response from Reynolds.

"Didn't think so."

"My men will be checking out the weaponry, you do understand?"

I batted my hand. "Go ahead, knock yourselves out. Everything that's fitted to the *Nava* is well within regulations, and anything that ain't, well I'm always certain to disable it whenever I enter Fritten territory." I twitched my nose, thinking that I could feel a sneeze coming on—all this air conditioning necessary, I guessed, with all these men marching about in snug-fitting suits. "You must be getting really desperate if you're down to checking over my ship for regulations. Even if you do find something slightly over, there's no way it'll be something you can legally hold me for."

"Who said anything about doing this legally?"

"Well, why else have you been so reasonable so far?"

"Maybe I'm just a nice guy."

"Nah, you're only doing the bare minimum when it comes to courtesy—I know if it was up to you you'd have flushed us all out into space right away."

"Is that what you think of me?"

"You're an FSA captain, aren't you? Which, if you ask me, isn't really much of a captain at all."

Reynolds went real quiet after that and I could see that I'd touched a nerve. If there's one thing a captain really hates it's being told that he doesn't deserve his rank. And I know, from my own time in the FSA as a cadet, that the captains have a huge chip on their shoulder. When push comes to shove they'd much rather be off with the navy, flying into new territories, doing battle with rogue factions—anything not to just go trolleying around the Fritten System picking up small time crooks like me.

He did some more of his standing there silent and then turned on his heel and bucked back out of the holding area, not looking back once.

"Well," I said, to no one in particular, "looks like I've made a friend for life right there."

————

As it turned out, from the state of our dinner, I really hadn't. We each got given our energy pill after the mandatory five hours incarceration, but mine—and I guess Foy and Wood's too—tasted like ash in my mouth. I have no idea what they did to it, but I was sure that Reynolds was behind the treatment. Still, I got it down, not wanting to make any inroads into my belly—I wanted to stay as portly as possible. Then I looked to Foy. "Got any ideas about where that stone might be?"

Foy gave me a slight smile. "I've got no idea what you're talking about."

"Thought so. Have to say I'm getting to like you more and more."

Around what I presumed to be seventh or eighth hour,

Reynolds showed his face again, this time flanked by two particularly fresh-faced guards. Reynolds kept his arms down by his sides and shot me a handful of scowls.

That cheered me up no end. "Found what you were looking for?" I said.

He ignored me and turned to Wodd. "You. You're to come with us."

"What?" I said. "Why?"

"He's been confirmed as a citizen of Hortenine-6, and it appears that he has no clearance to have left the planet, much less to be here in the Fritten System."

"Oh no," I said. "He's staying with me."

Reynolds gave me a sliver of a smile. "Sorry, regulations are regulations."

The guards deactivated the laser bars and stepped through. Both of them took up their positions beside Wodd, ready to cuff him.

Something in the base of my stomach tweaked. Perhaps, most likely, it'd been that stodgy energy pill, but I like to think it was some sort of emotional response to Wodd's predicament, at least I think that's why I said, "You stand down, officers. He's with me."

"What did you say?" Reynolds said, looking a touch amused.

"I said he's with me, a member of my crew."

"Impossible, he has no registration to your ship, which is also true for this young lady here," he said, inclining his head in Foy's direction, "but at least she's from Trivus-3, Corfian, so she has permission to be *in* the Fritten System. What exactly she's doing on your ship is none of my concern, although it does implicate her in your affairs somewhat. As far as I'm concerned she's cargo."

If looks could kill Foy would've burnt a hole right through Reynolds's chest right then and there. I could see that Reynolds didn't quite know his way around women—because even I, as a body-odour-reeking smuggler, know that women don't like to be referred to as 'cargo.' Still, I had more pressing matters to see to, apart from defending Foy's honour.

"According to Protocol Eighteen, Section Nine, Part B, Subsection L: The captain of any interstellar vessel may commandeer, depending on his personal necessity, as determined by him or herself, the need to contract, up to a maximum of three, any crew which he believes to be of use in the safe operation of said ship—"

Reynolds opened his mouth to offer comment.

"Wait, I haven't finished," I said. ". . . Further along in the regulations, footnoted as 'Additional Information for Clarification Purposes,' it states that any such person who is taken on by said captain shall be exempt from any such rules on immigration or emigration provided that on entry to any port they present themselves in an official manner and pass through the regular channels for acquiring proper permission to be present in the appropriate authority—"

Again, Reynolds tried to break my flow, but I wasn't having any of it.

". . . And said crewmember's status shall be the responsibility of the captain, and the captain shall be responsible for all due clarification of the crewmember. Now," I said, starting to feel a little smug that I was out-regulating the regulator, "as I've seen fit to take on Clive Wodd here, then I'll be pleased for you to drop your threat to send him back to Hortenine-6."

Reynolds frowned, what was becoming his default facial expression. "The regulations also state that the captain must register such a new edition to the crew within a timely manner."

"And how would you define that? A 'timely manner?'"

"Well, I'd say it's open to interpretation."

"And, Captain, do you anticipate going through a lengthy tribunal to be a fun thing? Because I'd be prepared to do that if you *do* decide to send Mr Wood back to Hortenine."

"You won't have much chance for that when you're in Krykelseare."

"So why ain't I on my way there right now?"

No reply from Reynolds.

"That's what I thought. You've got nothing on me. You might as well let me free right now. If the only reason they made me 'most-wanted' out here was for that stone thing, then I guess you're going to have to spring me sooner or later, or do I need to get myself an advocate droid?"

Reynolds remained steeped in silence for several moments, meanwhile his inferiors awaited their commands, still not having been given their orders on what they were to do with Wodd. He called off his officers and left the holding area once more. Unfortunately he was of clear enough mind to reactivate the laser bars before he headed out.

———

To say that Wodd was gushing at my sticking up for him right then is really not to put too finer point on it. He was opened up wide, just about kissing and hugging me, leaping about me like a puppy just given a ninth hour reprieve from neutering. I did my best to be humble, telling him that, really, it had been nothing, and that he was more than welcome—and really I was honoured to have someone of his technical prowess aboard the *Nava*. All things considered, what with Foy's shooting skills, Wodd's hacking and my all-round nous as a weathered space smuggler, I thought I was getting a pretty nice little team together. The only missing piece of the puzzle was the small matter of the ship itself. But, as it turned out, things were taking care of themselves.

Well, it was just a case of waiting out the ten hours, and, sure enough, just like the stickler for rules Reynolds clearly was, he popped up with his same two officers and let us out of the holding cell. Sometimes I just love the liberal system of the Fritten. Yeah sure, there are some bad things with that threat of Krykelseare hanging over everything but they're pretty good about not holding people when there're no charges. And, since there was no evidence of what I'd done, and it didn't look like they would turn up anything any time soon, they had to let us go.

It was weird to walk back through the *FSA-0106I* without the cuffs from before, as a free man. Reynolds actually got pretty talkative on the way back. He gave me a sidelong glance and said, "I looked over your service record. It was a while ago but it's pretty impressive. There might've been a good job waiting you in the FSA if you'd wanted it."

"Well, thanks, I appreciate it," I said, feeling a degree warmer towards Reynolds.

"Just makes me think why someone with such a bright future as you would throw it all away."

We reached the walkway which led off to the *Nava*. I glanced down it, really wanting to get back at the controls to my ship and to fly away from this FSA fleet as quick as I possibly could. But I knew that Reynolds wanted some sort of explanation, so I decided to give it to him. "I guess it depends on what your perspective is, don't it? I mean, for some it's working their way up through some structure like the FSA, getting all them pretty medals"—I nodded to the jingling shrapnel pinned to the chest of his uniform—"or maybe you can just go out and see something of the universe." I swallowed hard, knowing it was always difficult to admit when I'd overstepped the mark a little and said, "Look, no hard feelings about what I said about FSA captains, that was out of order, I think. Just want you to know that. I know it takes commitment to get where you've got to. I mean, wow, you've got a few hundred men under your command, that ain't bad going, is it?"

Reynolds cracked a smile then held out his hand. "Thanks," he said. "I appreciate it."

I accepted his handshake, a little taken off guard by its firmness. I'd expected Reynolds to be a sloppy handshaker, all limp-wristed and that. Guess he proved me wrong. "Be seeing you around, I suppose."

"Let's hope we don't meet again."

I grinned. "All right, Captain, thanks for your hospitality."

We marched up the walkway sharpish and got ourselves

back through the airlock, and into the *Nava*. As I sat back at the controls, taking up my place at the control stick, bringing down the navigational screen, I noticed that all the damage meters were back on green—that the ship had been repaired. Well, that just rounded off my view of Reynolds. I guessed I'd completely misjudged him. He was a good guy after all. A little stuck up, perhaps, but a good guy nonetheless.

Foy took up her, now familiar, position at my side, in the co-pilot's seat, while Wodd took up the position at the engineering panel, giving an overview on all the ship's wellbeing—looking after all that technical crap I'd never much ever paid attention to. If there's another thing you learn quick as a space smuggler it's that there's always a half-decent mechanic within a light year, or so, one that'll know why your ship's making that weird *clunking* sound. But having Wodd on board was totally different because, in my book, he was nothing short of a boy genius. He would go far I could tell and, I wagered, he might well get himself around to convincing me that we could lead a strike on Hortenine-6. I had to keep my guard up on that one, because if there's one thing I really hate, it's a suicide mission.

Just as I tested the thrusters, all in perfect working order, Foy gave me a nudge in the ribs with her elbow, broke into a smile and then opened her mouth. Right there, beneath her tongue was the Stone of the Angels, all nestled there, safe and sound. Wow, was I glad that they'd never thought to do a thorough cavity search, in fact, I wondered whether Reynolds had overlooked that at all. Something told me that Reynolds was a man doing his job, but perhaps it wasn't a job he quite relished.

He would probably cop a bit of flack for letting us go, but his hands had been tied. Fritten System regulations bound him.

I slumped back in my chair, feeling all confident and full of beans. I glanced at the vidscreen as the FSA fleet disappeared off behind us. Not bad for a day's work, all told, I'd managed to get my name scratched off the most-wanted list and made some headway on working out who was behind all this business with trying to kill me. With any luck, working together, we could make some further progress on this Stone-of-the-Angels thing or, at the very least, work out how we might be able to make a buck or two.

6: FRONTIERS OF FRITTEN

THE *NAVA* JUST POUNDED through space, as she's wont to do, and we put some serious distance between us and the FSA fleet. While my appreciation for Reynolds had grown I had no illusions that high command might send him orders to pursue us, bring us in again for another grilling once the mandatory recapture period of ten hours had elapsed. The least we could do was make it difficult for him to find us. As it happened, after Wodd ran a scan on the message to Susie from Kools, we followed the trail all the way to the frontiers of Fritten, where it would take a whole FSA fleet quite a while to get organised and shoot off to. I was pretty happy that we'd be safe around there . . . for the time being.

The navigational screen showed up that we were approaching Yightly-21, the last planet in the Fritten System. It seemed that lonerism ran in Kools's family or whatever relation Susie had to Kools. We got accosted by a small pilot ship, barrelling out up to us from the atmosphere. I have to admit I was so jumpy at that point that I had Foy on standby, crosshairs set on the ship approaching us. Once they'd checked out our info, though, we were good to go. I'd actually put through Wodd's registration to the *Nava*, had him struck off from his old job, during the journey to Yightly—so he was all good to go, my responsibility now. It was kind of like being the president of a three-person country. Not that I was getting any ideas of false grandeur.

All things considered, Yightly-21 being right out there in the sticks, they had a pretty nice terminal. In fact I guessed that it saw a bit of use considering they had no less than a dozen ports. We got our clearance for Gamma Port, lucky number seven, I hoped that would be a good omen, or something. As I set the *Nava* down I was pleased to note that they had none of the customs officers which had plagued Hortenine, then again our navigational computer showed we'd just got in from within the Fritten System, so ostensibly they had nothing to worry about.

Wodd stopped me in the middle of locking up the *Nava*, broke off one of the electronic panels and scrabbled away there, meshing wires together and dialling stuff on the keypad. I was beyond bothering to ask what he was up to now—I could simply assume whatever complex and tedious thing he was doing it was for the benefit of the *Nava*, and her crew.

We left the *Nava* behind and emerged into a thick, humid day. Almost immediately I started sweating. Beads of sweat rolled down the wrinkles in my forehead and sticky patches formed themselves at my armpits. I supposed that the atmospheric controls were on the blink, or something. As is often the case in places out of the way like those, it's harder to get hold of a good engineer for the really complicated stuff—like atmospheric regulators. Still, it's a wonder that those outer planets don't invest as much in education as the central sections of the Fritten. Then again, different values, different people. It's what makes us all great. Or that's what they say.

At the side of the port an elderly man was making demon trade with a bunch of moisture decanters—self-sealed bags of water. We immediately bought a dozen. I knocked back three or four in record time. That's the problem with having a bit of sag about you, makes you sweat by the bucket load. We proceeded to ask directions off one of the assistants in the terminal, waving the address Wodd had managed to garnish from the handheld communicator. She gave us a bunch of almost unintelligible instructions—that we'd have to get the magnet railway to an outer district, almost all involving different coloured lines, and her including every little detail about how the schedule worked and how the blue line wouldn't necessarily take us to our first change, depending on whether or not it was before or after fifth hour. In the end I opted for my well-worn approach: fling it all and hope for the best. It's also, usually, a trustworthy way of running into trouble. And we did that too. Quite quickly, even by my standards.

What happened was we were standing on the platform, waiting for the magnet train to swoop in—with that satisfying *zip-bop!* sound it makes, well I find it satisfying anyway—when we were accosted by a kid about twelve or thirteen. I was standing there, trying to make head or tail of the screen showing the arrival of the next train, minding my own business, when what do I know but I feel a tiny hand patting its way up the side of my jacket then, swiftly, snatching hold of my blaster, tugging it free from its holster. I watched as the kid made off through the people, blaster and all.

Now, different planets have different regulations on weaponry, whether it can be carried or not, and although I got the impression that Yightly might well be the former, that even if the blaster fell into the hands of the authorities and they traced it back to me, I decided that I couldn't face down having had a kid run off with my blaster. Not to mention that I might need it at some point of this current excursion, I knew that I'd be a laughing stock when I returned to *The Bitch's*, if I ever got the chance to do so, if Radley's hatred of me was to be believed.

The kid had long hair, down in a plait so that when he ran it bobbed against his lower back.

I just about emitted something along the lines of a "Yaw-kaw!" when I set off running, hearing Foy and Wodd beating along behind me, following close on my heels. The little bugger had some serious dodging skills—I guessed that I wasn't even his first target that day. And, all the more annoyingly, he knew the terrain well. He led us away from the platform, up spiralling automatic staircases, then back around again. I kept sight of him despite my heart bobbing in my chest, warning me that I might keel over at any given moment. I had to get my hands back on that blaster. No way in hell was I going to get beaten by a kid. And just as those thoughts lingered on my mind, we lost him in the crowd.

Wodd sidled up beside me, panting away. "What did he take?"

"My blaster," I said.

"Damn."

Foy batted her fringe from her eyes. "Does it really matter? I mean, don't you have others on the ship?"

"Yeah, but it's the principle. What happens if I start letting little kids getting away with mugging me, what's next, eh? Will they be bouncing about all over the *Nava*? Pinching my energy tablets?"

Foy twitched her mouth. "He's probably taking it to a fence —some older guy who's told him—"

"I'm a smuggler!" I said. "I know what a 'fence' is!"

"All right," she said, rolling her eyes. "Just trying to be helpful."

Wodd pointed through the thronging crowd, mostly businessmen and women dressed in uniform—what kind of business they got up to on Yightly I have no idea, but I know never to underestimate the Man's ability to create office work. I saw where Wodd was pointing to, a conspicuous-looking ventilation duct. I had a moment's hesitation, running through all the mental calculations, trying to work out whether I could squeeze my sizeable mass through that space. I decided that, with my pride at stake, I would have to. Now I'd made a scene, that Foy and Wodd had witnessed me getting robbed by a kid, and subsequently chasing after him, I had to show that I wouldn't be pushed around. I was their captain after all.

And so, to the sound of much dissuading in my ears, I made for the tiny ventilation duct—growing tinier with each step toward it—I whipped out my multi-tool and prised it off. As it turned out, it was only hanging by a single screw so it wasn't hard going. With the assistance of Foy and Wodd pushing my buttocks through the gap, I got myself through, emerging—thankfully—into a slightly wider area: the ventilation tunnels.

I looked around in the blackness. When I spoke the tunnels gave each word a metallic *twang*, I kind of liked it—made me think what it might be like if I was a robot. "Which way do we go, then?"

Foy and Wodd descended into silence.

"No suggestions?" I said, then squinted through the gloom, trying to make out something that might give us a clue as to where the kid had disappeared off to. Again, with nothing forthcoming, I resorted to my old reliable decision-making paradigm. "This way," I said, sounding way more certain than I actually felt. And the funny thing with confidence is—if you fake it—most people just go along. I really should get to writing that book, shouldn't I?

We carried on along the ventilation tunnel, me, in the absence of a blaster, holding out the old-fashioned steel blade to fend off any attackers. I don't know how many hostiles I thought I'd encounter in that ventilation unit, but I stayed on my guard all the same.

After a certain point the ground sloped away from us. Unperturbed, I carried on. Neither Foy nor Wodd thought to complain either, and I got to thinking that they'd make decent inferior officers at that rate. We kept going down, further down, until we got to a wide open space. It took a couple of sniffs to confirm where exactly we'd arrived, and my nostril hair was greeted by the stench of raw sewage. Why is it that I always end up in the sewage works just about everywhere I go?

We kept to the side of the ruddy-brown coloured canal. Every so often a heaving, great wave burbled along and soaked our trouser legs. I murmured a few words of apology each time it happened—feeling more than a little responsible for having dragged us all down here after my blaster. However, before our spirits got too deadened, we happened upon a light at the end of the tunnel—after all we'd been through up to that point I wondered whether it might be heaven or some such. As we got closer I observed that it was a flickering light. Whoever was down here was using a dodgy fluorescent, one of the cheap, old models. The ones that burn through energy like there's no tomorrow. That kind of waste always pisses me off. I mean, I might not be the most moral person in the galaxy, but the new, efficient technology is pretty available, and no more expensive than the older stuff, so why not save a tree or two? Some people just don't give two shits about the universe, that's what it boils down to.

I murmured for both Foy and Wodd to be quiet, to follow my lead, when, in truth, it was my boots that were making a pretty ridiculous *squelch* sound. I guess I must've taken on a bit of the sewage during one of those tidal surges. Nonetheless, it didn't look like the headquarters was that guarded. But why would it be? It's not like a spaceport where you've got to lock down your ship considering the amount of traffic passing through—pretty much all you'll find in the sewers are cleaning droids.

We stole closer to them and turned the corner. I caught

sight of the place up ahead. It was no more than a gap in the wall, which the flickering naked bulb lit up. I guessed this was where the kid hid himself away. I held Foy and Wodd back, counting on my fingers, grinning a touch in anticipation of the surprise we were going to give this kid, and then I burst into action, rounding the corner, multi-tool outstretched.

With a *whiffle* of material a large, thick sack descended on all three of us and everything went dark.

———

An ominous *cackle* accompanied the lifting of the sack. My first thought was that all the lights had gone out—or the *one* light. I looked about me, intent on finding out who was doing all the laughing, and maybe sticking his teeth down his throat for good measure.

"What're you doing down here, laddies?"

I spun around, locating the source of the voice, up above our heads. I picked out the vague silhouette and stepped toward them.

"That'll do you, right there, I wouldn't take another step unless you want me to plant you one right between the eyes."

So this guy had my blaster. At least I'd established that much. Then I caught sight of the kid, standing beside the main figure.

"Me and my boy have been down here a long while without visitors—might I be so bold as to ask what you want down here in our domain?"

"Your *boy* stole my blaster."

"Too bad."

"Well, no, that's not the thing, is it? You're going to hand it back over or I'm going to make you."

"You got another blaster between you, then? Because all I saw of you coming in here was with that piddly little multi-tool. If that's all you've got to bring to the table I'd hop it if I were you."

"Not till I get my gun back."

Foy spoke up. "Look, isn't there something we can bargain with? You must want something we've got. It's not like that blaster's worth much anyway."

The man kept still, continuing to point the blaster down at us. Right around that time I wondered whether he'd had the sense to click the safety off, if I'd even thought to click it on in the first place. I decided that it might be just a little too risky to try and work that out. As I said, I'm not really one for experimentation where firearms are involved, better to play it safe, especially when unstable individuals are thrown into the mix.

"Okay," Foy said, stepping out in front of me. "How's about the Stone of the Angels?"

"Say what?" he said.

"You heard me fine."

There was a pause and then he said, "You're bluffing."

"Can you be sure?"

The man spoke to his boy in his local dialect and the boy skittered off somewhere into the darkness. Moments later, the light bulb flickered on and I could get a good view of our assailant. He wore a tatty black robe which exposed a chest of black hair failing to conceal bulbous man bosoms. He held the blaster in his crooked hand, his fingers skeletal as they gripped it, primed to squeeze the trigger. He had a twitch. Every ten seconds or so, he would shake his head and erratically rub his face against his shoulder. That might well be our opportunity right there. Or a very palpable danger. We'd have to wait and see.

True to her word, Foy removed the stone from beneath her tongue and held it flat on her palm. She looked to our assailant and waited expectantly.

"Bring it up here," he said.

"You'll shoot me," she said.

"Nah, promise I won't if you step up here. But if you don't bring it right now I *can* promise that I'll shoot one of your friends here. How's that sound?"

Foy shrugged and climbed the steps up to where he stood. She held her hand out for him to see.

The man leant in to look closely. His eyes flicked up to meet Foy's. "Man, you're not joking at all, are you?"

"Would I lie to you?"

"Well, I don't know, I've just met you, haven't I?"

Meanwhile, during this exchange, I watched the kid keeping himself to the fringes of the area, up against one of the concrete walls. I decided that this might be my opportunity to make a move—something to work as back up if Foy's idea didn't quite go to plan. Slowly, I trod my way around the arena, trying to make it look like I'd found a particularly interesting piece of brickwork.

The kid continued to watch on, head tilted back to watched his father pawing over the Stone of the Angels, holding it up to the light. He was utterly transfixed. Then, in a swift movement, I grabbed the kid from behind, taking hold of his sprawling limbs as quickly as possible. The kid cried out and, in the panic, his father dropped the Stone of the Angels. I watched on as Foy scooped up the stone and rushed back down to where Wodd stood, leaving the kid's father up on his own—only clutching my blaster.

This seemed to bring out something of a nervous fit in the guy. He flinched several times over and did his head jerk thing. Finally, he got a hold on himself, shakily pointing the blaster at me and the boy. "You . . . you tricked me!"

I held on strong to the kid, anchoring him with my weight. He was going nowhere. His slender frame, and malnourished form were no contest for my tonnage. I looked up to his father. "Blackmail's not very nice when it's put the other way around, is it?"

The man blinked several times. "I . . . I . . . I'll shoot you all!" he said.

"Easy now," I said. "No one's going to get shot. Now this is much fairer. I've got the kid, you've got my blaster. Let's make a trade."

"No!" the man said.

"What do you mean, 'no?' I've got your kid here. Don't you want him?"

"No," the man said, sounding more in control than he did before. "He's just another mouth to feed, more trouble than he's worth."

I squirmed a little at his words—even if he was acting out of some sort of desperation, not wanting to be made a fool of, I knew that the kid would remember what his father had just said for years to come. I know that my father's words about how I'd thrown my life away by leaving the FSA still stung me for years later. Still sting me even now.

"Na—now hand him over or I'll shoot you all dead!"

I studied the quivering features of the man, trying to get a hold on whether he really had what it took, whether he was truly out on a limb. He must've been coming down off something. What else could've got into his warped mind that he could possibly have the upper hand here?

And then, all of a sudden, the man let off a shot. The beam sizzled through the air and I felt its heat sear past my shoulder. If I had moved an inch either side he would've got me. That first shot seemed to release the floodgates, because after that he just went wild. He shot off the blaster every which way, sending us all scattering. The kid turned from my hostage to being my protectee. I dived to the ground, out of the line of fire, and I watched on as Wodd and Foy did the same. The maniac's cackles resounded around the area, sending shivers down my spine and blood rushing to my head. I got a hold of the kid's wrist and managed to drag him from the area, back out to the sewage canals. Once I had us safe, I checked back for Wodd and Foy, who were making a good job of dodging the beams. They got themselves out too, drawing the fire toward where we all stood.

There was a nasal *whirring* along the tunnel and I looked up to see a cleaning droid, as large as four refrigerators, making its way towards us, its mechanical arms outstretched, wiping the walls and dabbling its feet into the stream of sewage. Despite all the action I had a humanising moment of sympathy—who would be a cleaning droid?—before snapping to my senses and ordering us all to jump aboard.

As it hummed up beside us, its fans obliterating the sounds of the blaster firing away, I tugged the boy up onto its back and set him down beside me. Foy and Wodd hauled themselves up too. The cleaning droid made its way gradually along the tunnel, gradually enough for us to see the boy's father emerge from the gap in the wall, blaster still firing, eyes still crazy. Luckily his aim was pretty off and he shot the dirtied water mainly. The boy tried to jump off a few times, but I kept him still. No way was I going to let him go back to that maniac, not yet anyway. Not till I got my blaster back and he calmed himself down. Most people *do* calm down considerably once they've been disarmed—especially if they're not used to carrying weapons.

The cleaning droid carried us up and away, out of the sewers and, after a series of labyrinthine tunnels, into the clear light of day.

7: YIGHTLY-21

BRIGHT DAYLIGHT STUNG MY EYES. I held up my arm to shield them, still grasping the kid with my other. We emerged into a flat area busy with hundreds and hundreds of other cleaning droids, all swooping back and forth, programming and reprogramming their destinations. They deposited their waste into the trenches beneath us, to be washed away and processed out of sight. As our own cleaning droid approached its drop-off point, we hopped off and skittered around the edge of the sludge fields, doing our best not to fall in. The kid seemed to have quietened down somewhat. I supposed he hadn't much been out of the subterranean world his father kept him cooped up in, so he was probably struck by the magnitude of the outside. When I was sure he wasn't going to do something stupid, go running off, trying to get back to his father through the tight, and grotty, tunnel we'd just emerged from, I released him. He wobbled a bit as if he might be about to faint, and then he found his feet and took his time in looking around him.

I looked over Wodd and Foy. "What do we do now?" I said.

Foy crouched down and touched the boy on his forearm. "Would you like to stay with us for a while, come with us on a bit of an adventure? We promise we'll take you back to your dad later. It's just"—she looked to me and Wodd for support, but obviously, us being pretty useless men without any real parental skills, she didn't find what she was looking for—"just that we can't take you back to him just yet. He seems to be having a funny episode, doesn't he?"

But the boy remained transfixed by the plethora of droids bumbling back and forth. I guess his world was pretty small down there with his father. His child's mind might never in its wildest imaginings considered there could be more than the single cleaning droid which passed by their home. And now his eyes were truly being opened.

"What's your name, kid?" I said.

"Milky."

"'Milky?'" I said, somewhat perplexed.

"Yeah."

I guess, with a drug-addled father like he had it followed that he wouldn't be called something normal, like Jake or Tom. But, still, 'Milky?' Really? Before I got the chance to make some out-of-place crack about it, however, Foy got her own comment in to the boy.

"We're off looking for someone," she said. "Her name's Susie. Do you know anyone called Susie?"

Milky shook his head.

"Well, that's okay. We've got her address already, maybe you can help us with that."

A glazed look passed over Milky's face and my suspicion that he might not be the best person to ask when it came to information on Yightly-21, at least the area above ground, proved true.

"All right," she said, readjusting her expectations. "Then I guess you can just tag along and we'll see if there's something you can do to help out on the way."

"Okay," Milky said.

Throughout all this I thought about the kid's previous reaction, how he'd near enough broken my arm trying to get back to his father. Now, though, he seemed much calmer. I'd have to keep my eye on him, but I was beginning to think that, most likely, he was okay. Only time would tell, I supposed.

Thankfully we had no need to take another magnet railway and we hailed a private hire hovercab which carried us right to Susie's front door. Right there and then I told myself that I wouldn't be taking public transport for a while. Taxis on unknown planets seemed to be the way forward.

I don't know what I'd been expecting of Susie's house—I guess, having been to Kools's place I was thinking that it would be all raggedy, have that lived in feel—so imagine my surprise when it appeared as nothing less than a mansion, painted a pleasant light-yellow, with thick marble arches either side of the front door. There was a series of animal shapes sculpted out of the garden hedges: turtles, monkeys, dolphins, a horse. You can tell a lot about a person by their garden, usually the most basic analysis is whether or not they've got one—I don't have one. Anyway, we slogged our way up to the front door, rang and were promptly invited inside by someone who I guessed to be the butler: what with his beady eyes and smart suit. He escorted us into a sitting room near the front of the house and served us all water, *in glasses*, before mumbling something about Susie being occupied and wandering off into the house.

The room contained a sitting room set: sofa, armchairs and a tidy coffee table. Bookshelves, stuffed near to bursting, lined the walls, and the air had that woody smell of warmed up paper. With nothing else to do while we waited for Susie, I decided to peruse the collection. Most of the names were unfamiliar . . . okay, all of them were unfamiliar to me, but with a space smuggler what were you expecting, a university professor? Nonetheless, one of the titles did catch my eye. It was lying on its side on the shelf, obviously not quite fitting with the other books, and it seemed that it had just been left there and forgotten. I read the name off the spine: Fonch. Same yellow colour scheme as that wrapper I'd found in *The Bitch's*, what Gus and his guys had left behind, and beside Kools's body. I reached for it and opened it up. As it turned out it wasn't a book at all. Inside was nestled an electronic document reader. I glanced around the room to see Wodd, Foy and Milky all over by the window, looking out over the remarkable view—all rolling green hills, spotted with cattle and sheep—and then clicked the reader on.

The first few pages were nothing noteworthy, just some dull accounting information, overviews of various financial years, until I recognised a name listed there: Lionel Fox. I scanned it back and forth, thinking it over. Lionel Fox, otherwise known as Kools. The entry listed a number, which I recognised as the format for naming a moon, and it specified its transfer to him. So Kools had owned that moon?

Just as I was wondering what Kools might have to do with a sweet manufacturer, a voice with round, dulcet tones carried from the door. "I'm terribly sorry to have kept you waiting, but, I suppose, I had no knowledge that I might be having visitors today."

I near enough dropped the Fonch tome, but I kept myself together enough, still with my back to the voice, to replace the document reader—and its case—back on the shelf. I think I was subtle enough about it, but who can ever be sure? When I turned around I took in the woman standing there. She wore a purple gown and had on long silver earrings. Her hair was dyed a cosmic-blue to match her eyes, while her skin looked unnaturally fresh, tight, for a woman of her age—surely around fifty or sixty. Susie.

She stepped forth into the room and approached Foy, who was smiling away, generally being as charming as possible. "Pleased to meet you, dear," Susie said, swooping to kiss her on both cheeks. Then she turned her attention to Wodd and did the same before administering a pat on the head to Milky. When she caught a glance at me I noted a quick flash of disgust—gone in the blink of an eye. I'm used to that. I'd be first to admit that I'm not the most-presentable of men. But, then again, in my business that's really not all that important. The longer your beard, the larger the gut and the muskier your body odour the better your pay rates. Or so goes the joke.

"And you," she said, looking me up and down, "you must be the *captain*."

The way she said it, drew out my title, made it sound exotic, out of the ordinary—as if I was some sort of buccaneer who'd just dropped anchor in port, ripe for adventure and debauchery. I have to say that I kinda quite liked it.

"Susie, I presume?" I said, noting that she didn't make any move to grace me with kisses, as she had done with Wodd and Foy. And I'd gone to all the trouble of washing that week. Still had the scrunchie beard and lardy gut though.

"Yes," she said, her eyes wandering over the bookshelves, no doubt wondering whether or not I'd pilfered something. She turned her attention back to me. "And so, how might I be of service to you?"

"I've come to ask about Kools."

"I'm sorry, who?"

"Lionel Fox."

Her skin blemished a touch and her eyes ebbed away into the middle distance. "What"—she paused, batting her eyelashes —"would you like to know about him?"

"I suppose you've heard the news?"

"'News?' What 'news?'"

Now coming all the way out to Yightly-21 and making an old lady cry just really wasn't my biscuit. But it seemed, now I had piqued her interest, I really had no other option except to continue. "Um," I said. "Lionel's dead, ma'am."

She blinked a couple of times in rapid succession and then

looked down to a hand-woven rug. "I see," she said. "Yes, I did think it might only be a matter of time."

I cleared my throat. "I was a colleague of his, in a way, and I wondered what your connection might be. You see, we found his handheld communicator at his side," I said, pulling it from my pocket and handing it over, "with this message addressed to you. We followed the coordinates to your home right here."

She took the handheld communicator from me and ran her eyes over the message. She coloured slightly. Her eyes watered. "And what business is this of yours?"

"Well, ma'am, you see, the thing is that I believe those men, the ones that killed Lionel, want to kill me too."

"How ghastly."

"Yes, but that's just the nature of the thing, ain't it?"

She glowered.

"I mean, 'isn't it?'" I waited a beat and then added, "So, do you have any idea of what those men might've been up to, who might've had reason to kill Lionel?"

"None."

"I see."

Susie gripped the handheld communicator tight and pressed her lips together. Just as I thought she might be ready to beat a tearful, hasty retreat, and to have her butler turn us out of her home, she looked back up at me and said, "You know, I was always telling Lionel that he was better not getting mixed up in all those things."

"What 'things,' ma'am?"

"Oh, he said that it was a good job—a safe job. All he had to do was take up a post on that Godforsaken moon and wait until he was called for, like a dog. He told me all about the money, that he would be making a killing doing nothing. But it was never about the money. If he'd wanted money he'd only to ask me. I guess he just liked what he was doing being involved in all of *that*."

"And what's 'that?'"

"Those *gangsters*."

So I guessed that my initial thoughts on Radley being behind this was being proved true. It was all beginning to add up to me. I had to ask the question that had been itching away at me throughout the whole icy meeting. "Was Lionel your husband?"

She snorted a laugh and then shook her head. "Oh no, thank goodness. No, he was my brother-in-law. My sister, she died a long time ago, as did my own husband. So, I suppose you could say that we always looked out for one another, despite being very different people. We were drawn together over our linked tragedies."

"Forgive me asking."

"Not at all," she said, brightening a little. "The memories are all I've got left now, so it's nice to revisit them once in a while."

Thinking about dead people just about gets my stomach knotted right up to my chest, but who was I to interrupt this old lady's sadness?

I glanced around my troops, to Foy, Wodd and Milky, then I nodded to Susie. "Thanks for your time, ma'am, it's been great to get your thoughts on all this. Helped me a great deal."

"You're welcome, Captain."

"We'll be going now, leaving you in peace to your afternoon."

"I'd offer you all a bedroom or two for the night but, you see, my house staff are on leave for the week. It's all a bit of a state up there."

"That really would be too kind and I appreciate the sentiment. We'll be going now."

I was last to leave the room and, as I did so, I got a glance back over my shoulder.

Susie stood with her back to me, looking at the bookshelf. It took me a second or so to realise that she was inspecting something there—the tome on the Fonch accounts. Had she seen me leafing through it or was I just being paranoid? What did it matter anyway? From what she'd told me, perhaps she was accustomed to Kools leaving stuff around her. Most likely she'd never even seen it before. She'd probably go around for a fair few months finding various relics of Kools's involvement with Radley scattered about the house. In some way it makes me glad to think that I have no ties, not in this whole universe. No loose ends. Nothing for anyone to get sad over.

———

"Well, where to now, Captain?" Wodd said, as we stepped out through the neat garden gate and onto the road leading back up to the magnet rail station.

I chewed on my tongue and looked to the sky. Perfect weather. All clear. White rose-tinted sky and the smell of freshly cut grass lingering on the air. And I'd have had a chance to enjoy all of that if I wasn't certain that someone, somewhere, was determined to see me dead.

We wandered on through a series of market stalls, multi-coloured canvas with hawkers mumbling at us, trying to get us to buy their wares. We got through the markets having bought a bag of some slimy snail-like bugs which the hawker had assured us were 'delicious.' If nothing else, for all my travelling through the universe, I try to keep an open mind, to try new things, to sample new cultures, but those bugs. Damn. They were something else. Call me crazy, but when I popped one in my mouth I presumed it was dead. How wrong I was. That damn bug leapt to life and bit the side of my mouth. I doubled up and stuck my fingers in my mouth, trying to drag the thing out, without much success. Only after I'd had help from Milky—if not initiated in Yightly-21, at least used to these bugs—did I manage to get it out of my mouth. I spat it out in a splatter of blood then left the rest of the bag to the others. If they wanted to risk their lives that was their prerogative.

As we returned to the central station, the magnet rail station where I'd been pickpocketed by Milky earlier on that day, I brought us all off in the direction of the ventilation duct and we headed off down into the sewers to reunite Milky with his daddy. Another, saner, man might've decided to simply hop onto his spaceship and jet away, but I felt a sense of responsibility for the kid. Since I'd argued with myself that I had taken him away from his daddy in the first place for his own protection, it only made sense to bring him back now to see if things couldn't be patched up now his daddy wasn't high as a kite.

We stomped along the sludge canal, while Milky perked up,

clearly glad to be getting home. One thing I've observed from a distance, not being a parent myself—at least to my knowledge—is the incredible capacity kids have to forgive their parents. Just about anything. I've seen kids slapped about, sent out to work all day, not given enough to eat, and then they just go crawling back when it's all over. Hell, even I forgave my parents for making me do military service. Guess I had the last laugh on that one.

As we turned the corner into that blasted-out area where we'd had the standoff with Milky's dad, something didn't feel right. I guess it was the quiet. By nature I'm quite a loud person, I'd be the first to admit that—what with all manner of burping, farting and other body sounds from orifices unknown—but even I felt that silence. Now, thinking about it, it was just that. The sound of death.

So when we looked in on the area and saw Milky's dad lying there, prostrate, arms taut and face curled into an eternal scream, it was more or less what I suspected. Milky was desolate, of course. In fact he went ape shit.

Milky clawed at his dad's chest, the blaster hole which, I couldn't help noting, was identical to the one I had seen in Kools—the same gun. And then, when he'd worn himself out sobbing, he just lay across his father's body shivering.

While Foy and Wodd consoled Milky, I had a look around the area, trying to find my blaster. Although I couldn't find it anywhere, I did find what I supposed to be the living quarters of Milky and his dad before. There were two soiled, brown blankets—screwed up sacks really—lying across a pair of mattresses which had surely been salvaged from the sewage channel, and had a stench to match. Through all the emotion pouring out from Milky, I knew that this had never been the life for him. Who would put their son through something like this? I knew that I could offer him a better life than he would've had with his father. I would accept him as another member of my crew—bringing our number up to the more standard four, for a ship the size of the *Nava* anyway.

And then my thoughts turned to more urgent matters, to wondering who in the universe would have decided to come down here, into the particularly unpleasant belly of Yightly-21 and murder some burnt-out junkie in cold blood. Okay, so the guy had a blaster—my blaster, but would they really have killed him for it? Just a standard gun like that? Maybe that was possible but there was really only one conclusion I could reach, and that was that someone had been following me—and had meant to kill me.

I gathered the others together and we made our way back out of the sewers. Before we could, though, Milky insisted that we place his father's body on the manky blankets they'd used to sleep before and wrap him up. With that done we carried him between us up to the side of the canal where we deposited him on the waging sewage, frothing away below us. I watched as Milky's dad slipped below the grungy tide and felt bad for Milky. As for me, though, as I've said before, I find it difficult to empathise with those that have tried to kill me. Perhaps I've got some inbuilt, out-of-whack sense of karma. Or maybe I'm just a rotten, cold-hearted bastard.

———

With Milky's dad dead, there was only one thought on my mind, that we had to get back to the old lady's house, to go and see Susie. It seemed logical to me that they would come out to take care of us both—to try and paper over the cracks of the job they'd botched before. So, we found ourselves, again, shooting around bends at hundreds of kilometres an hour, whipping up and down slopes toward Susie's house. Everyone was silent. I watched as Foy held Milky's head to her chest, running her hand through his hair like a surrogate mother. Wodd, on the other hand, looked tense. And, to be honest, I couldn't blame him. Looking back it might've been an idea to leave the three of them back on the *Nava* while I made my inquiries, but I just didn't trust that they'd be safe there. These guys had attempted to blow my ship out of the sky once already, so they had no reason not to do it again.

We got to the station, moved quickly through the markets—past the salesman looking to sell us another bag of those snail bugs—and bombed along the pavement, headed for Susie's house. And, just like a nightmare, it unfurled right before my eyes.

The pepper of blaster fire cut through the otherwise tranquil atmosphere clinging to Susie's street. I stood my ground, blood frozen in my veins, at the same time knowing that I myself was unarmed. I looked about for any sign of police, but there was none. We'd got here too late. The best thing to do now was to turn around, go back to the terminal and take off into space. I could steer clear of the Fritten System till all this blew over, that would've been a coward's plan, but a plan nonetheless. Instead, though, being as stupid as I look, I ventured along the pavement, drawing closer to the house. I told the others to hang back, but none of them obeyed me, following on my heels.

I weaved my way up the garden path to the front door, which I found to be hanging off its hinges. The distinct smell of fried electrics—blaster shots—lingered on the air. Everything else looked pretty much as it had when we'd left earlier. I heard voices through the house, someone obviously alarmed. Perhaps they'd heard my footfall on the garden path. Then the sounds of scrabbling as they passed through the house. All right, I might be stupid, but at least then I saw enough sense to hold back, not to chase them out of there, unarmed as I was.

Glass tinkled as they broke their way out the back and beat a hasty retreat. I counted off the seconds, not wanting to run into them—for them to see who I was. Not yet anyway. Sure that they'd got away from the house, I proceeded into the sitting room, the one with the bookshelves, where we'd met Susie. Instinctively, I eyed the shelves and realised that the Fonch tome was gone. The guy, or guys, who'd come here had swiped the accounts log.

I steeled myself, glanced back at the others still following my lead, then I ventured upstairs, to where I was sure I would find Susie's body. I found her lying in the master bedroom. Inside there was a four-poster bed, cream, silk sheets with several very plump-looking pillows. And on top of it all lay Susie. They'd shot her in the gut. Her eyes were closed. I guessed that they'd given her prior warning of what they'd intended to do. The bastards.

I shepherded the others out before they got the chance to see the body. If there's one thing that has a habit of messing with crew morale it's dead bodies. And, right now, we had to keep things up—what with the death of parents, the loss of a planet to mobsters and the lingering scourge of kidnap. One thing was for certain, I had picked up a crew with no small amount of baggage attached—not that I was complaining.

8: EMPTY SPACE TO OBLITERON

I GUESS following the pretty disastrous trip to Yightly-21, having left the place with the blood of a boy's father on my hands, not to mention that of an old lady, I decided to slip back into protocol, to allow those well-ingrained processes to take over. And so I did what comes natural to any captain, I delegated.

As we set course for a blank piece of space, a destination intended to give me time to think, to plan our next move forward, I set about assigning my crew to the various duties aboard the *Nava*. Now, I'd already given Wodd responsibility of basically the entire electrical system, navigational systems— really had him performing all the duties of an on board engineer —and so he was pretty much occupied. Foy, however, only had the gun turret thus far, and although she was doing a commend-able job on comforting Milky, if she really wished to be a fully-fledged crewmember of the *Nava* she'd need to take on a little more of a workload. As it turned out, she had ideas herself. She told me that as part of her training back on Trivus-3 for the Protectors she'd been trained up as a medic. That gave her something else to concentrate on, though I can't say I was totally happy with it—given that injuries on board are about as common as fire fights. So I also gave her the role of co-pilot, whenever I was off the bridge she'd be in control. Milky was a tougher proposition. The truth of the matter is that the *Nava* really isn't the biggest ship in the universe. Hell, I managed her myself for a long time without much sweat. But I had to make up some jobs fast so I gave him the job of programming the cleaning droids, his job was to keep them efficient, to their protocols and generally tasked with their upkeep. I suppose it was more responsibility than he'd ever been given by his 'father.'

With everyone having a job to do: Wodd tweaking some bit of code or other, Foy setting up her doctor's office, making an inventory of supplies we'd be needing if we were going to be serious, and Milky typing away, playing, with the maintenance droids, sending them scurrying about the ship at his whim, we barrelled onward, deeper into space, out of the Fritten System.

About three quarters of the way to our pseudo destination, I decided to step away from the controls and go give Milky a proper man-to-man moment. Someone had to say something to the kid, all that mollycoddling from Foy would drive the kid nuts. I gave up control to Foy, who seemed quite pleased to be getting her hands on the control stick for the first time since taking on her new responsibilities.

The door to the utility cupboard, now Milky's quarters, was left ajar. I peaked in around the doorframe and saw him there, slouched on his bed, fiddling with one of the maintenance droids. When I coughed, announcing my entry, he set the droid to one side and peered up at me, smiling weakly. I scratched my arm and thought about how I was going to get this conversation started. Then I decided it'd be better just to jump in—feet first.

"You know," I said. "I left my parents a long while back. I was a little older than you, sure, but I left them all the same. Not like they were killed or anything, though. Wow, I mean, I can't ever imagine what that was like."

Milky swallowed hard and his Adam's apple bobbed in his throat.

"Look, kid, I'm not great with these things—probably why I never had kids of my own—but I just want you to know that I'm truly sorry, that what happened was a terrible thing. And"—I paused briefly—"I just want to say that you shouldn't beat yourself up about it. What I mean to say is that there was nothing you could've done for him. If you'd been there, at his side, then they would've killed you all the same. They were after me, see?"

He narrowed his eyes. "They killed him because of you?"

A little uncomfortable at the direction the conversation was heading, I attempted to redirect things. He was cutting a little close to the quick here. "Well, they killed that old lady too. Because of me? I don't know about that. What I do know is that I'm going to find whoever did this thing and I'm going to punish them for what they did. That's what I've learnt out here, the universe is just one big cold, unforgiving place. Too much space for evil to roam. It's the responsibility of each one of us to make sure we look out for the other, that's what being a crew means. We're your family now."

At this remark, Milky tilted his head back and eyeballed me. "And you promise me that we will find them?"

"Oh yes, boy, I can promise you that, cross my heart."

———

I don't think I was all the convincing with my acting when we reached our destination. I made a face and told the crew that I must've got my calculations wrong. Wodd and Foy shot me side-long glances, but, like all good, obedient crewmembers, they held their counsel.

"Where to then, Captain?" Wodd said.

I thought over what we'd been through, how we'd reached a dead end with Susie—quite literally—and let out a sigh. "Check out the communications portal, will you?"

"Sir?"

"Let's see if any job offers have come in, I'm gonna have to work extra hard now I've got a sizable crew to feed."

Job offers are sent to the *Nava* through a secure system—a system, I'm sure, that since Wodd set foot aboard has got even more secure. As a group, us smugglers are surprisingly well organised. Job offers plunge into a pool and the first to grab the job gets it. Simple as that. Once we almost had a smugglers' union. I shit you not.

In the event of the contractor wanting to employ a specific smuggler—as was the case when I got the innocent-looking offer to pick up the stone from an unknown moon and fly it to Horte-nine—then they contact the smuggler directly, not bothering to deal with the pool. Contraband is big business and it needs a sturdy infrastructure to support it.

Wodd set the localiser on the job offers to bring up all the feasible options available, those within ten hours flight and suitable to the size of our ship. This too, I saw, he'd tweaked, because there was a whole host of extra criteria getting chewed on, I just caught sight of a couple as they spun about the screen: maximum speed, fuel type, shield state. Those were all criteria I'd have had to trawl through before accepting an offer and now it was all done automatically. Maybe whatever I would end up paying more for in excess baggage, what with the extra crewmembers, I'd make up for in efficiency.

Going by another of the smuggler mantras, I picked the second job offer available—this mantra may well be circumvented should said first offer be about twice the value of the second, also depending on the penchant for superstition on the part of the smuggler, I don't consider myself especially superstitious, but enough so to abide by this rather silly tradition. The job was on a nearby planet named Obliteron. A lonely planet with a distant star. The only one in its system, hence its jolly name. It seemed quiet enough so I set the course and we were away.

As we drew closer we got a nice view of Obliteron. It was a deep blue colour with a brooding neon-purple glow surrounding it. This had all the makings of being a scientific outpost, because I could initially see no other reason for anyone wishing to set up a colony there. However, as we descended into the atmosphere, it became apparent that there wasn't only a colony outpost there, but a sprawling metropolis.

The city, which the navigational computer identified as Obliteron City, sat on expansive steel struts, its buildings perched several kilometres above the base of the planet, which, as far as I could tell, consisted of a tar-coloured sea, lashing back and forth. The navigational computer identified the terminal and had us assigned for landing at Port O. The 'O,' I supposed, stood for Obliteron, and I was starting to get the impression that these people, these Obliterons, had something of a fetish for their own name. Nothing wrong with that, though. Everyone's got a fetish for something, at one time or another.

I brought the *Nava* down and parked up. As I stepped down the landing platform, I couldn't help but cast my eyes skyward, half-expecting to see a ship pursuing us, to see the hoods that had followed us to Yightly, done in Milky's father and Susie.

A stench crawled up my nostrils. It wasn't all that unpleasant, not at all, really. But it was pungent and clung to everything. If I had to describe it, it would've been somewhere between kidney beans and burnt-out electronic equipment. Not being much of a restrained fellow, I collared the nearest Obliteron and asked him what it was.

He had a marble-like sheen to his eyeballs and his mouth was formed like an especially smooth marshmallow. He examined me as if I was half-mad, then said, "That, sir, is the distinctive scent of hench."

"'Hench?'" I said. "What the hell are you talking about?"

"It's what our city, our world's built on."

"Uh huh," I said, resisting the urge to roll my eyes, in my attempt to scavenge more information from him.

"A wonderful energy resource." He waved his hand upward to indicate the streetlights which blinked a greyish green all over the place. "Hench powers everything on Obliteron."

"I've never heard of it, and I'm a spaceship captain."

He smirked. "That's because it's prohibited to sell the hench. Only the government may do that. Then they bring the money back to us, put it into our city, back into our planet. *That,*" he said, as if he were making an especially persuasive point, "is why Obliteron is one of the greatest worlds in all of the Fritten System. We have brilliant education, a first-rate medical system, a—"

"Yeah, yeah, enough with the sales pitch already, okay? So this 'hench' stuff, it's basically the shit?"

The Obliteron scowled. "You might choose to phrase it like that."

"Right," I said, flexing my eyebrows, then withdrawing my handheld communicator and showing him a map of our rendezvous. "And would you mind showing us the best way to get here?"

———

It seemed like a real hike to get us to within the rendezvous's neighbourhood. He certainly had decided to place himself right out of Obliteron City, I mean right out in the sticks. My communicator indicated that his house was the next on our left so, with no further instructions provided on the job offer, no preference for us to be subtle, I gave the door a couple of thuds with my fist.

A vacant-expressioned youth peeled open the door. He wore a string vest and had a few days' stubble sprouting from his cheeks. A slight smell of opium pervaded the whole place and I guessed what might well be happening to the urban youth on Obliteron—what with so much spare change floating about.

"We're here for the job."

The youth grunted and then shut the door in our faces.

I stood there on the doorstep, thinking about how I should get that smugglers' union back together, have us all demand to be treated like the reasonable professionals we are. But, before I got the chance to reach any pragmatic conclusions with those thoughts, I found myself face to face with a large man, he could've been a carbon copy of the youth—if the carbon copy had somehow slipped onto the floor, been dragged through several puddles and left on a windowsill to gather mould for between twenty and thirty years. And so I deduced that this must be the boy's father, and our employer.

I loosened a chunk of energy bar caught between my lower teeth and then gave the man a smile. "You called," I said.

The man looked beyond me, to Wodd, Foy—pausing a second or so on her breasts—before turning his attention to Milky. He looked back at me. "Don't work with kids."

"Oh," I said, "I can assure you that this one is extremely professional. In fact I'd wager that in a few years he'll be flying the ship in my place, strapped to my seat."

The man snorted. "If you're a FSA agent you're not doing a particularly good job—I'm seeing lapses all over the place. Doesn't look like you've much done your research."

Now, if there's one thing that's sickening above all else for a smuggler, it's having the insinuation that you're working as an undercover agent for the authorities bandied about. Our job is dangerous as it is without being called liars on top of everything else. So I simmered for a few seconds, not wanting to respond to this oaf.

The man broke out into a smile then slapped me on the upper arm. "All right," he said. "Just testing. Wanted to see how you'd react. You can come in now, it's all cool."

I cast a glance back over my crew, doing my best not to show that I'd been somewhat peeved by our employer, then gestured for them to follow me inside.

The inside of the house was pretty much in keeping with the personal hygiene of the two specimens I'd already encountered, which was to say, drab and could-do-with-a-wash. Don't ever let anyone tell you that smugglers are a dirty breed. I can assure you that, for the most part, the people who employ us are much worse.

The man led us down a hatch in the middle of what I supposed to be his sitting room—from the battered sofa and vidscreen spewing out some incomprehensible game show in Obliteronian, or whatever their language is called. A baby suckled at a large woman's breast, and she paid us no mind as we approached the hatch—temporarily blocking her view of the vidscreen—and then descended a flimsy staircase, its wooden slats creaking below our feet, following after the man.

A fluorescent bulb blinked on and we found ourselves surrounded by barrels upon barrels, all stacked up.

The man snorted and wiped his nose on his sleeve. "You

gonna be able to get this all out? I put in specs asking for a big capacity."

I checked out the payload. "This'll be fine. It'll fit in the cargo bay."

He nodded to me. "Bring your ship around then."

"What is this?"

"Whadda you think?"

"Hench?"

"Right-o, can tell you're a proper bright spark." He squinted at me. "Listen here, fatty"—

I decided not to launch a protest at that point. Most of the time, when I get met by a rude employer, I just suck up whatever abuse they doll out, telling myself that I'll be the one laughing when I get the paycheque. Maybe it's another issue the smugglers' union could fight for.

—"this took me years to get together, see? All this hench. The government keeps a tight fist around it all, keeping us from it. But some of us don't want to be on Obliteron our entire lives. Some of us have got aspirations and that."

I didn't think to prompt him for what those aspirations were, although I guessed that large woman in the sitting room suckling a babe was looking for him to provide.

He snorted a trickle of snot descending from his left nostril. "Don't wanna spend our lives living on hand outs, see what I mean?"

"Yeah," I said, taking the opportunity of the slackened social graces to give my arse crevice a good scratch.

"This'll be safe in your hands, I hope?"

"Absolutely. We're the most professional crew in the universe."

"Just get it there, buddy, all right?"

And so, without any offer of a private transporter to take us back to the terminal—I had had my doubts that our dear employer would have had one in the first place—we tracked back to the *Nava*, evaded the local authorities' checkpoints and put her down in a municipal park nearby our employer's house. Usually it's not that easy to bring a fully-fledged spaceship through a city, but I guessed that the work Wodd had done on the cloaking system had helped us out somewhat. To be honest, I really didn't feel like suffering through a detailed, techno-crap lecture on whatever clever thing that he had done, so I settled on a swift 'attaboy' and ruffled his hair. He seemed to appreciate the sentiment.

Our employer definitely took his role seriously, which was to say, he stood about, arms crossed, sucking back snot, while watching us load barrel after barrel of the hench—content not to lift a finger to help. I would've thought he'd be afraid to get his DNA on the stuff if I hadn't known that he'd been responsible for trucking the stuff down to the basement and stockpiling it in the first place. Finally we got all the hench packed into the cargo bay of the *Nava*, gave our faithful employer a heart-warming farewell-wave and then shot off, back into space.

———

I dialled up the navigational computer to find that we were headed to planet just outside Fritten to make the delivery. The planet turned out to be called Phoenix-13. That's another little quirk us smugglers have got: the number thirteen. Me less than most, though. I did have a bit of a quiver to my fingers as I guided the *Nava* down through the pitch-black atmosphere, to the completely unlit terminal—good thing Wodd had done a job on the proximity detector calibrations—and set down on what I presumed to be the principal port, not that I could see anything to confirm it by.

Just as I glanced out the front window of the *Nava*, expecting only to see more darkness, a series of multi-coloured flares fired up to reveal a whole damn procession waiting for us. There was a brass band tootling away, a pair of scantily-clad ladies, in swimming costumes, and, at the front of them all, pretty much inevitably by this point, a man with a sash over his shoulder and a golden medallion hanging from his neck—the President of Phoenix-13, I presumed.

Now, I've got nothing against a stately welcome, being greeted by the great and the good of whatever planet it might be. But I do have a certain profile to keep under wraps. Sure, smugglers are a known annoyance of the universe, but that doesn't mean we're the first to slap our mugs all over every media outlet around. So it was with a little foreboding that I stepped off the *Nava*, shook hands with the President and showed his handlers the way to the cargo hold and the hench.

With my crewmembers in my wake, I traipsed along with the President—who demanded that I call him Phil—back toward the terminal building. "You know," he said, "you're the real heroes of this universe—people just like you." He jabbed me in the chest with his index finger—actually jabbed me, as if I was someone who enjoyed that sort of thing. "Those Goddamned Obliterons are holding out on the whole damn universe. There they are, they've got just about the most proficient energy source ever discovered in the history of man, a supply they couldn't use themselves for a million years, and they've got the gall to let it dribble out into the market just so they charge an arm and a leg for it." He shook his head. "Always have to go through the unofficial channels if we want anything approaching a fair deal. But," he said, eyes glazing over, "things have been tight over the past few months, had to ration. As you can see from the state of our terminal here. Sorry state of affairs. Still"—he turned his attention back out the window to the *Nava*, being unloaded by his trusty men—"this should see us through another year or two. Good solid supply by the looks of it."

"Right," I said, glancing about.

Then he put his arm around me, that arm-round-the-shoulder that says a bombshell is about to be dropped. "Look here . . ." He paused, waiting for me to give my name.

"Captain Arkle Wright," I said. "Call me Arkle."

"Right, Arkle, you see, we've got a little bit of a problem."

My heart sunk. "Oh yeah?"

"Nothing serious, just a bit of an issue with cash flow. Should be sorted out soon enough. You don't mind waiting around an hour or two, do you?"

Oh, brother.

9: PHOENIX-13

TO BE FAIR TO PHIL—the tightwad scumbag—he put us up in a pretty nice suite: four bedrooms, hot tub and a twenty-four hour service from the kitchen—which I made good use of. But it wasn't getting paid. And I knew, from those situations, that the longer it went on, the less likely we were ever to get paid. The trick was knowing when to pull the plug on the whole deal, not that our bargaining position was any great shakes given they'd already seen to unloading the hench.

I stood at the window, looking out over Argonate—the capital of Phoenix-13. Slowly, streetlamps blinked on, transports started up, in short the planet was coming back to life, and all because of that hench we'd delivered. I thought about the lies Phil must've told his people to keep them placated during the times of rationing. If there's one thing that people hate to be told, it's that they can't use all the power they want. Holds true on any planet in the universe.

A troop of maintenance droids buzzed their way up the street, all having been reset, ready to return to their programming hub where they'd receive their latest orders. I noticed Milky taking a special interest in them and announced to myself that this was a good thing that he was showing an interest in bettering his craft—getting to know his area. Wodd and Foy had taken up a virtual card set and were laying out an epic battle—well, the game had taken longer than thirty minutes so, by my standards, it was an *epic* battle, there are probably gnats that put my concentration to shame, and if there's one thing I hate more than anything else, it's waiting.

I strutted about nearing the window, getting more and more wound up, feeling more and more tense with each passing minute. Any moment I expected Phil to arrive at the door to the suite, cash in hand, for us to deliver back to our employer. It really was no joke because if we didn't get paid, then neither did our employer, and employers have a nasty habit of blaming the smuggler in situations such as those. They're quite quick to reach for a communicator and find a good-quality assassin from a similar pool they found the smuggler. Sometimes I wonder if assassins have seen enough sense to organise themselves into a union.

We idled away yet more hours, watching more and more of Argonate break from its gloom. Before I knew it the whole place was lit up and looked a sight jollier, not that I could feel all that good for them—not till I had cash in hand. I watched as grinning school children skipped along the street, no doubt heading to school for the first time in months, now that they had power. It always makes me wonder why these colonies get started up in places where human life is just so implausible. On the way to Phoenix-13, I did some research and came up with the fact that they receive precisely zero daylight from their star. Call me a traditionalist, but I prefer to set up a colony where there's actually a decent level of basic pre-conditions for human life. Too late now, though, everyone's there. Humans are all set up on Phoenix-13.

Phil did make an appearance later on, a good ten hours since the lights of Argonate had been shining brightly, everything working fine. No doubt he wanted to check that our hench was of good stock—not that it would've been my fault if it wasn't, but, hey, I don't think the expression 'Don't shoot the messenger' has penetrated certain, darker areas of the universe.

He had a grin spread across his cheeks—always a bad sign, especially in a politician—as he marched into our suite. He strode up to Milky, pinched his cheek and said, "How're you, my lad? Enjoying it here, eh?"

Milky exchanged glances with me, clearly unsure what to do in this situation.

I just gave him a vague smile and a slight shake of the head.

Then Phil made a spectacle of watching over Foy and Wodd's game of cards, hands in pockets, bending down and whispering in each player's ear, before straightening up and grinning to himself. Once he'd finished with all this pretence, still smiling, he rested a hand on my shoulder and said, "Captain Wright, let's take a walk, shall we?"

I resisted the urge to peel off each and every one of those slender, sly fingers.

He escorted me down a long corridor and then into an

expansive room—an observatory, judging by the ceiling which peered upward into space, visuals working to identify the various star signs in the sky. A pair of guards followed behind us, both of them looking fairly bored, but their guns looking pretty alert.

Phil closed one eye and pointed upward. "You see that, there?"

"No," I said.

"That's where I was born, on Jek-7." He slipped me a side-long glance. "Seems so far away, doesn't it?"

Not really sure which planet he was pointing out among the millions, billions, up there, I just agreed with him. Sentimentality is another great diversionary tactic. And it probably worked just great with the businessmen he got there, the other visiting envoys from nearby planets. I had to admit that at that point I was ready to believe the worst, that I was dealing with nothing less than a crooked individual—then again, presidents who openly deal with smugglers often are . . .

"What's your planet, Arkle?"

I glanced up at the stars above us, wondering just how much information I should give this bozo, and then realised that, really, it didn't matter. If this guy wanted to go around the houses then he could do so. But I was determined that me and my crew were getting paid all the same. "Arkle-4," I said.

"Ah," he said. "So that's how you got your name."

"Dunno, I never asked. Most likely."

He chuckled and then led me around to the edge of the observatory, to a pair of chairs that had seemed to materialise there. Maybe he had some sort of materialising technology.

From what I had seen so far I could be sure that he had no qualms about using energy for his own ends—that observatory screen must've burnt through it.

I sat back in the smooth leather. I rested my arms and aching back. I still felt tense. All this waiting was taking years off my life.

As Phil took up his place beside me, he made a command to the observatory screen. "Computer? Zoom in on Arkle-4."

The observatory screen did as it was told. The focus barrelled its way along, smashing through stars and planets, taking whole systems in its bounding leaps before it reached Arkle-4. And my planet sat there, snug in space, twirling gently about its axis, basking in the warm light of Mertinon, our star. Its light tangerine glow sent a shudder of nostalgia up my spine —much to my disgust, seeing as I'd so nimbly concluded that this was precisely the tactic Phil intended to use on me. But, all the same, despite my logical brain stabbing at the weepy part, telling it to get a grip, I was quickly losing the battle.

"Sometimes we let it all get out of context, don't we?" Phil said.

Feeling a touch moist-eyed, I said, "Yeah."

"It just takes a few moments to remember exactly where we came from, reminds us where we're going to too, don't you think?"

"Yeah."

Phil remained steeped in silence for a long while, so long that I got to the point where I thought he might be about to pull out a bit of villainy from up his sleeve, shift back the camera to reveal that he had some sort of a death ray crosshair fixed over

Arkle-4, finger on the trigger, ready to blow it away if I didn't agree to give him the hench for no charge. However, he did something far more predictable. Something which turns my gut and makes me want to punch a wall. Phil reached across me, laid his hand on my forearm and said, "Arkle, we don't have the cash."

"Uh huh."

"But," he said, sticking his finger up in the air as if he'd thought of something even better, "I do have something else that you might be interested in."

Already wondering how I was going to explain this turn of events to my noble employer, I turned to face him.

"We got our communications back online about an hour or so ago, really doesn't do them any good to go dark for such a substantial period of time, as I'm sure you'll empathise with."

"No one can live with broken communications."

"I knew you'd understand." He flapped his hands. "Anyway, point is that I have it on fairly solid testimony that you're a wanted man—that you're being followed. I saw it on the newswire, shared between all the presidents of the Planetary Federation."

"Tell me about it."

"You know about this?"

"Know about it? I've spent the past week getting almost killed by whoever. To be honest I haven't really been able to ignore it."

"And do you perhaps have some idea of who might be behind it?"

"Got a few. None that I'm going to share, though. No offence."

Phil smiled. "I've given you no reason to trust me, why should you? Is there anything worse than a customer who doesn't pay?"

This guy was starting to come around to my way of thinking.

"Really, Arkle, I feel terrible about the situation and would like to see some way past it—a way that might see us right. It's my understanding that your life is in danger, under threat by whom we shall not say, and I should be as glad to leave it a secret as you are, but, please, tell me Arkle, have you happened across any of these new Fonch sweets on your trips throughout the universe?"

"I have actually."

"And have you put any thought into what they might mean?"

I thought back to the times I'd been close to getting killed: back in *The Bitch's*, then at Kools's deathbed, that tome of accounts in the sitting room at Susie's house. And now here was the President of Phoenix-13 bringing it up once more. "Nope, not really the thinking kind of guy."

"Please, Arkle, I'm sure you've got an astute aspect to you, what with being a captain and all."

This guy really didn't know me at all.

Phil flexed his fingers, as if this was a case of him doing *me* a favour, like this wasn't the pitiful attempt to duck a debt that it was. He smoothed out his sash—it appeared that he never took it off—and then said, "All I can say is that if you were interested in where those Fonch sweets come from then you might think about going to this location." He clicked his fingers to a point he'd obviously bookmarked previously on the observatory screen, and it brought up a planet out in the middle of the Fritten System. A label informed us that its name was Tetrahedron-2. He glanced at me expectantly. "So, Arkle, what do you make of that?"

"And you think this'll make up for dodging payment on this deal?"

Phil sniffed a couple of times, as if the very idea of getting down to brass tacks was an unpleasant business, and that was all very well for him but *he* wasn't the guy who wasn't getting paid here. He'd already provided for his planet, got them the hench they'd so badly needed, so he had no need to worry—what should he care about my crew?

He straightened in his chair and then checked over his shirt sleeves, as all guys in suits like to do from time to time, especially when in less-well-dressed company. "I'd be careful about the threats you make toward either myself or Phoenix-13, Captain Wright. That hench you've so kindly provided has seen our laser defence system back online into *extremely* operational condition. It would be a shame if one of the operators were to get a little over excited and decide to test out the restored capabilities on your spaceship, wouldn't it?"

Now, if there's one place you don't ever go with a captain, it's his ship. Insult his mother, sister, swear his aunts and grandmothers out of existence, but, dammit, leave his ship out of it. That's a sure fire way to land yourself onto said captain's List of Eternal Ire and Damnation for life—and don't believe any captain who claims he doesn't possess such a list, lists don't always have to be written down, captains are known for having an exceptional memory for grudges, and I'm no exception.

I lurched to my feet, stared him down, thought twice about giving him a thorough shove—considering the guards standing with their trigger fingers looking especially twitchy—and then stormed away from the observatory. As I ploughed on down the corridor, back toward our suite, I was sure that I heard a peal of laughter, and I wouldn't be at all surprised. If there's one thing these power-hungry presidents love more than anything else it's getting off some bill they'd rather not pay.

I swept through the suite like a chubby tornado, grabbing hold of all the crewmembers I could get my hands on, all of them, as luck would have it, and then we stumbled onward to the terminal, back to the *Nava*. I had her all powered up when I saw a transmission burbling onto my screen. Under any other circumstances, if we'd been out in open space, I would've ignored it, but, unfortunately for me, in accordance with various different interplanetary laws a captain must accept all communications made by the central terminal while the ship is either approaching or taking off, and certainly while it's standing waiting on the dock. Nonetheless, the idea of simply ignoring it did cross my mind, but I recalled 'Phil's' vague threat to have me blown out of the sky by a freshly powered up laser beam, and I've learnt from experience that it's better not to test presidential paranoia—no matter how paranoid it seems. And so I accepted the transmission. And guess just whose face appeared on the vidscreen? No prizes.

With a presidential smirk riding high on his lips, Phil looked out at me. "Remember, Captain Wright, go and check out Tetrahedron-2 if you want answers. Later I'm sure you'll come to realise that it's better than any pay packet I could've offered—"

Although there's a lot of regulation on accepting incoming transmissions under certain circumstances, there's nowhere near as much on when or when not to cut them off. So I take quite a few liberties with that loophole, as I did then. If a president has me beat because of the flexing of military muscle, fair enough, but don't expect me to sit about allowing him to gloat.

We jetted off upward into space. Just as we broke through the atmosphere and entered our cruising pattern—navigational computer set to Tetrahedron-2 more out of not wanting to face up to our employer than wanting to go through with whatever titbit Phil had felt like throwing me—Wodd perked up from his control panel. "What was that about us not getting paid?" he said.

"Nothing to worry about," I said. "Just an everyday risk of the business."

"Are we going to be all right for supplies?"

"Yeah, I saw that our mate Phil at least saw fit to stocking us up with energy bars and other vitals, I think we're going to be okay for the time being. No money, but okay."

Wodd nodded and went back to his work, hassling whatever part of the ship's computer he was hassling.

I ducked out of the captain's chair and dodged through the *Nava*, headed for the toilet. Whenever I find myself at a crossroads I always make for that place, and goodness knows with all those people aboard it was just about the only place I *could* be alone. I shut the toilet lid and sat there, just staring at the blank wall, thinking about this blithe mess, and wondering whether there might be *any* substance to what Phil had said about going to Tetrahedron-2 being worth my time. Surely it had all just been political spin, just a ruse to get us out of his hair. Maybe even a poorly concealed threat. Very poorly concealed seeing as he did actually threaten me with lasers.

Once I got off the pot and back out into the *Nava* I had little motivation to get myself back into the cockpit. Foy was more than competent at the controls—well, from what little I'd seen of her piloting so far she was better than me. Whereas I jerked the stick about all over the shop, she was gentle—that woman's touch I guess, and don't you dare call me sexist, I know I am. I can do all the calling fine by myself.

I looked in on Milky, seeing him lying on his bed, tweaking a droid, bits of it sprayed all about. I felt a bit like a parent looking in on his son, and then I drew away before I started to get all moist-eyed and get to wondering why I'd never seen fit to have a family of my own. As I tell myself everyday: my ship is my wife, kids and mortgage.

And wouldn't you have just known it? As I lay back on my bed, head smushed into pillow, eyes shut, a concussion rippled right through the ship. We were under attack.

Again.

10: EN ROUTE TO TETRAHEDRON-2

ALL THE ALARMS JANGLED AWAY, of course, so it would've been impossible to drift off back to sleep. In any case, I knew I'd have to get up. For all I knew Foy and Wodd would be freaking out about this attack without their captain on the bridge to instruct them. Actually, I have to admit that I was a touch disappointed that, when I did arrive on the bridge, they were holding things together quite nicely indeed. Wodd had got the shields up ever since that first shot and it looked like Foy was doing a nice job of steering the ship while bringing the enemy into range with the blaster. To be honest, I felt a little out of place taking up the captain's seat to look after the steering side of things.

"Closing, Captain," Foy said, eye to the weapons system.

"Right," I said.

"No damage to report," Wodd said.

"Good, good."

Milky appeared in the doorway to the bridge. I turned in my chair and said, "Kid, you might want to take up that chair back there, get yourself strapped in. You never know, you might learn something."

Foy glanced at me. "Wouldn't it be better if he stayed in his room?"

"Nah," I said. "Captain's orders."

She hesitated a moment before returning her attentions to the weapons.

The ship appeared quite small on our navigational screen. It had to be half-mad to be attacking us out here in the middle of nowhere. Or desperate. This had all the signs of being one thing and one thing only. Space pirates.

There's nothing jolly about space pirates, no rum or singsongs. These are desperate people, usually from impoverished outer systems of the Fritten. They snatch themselves a spaceship and go around wreaking all manner of havoc on the universe. They've been known to attack whole fleets of FSA ships, and go down in flames doing so, not wanting to get captured. Quite simply put, they're an unknown entity. Complete mavericks who don't hold to any sort of code or obvious strategy, and that's their danger. Poor bastards. Best you can really do for them is put them out of their misery.

Foy got them in our sights and looked to me for the order. They'd fired on us so we had every right to retaliate to save ourselves. I was on the point of nodding in response when our incoming communication light blinked away. Pirates weren't known to use communications much, so I was wary. This might be some sort of a trick, a way to catch us off our guard. But always having been a deeply humane and moral person—yeah right—I decided to hear them out. That did please Foy no end because, as she pointed out earlier to us, she wasn't a big fan of mindless killing.

Their image fizzled onto the screen. A pair of skinny looking kids, maybe a few years older than young Milky. They looked scared. Their clothes were ragged and their faces looked like scooped out skulls. It's true what they say about letting an enemy onto your vidscreen, it's like naming a dog, you get attached to them.

Trying to maintain some semblance of threat, I said, "Arkle Wright of the *Navaplastas* here. What in hell's name do you think you were doing shooting on my ship? Give me one good reason why I shouldn't just blast you right out of existence right here and now?"

Strangely, one of the boys broke into a grin and nudged his companion. When they turned to look back at the camera they were both grinning—wide, great serious grins. I wondered whether they had some drugs stashed away on that ship. "Mister Arkle—"

"That's *Captain Wright*, sonny boy."

"Yes, sir, Captain Wright, sir. Please, forgive us, there wasn't any other way for us to get your attention. The *Navaplastas* is far too quick for our piece of junk, it would never compete with you."

"What did you want my attention for?" I said.

"Sir, we've come from halfway across the universe to find

you. We've heard stories about you, what a famous smuggler you are, and we wondered, well . . ."

"Spit it out."

"We wondered if you might accept us on your ship."

"Ship's full," I said.

"Or as part of your fleet."

"Ain't got no fleet. I travel light. Like you said, your ship would only slow us down. And I don't tend to trust people who try to kill me."

After making that comment I made an effort not to catch any glances off Foy.

The boys' smiles disintegrated and the talkative one continued, "But, sir, please, you have to believe us. We've come to find you. We need your help."

"Sir?" Wodd said from behind me. "I've got the report on the ship."

"Give it to me."

"Well, using the newly cross-referenced FSA database for reported ship jackings, I've found that their ship belongs to a certain Milot Yaught, and was stolen recently. The case is reported as unresolved, sir."

I turned back to the vidscreen. "All right, and I suppose that neither of you is Milot, that correct?"

The boys visibly quivered in their seats.

"Thought not," I said, then looked to Foy and said in a loud voice, so the boys would hear, "turn them to toast, will ya?"

Foy, of course did nothing of the sort. In fact, I noticed that she had long ago retreated from the laser crosshairs and she had been watching the conversation play out.

"Wait!" one of the boys said. "Please, you've got to believe us, we did the right thing. This is my uncle's ship—we asked him if we could take it and he said no, but we needed it because we had to find her."

I rolled my eyes. "And who's 'her?'"

"Our cousin. She got taken a while back by gangsters, or that's what Dad and Mum say."

Foy leapt out of her seat. "My god! I knew I recognised them." She leant over my lap, quite forgetting all protocol, who was supposed to be boss around this cockpit. "Brian, Terry, that's you two. I knew it was you. You looked so thin, that's all, I was sure it was just my mind playing tricks on me." She glanced back at me, fury etched all over her face. "And to think that I almost blew them into tiny pieces."

I held up my hands. "Look, I was just acting on instinct. From experience let me tell you that ninety-nine times out of a hundred you're better off shooting back at something that shoots at you. At least it's kept me alive so far."

She flung her hair back over her shoulder and looked back to her two cousins. "Hang on," she said. "You two look half-starved. But don't worry, we'll get you on board and get you fed up."

I'd obviously left this conversation—or at least the decision-making component of it—so I sat there quietly with my arms folded, waiting out the inevitable. Two more mouths to feed. Just what we needed. And more kids about the place. Knowing my luck they'd all get together and decide to put on a mutiny—get rid of that grumpy captain bossing everyone about, ruining everyone's lives. Not much I could do, though, Foy was already putting the ship through all the motions, bringing the other one closer to us.

As we'd recently dumped the hench, the cargo hold was empty, and it turned out to be large enough for the boys' small craft. I marvelled at how they'd set out into deep space in such a tiny little tin can. Then I realised that they were kids, and if there's one thing you can always depend on kids for it's lack of forethought, or stupidity, as some might call it—not saying I'm a master planner or anything.

Brian had a bushy afro with a single curl twirling down over his forehead, while Terry had matted, straw-yellow hair. I guessed they must've been brothers, but they looked quite different. In any case I got them all set up Foy's room, having them make up some beds on the floor there. The way I saw it, it was her family so it was her responsibility.

After we'd got our new passengers / freeloaders on board, we jetted onward to our destination: Tetrahedron-2.

———

There were only two planets in the system: Tetrahedron-1 and Tetrahedron-2. They reminded me of twins with their equally, almost triangular-shaped forms and similar blue-grey colour. The navigational computer pointed out which was Tetrahedron-2 and we headed right for it. As I put in the request for landing permission at the terminal I was greeted with a somewhat predictable corporate message:

"Fonch Confectionaries welcomes you to Tetrahedron-2,

production centre of the famous Fonch Chocolate Swirl, the Fonch Fondue Supplement and the—"

I decided to interrupt this merry jingle. "Yeah, yeah, I'm just looking for permission to land, you gonna give it to us or what?"

The jingle subsided and there was a series of clicking noises as, apparently, the communicator was handed over to a human operator. How most terminal controls work is to have a series of droids answering calls, putting ships into position for landing, but there's always a human on hand. In this particular case I decided that the droid controllers would only function at the end of the welcome jingle so if someone wanted to land with any urgency, or just didn't want to listen to that unbearable piece of propaganda the whole way through, then they needed to get antsy.

The human operator got us landed without any trouble and I put the unpleasant business of that marketing pitch, that ungainly happy voice from my mind, as we strolled through the terminal where we were met by a man wearing a light-blue suit with a silk-grey tie. He had a smile plastered across his lips and a flashing badge which declared: Welcome to Tet Two! Home of Fonch Confectionaries!

One too many exclamation marks for my liking.

He shook us each by the hand and I was beginning to wonder whether this guy might be a distant relative of Phil— what with his politician's touch. He examined me and said, "You must be the captain of this whole enterprise."

"Uh, that's right."

"Forgive me, I read off your ship's registration as you landed,

and it states that you are a free cargo ship. At Fonch Confectionaries we are always looking for excellent employees to add
to our family."

Now, one of the perks of working freelance is that you are
never, technically, an *employee*. However, in this circumstance I
decided it wasn't really worth taking offence. After all, we were
here to get an idea of what it was exactly that Fonch Confectionaries did. And so being in the role of prospective 'employees'—God that word makes me want to spit—meant that we
should get a more thorough tour of the enterprise. In theory,
anyway.

"Name's Mr Clark," he said, offering me his hand, yet again.

"Captain Wright," I said, deciding to keep things formal.

Mr Clark led off down a series of weaving corridors, past
great big steel liquid tanks and through mountainous ware-
houses staffed by seemingly hundreds of thousands of droids. I
caught a glance back at Milky—again he was fascinated by the
little machines. What is it with kids and obsessions? They
always get something up them, don't they? Well, seeing as he
was designated to looking after the maintenance droids aboard
the *Nava* then it couldn't do him any harm to show interest in
his profession. At least I wasn't complaining. He had a job to do
—if he liked to do it, all the better. Foy's cousins, Brian and
Terry just hung back on the fringes of the group, not speaking
much. I suppose they were still getting over the rush of actually
being in space instead of being stuck down on Trivus-3.

Mr Clark followed my gaze. "You've got quite a sizable crew
there, Captain, and quite a lot of children."

I shrugged. "Get them to do the heavy lifting. Kids work

harder and don't ask as many questions. Much easier in the long run. Once you've broken them."

Mr Clark failed to catch my irony, widened his eyes and generally looked pretty afraid. "Oh, I see. Yes," he said, forcing a smile. "I suppose I can see the logic behind that argument."

I bet he was reconsidering his offer for us to become one of the Fonch Confectionaries' family—if he was authorised to do any offering in the first place.

He brought us to a comparatively small room occupied with a single machine. Only when I gazed upward did I realise how expansive the apparently tiny space was. It stretched upward for what must've been twenty or thirty storeys. One long conveyer belt whirring away. I looked to Mr Clark, who was obviously enjoying my reaction to this particular component of the factory, and then back to the device.

"This," Clark said, "is where the Fonch bars all start off their life. Up there, out of sight, we have our special mixing procedure, where all the ingredients that make Fonch great are mixed up, before being passed down this device where they're formed into the distinctive disc shape." He shuffled over to the side of the machine and flipped the hatch to reveal a conveyer belt rattling along, pushing out those chocolate treats, brown on the outside and gooey pink on the inside. He snatched one up out of the line and handed it to me. "Go on, Captain, have a taste."

Although these damn sweets had plagued quite a substantial amount of my recent adventures I had yet to actually sample one. In a way I really didn't want to. I know it sounds a bit stupid but it felt like I would be yielding to something—letting these sweets get on top of me in some way. But, with Clark's eager eyes scanning me, I decided that I'd be better off taking a taste. Just a little one. And so I bit into the Fonch.

To be honest I wasn't all that blown away. It tasted a bit like those cakes toddlers make. You know the ones, where they bash up a chocolate bar and then pour in half a bag of brown sugar. 'Doesn't taste all that good,' does it a bit of disservice. Then again, I've always been more of a moiser guy, I can honestly say that I've never had a bit of a sweet tooth. In fact, right then, I had an urge to get a moiser down me, something bitter and alcoholic to strip away that unpleasant chemically-sweet taste.

"What do you think?" Clark said, leaning into me.

"Don't think it's really my thing."

"Oh?"

"No offence. But there meant for kids, right? Don't think I'm necessarily the intended market."

Clark flashed his eyebrows. "That's just where you're wrong, Captain, you see Fonch has been shown to be popular for both children and adults." His easy smile returned. "It's an extremely diverse product."

My this guy really was a one-man marketing machine.

"Perhaps the children would like a bite?"

I looked over Milky, Terry and Brian, all of them with their mouths latched open as they watched the procession of Fonch discs flying by on the conveyer belt. "Knock yourselves out, kids."

I just about got myself out of the way in time for the three kids to bomb past me and take up the position at the hatch to the conveyer belt. Clark watched on with, what I thought was, a bit of an evil supervision, like he was the linchpin of a drug empire watching a fresh bunch of druggies addle themselves on his product—making themselves addicts for life.

Whatever. I was their captain, not their parents, so I wandered off, into the next room of the factory. It was the packaging section of the place. Pipes jutted out from walls and snaked their way around the shape of the room. I guessed that there must've been several of those smaller rooms with conveyer belts for all the different types of Fonch available. But it was here where they were all brought together and shoved into those plastic wrappers that had followed me around the whole damn universe.

Several droids stood along a conveyer belt checking over the final product, occasionally snatching one of the Fonch bars out of rank and tossing it into a large chute to its side. Quality control. I approached the droids and looked over them. A couple glanced up a me briefly before returning to their work. I looked at the various different packets of Fonch and read off the flavours: Caramel, Fudge Sundae, Orange Zest, Cherry, Vanilla. They really had covered pretty much all their bases. I guessed that, no matter what the flavour was, they all came out pretty much the same—with that same gooey pink centre.

I followed the production line along as it shot past the droids, through a long tunnel and into another room where another group of droids bundled the sweets into large plastic bags, variety packs for the consumer to pick up at 'all convenient points of purchase throughout the galaxy.' I watched as the finished product, these variety bags, were lynched upward by a crane and then tossed into shipping containers—ready for the other members of the Fonch Confectionaries 'family' to haul away to the appropriate outlet. All this industry, all these machines, were making me a tad sick. If there's one reason for setting up a factory it's to make a tank load of money and I've never found myself able to see that point of view. Maybe I'm a simple guy but I've always been pretty happy with my ship, flying through the universe, doing my own thing. All that a ton of money brings is attachment and responsibility, and I've no use for any of that.

"Captain Wright?"

I craned my neck to see Clark standing there, heading my crew. The kids all looked like they would burst their stitching, while Foy and Wodd looked vaguely bored. I supposed they'd gone from fire fight to fire fight, and now they were coming down with this pretty tame tour of a sweet factory. Life as a smuggler can be unpredictable.

"I was just about to invite you up to the tower to take some refreshments, if you'd be interested in joining us?"

Glad to be getting away from all these machines, and attracted by the prospect of perhaps Fonch Confectionaries having moiser on tap—a pretty remote prospect granted, but a prospect nonetheless—I stepped away from the packaging machine, and made to follow the others.

Just as I was about to leave the room, I caught sight of one of the shipping crate lids cranking open. Curious, I stepped over to it and stood at its lip, staring into the contents inside. And what should I see but a humungous space blaster. Before I got a chance to inspect it more thoroughly a shower of Fonch packets rained down from above, covering up the laser completely. The lid came down with a metallic *slam* and the container shot off along on the conveyer belt.

"Captain Wright?"

A tingle ran up my spine and, still feeling a little queasy at what I'd just witnessed, I said, "Coming," heading in the direction of Clark's voice.

11: TETRAHEDRON-2

THE TOWER LOOKED OUT over the whole factory complex, which seemed to extend all the way to the horizon, maybe the factory took up the whole of Tetrahedron-2. As I sat there, slurping on what Clark had told me was a trial product—a, very non-alcoholic, Fonch milkshake—I considered how many guns they were shipping out of this place, and across the universe. Surely, the way this stuff worked, they would get the Fonch out to the various outlets and that was where they would distribute the guns. But who was doing the buying of the guns from the outlets? And why? In times of peace I could see no reason to have such heavy weaponry on a ship. Hell, not even the FSA packed hardware like that. Then it struck me. Whoever it was that was taking consignment of these guns was preparing for just that: a war.

"So," Clark said, addressing me while the others sat propped up at the window on the other side of the tower, peering out at the factory unfolding beneath them, the ships queuing up to access the terminal and pick up their shipping containers—the guns nestled inside, "what do you think of Fonch Confectionaries now?"

I did my best to put on a carefree aspect, because if there's one thing you want to avoid doing after discovering a weapons-smuggling empire, it's arousing some sense of suspicion that you really know what's going on. As a smuggler, I've always lived by the credo that you don't necessarily need to know exactly what you're carting from one side of the universe to the next, as long as the money's right—and I guessed it was pretty much the same situation for all these guys lugging the shipping containers of Fonch to the outlets. Maybe some of them had taken a peak inside the containers, found the guns, but I was sure—for the most part—they just took them to the destination and took the, what I assumed to be, tidy paycheque that went with it.

I stared out the window and said, "Yeah, it looks like a pretty well-organised operation you've got here."

"And would you be interested in signing a contract with us? To ship out Fonch to the furthest reaches of the universe. I must say that our pay scale for captains and their crew alike are extremely generous."

I had no doubts about that. If there's one rule for illegally selling off weapons it's that it pays *very* nicely indeed, and at least some of that needs to get back to the unsuspecting mules—just enough so that they feel good with themselves remaining unsuspecting.

I considered our options. One would be to blast ourselves off from here, get as far away from this operation as possible. I could find another job somewhere else, anywhere else, and just go on with it as if nothing much at all was happening. And then there was another aspect. There was that damn stone. It was still in my, or Foy's, possession. I wanted to know why I had been given it, well, in short, why someone had decided to make me a target. And I was getting around to guessing that it was because they thought I might endanger this operation right here at Fonch Confectionaries, at least that was where it all seemed to lead. Sooner or later those guys who wanted to kill me would track me down and, although I had ever confidence in Foy as a sharp shooter, and for Wodd to keep our defences up well enough, I was sure that they'd bring surprises next time—not look to take any risks. I needed to be more proactive, untangle my exact involvement with all this bullshit and as quickly as possible. Then there was that payoff. Hey, what can I say? First and foremost I'm a smuggler, not some private investigator. And I had a shipload of people to feed and clothe, even if it would mean taking on the mantle of 'employee.'

I eyed Clark closely then said, "Let's take a look at one of those contracts."

———

The contract was good, not knock-out good by any means, but good all the same. Like most contracts, I would just about make more on average than I would carrying out individual smuggling jobs—and the benefit of all this was that, officially, according to the paperwork anyway, it was all above board. So there would be no further run-ins with FSA fleets, unless they got the inkling that I did in fact have the Stone of the Angels, and there was no reason why they would get to wondering that, having already searched my ship. In fact, this would act as a good cover. Maybe show them that I'd decided to go straight after all, throw in the towel with the smuggling business and turn a legitimate profit with the *Nava*. At least it was a story that might fool the more naïve of the FSA captains.

With Clark still smiling away, hanging about at my side, telling us what a terrific choice I'd made for myself and my crew, we watched on as the droids loaded up the *Nava* with a couple of shipping containers of Fonch . . . along with those rather nasty-looking blaster weapons hidden away inside. As I stood there, tuning out of the crap pouring forth from Clark's lips, I thought over what my mate Phil, President of Phoenix-13, had meant by suggesting I check out this place—that it would be worth my while. I wondered if he'd only seen the surface, thought these good contracts for a dodgy smuggler such as myself, or perhaps his recommendation had come from a deeper place. He had mentioned that he knew all about me, so I got to thinking that maybe he knew there was more to this story than met the eye—and had some hint of my involvement in it all.

The droids loaded the crates onto the *Nava* in no time at all and I wondered whether I might've been missing a trick by not taking on some droids myself for that heavy lifting. Then I reminded myself that my crew was growing faster than a rabbit burrow and that I could afford to expend a bit of human muscle.

The best thing about getting off Tetrahedron-2 wasn't having a pair of massive weapons in our cargo, but being able to put distance between myself and Clark. If there's anything that bores me to tears worse than a salesman, I don't want to know about it.

As I set the navigational computer, Foy tapped me on the arm. "What're you doing?" she said. "This shipment's meant for Drokul-15."

"I'm taking your brats back to Trivus-3."

"Oh, no you're not."

"What is this a pantomime?"

She gave me a stern glance—the this-ain't-no-laughing-matter glance. "They came all this way to try and save me, doesn't that say something about them?"

"Yeah, they near enough starved themselves doing it, and now they're aboard they're doing their best to gorge themselves on the ship's supplies. No can do, got enough kids with Milky on board, and he was a pretty big exception. I think having your daddy killed qualifies you for service on the *Navaplastas*."

"If you send them back they'll be heartbroken."

"Oh, diddums."

"Listen, if you send them back they'll get into huge trouble with our uncle. In case you hadn't noticed, stealing a spaceship and flying off with it is taken fairly seriously back where I come from."

"I blame the parents."

"If you take them back then you might as well drop me off while you're at it."

I looked over to her, trying to work out whether or not she was serious about the threat. "But I thought you said you wanted to see a bit of the universe before you settled down with your man?"

"Maybe I'll bring my plans forward."

I did consider that long and hard. She'd proven herself not only a great gunwoman and co-pilot but also a trustworthy companion on board the *Nava*—so trustworthy that I was beginning to forget her carrying that gun on her, being ready to shoot me back in *The Bitch's*, and let me tell you that that doesn't happen every day: me forgiving people.

I stewed on her stubbornness a little longer and then decided to try a different tactic. "This mission's working up to be pretty dangerous. Wouldn't you feel better knowing that you hadn't put your little, fresh-faced cousins into the line of fire? Have you thought about how you'll explain how they got themselves fried to your aunt?"

"You wouldn't let that happen to them."

"Well," I said, hunching my shoulders, "I'll do my best, but I can't say I can make any promises. Shit happens on board smuggling ships, what can I say?"

All the lines on her forehead knitted together as she thought this out. Then, decided, she turned on me. "What if I make them my responsibility. Everything they do is my responsibility."

"Yeah, and how's that going to work out in practical terms?"

"Pretty simple. We'll share my food ration out between us. I'll be responsible for keeping them safe if we do come to a battle."

"Don't you think you're taking on quite a lot there?"

"Nothing I can't handle."

This really wasn't ideal. I had hoped that my argumentative skills might've been up to more than admitting defeat this quickly, but, that said, I knew when I was beaten. Foy was resilient, or stubborn, as I preferred to label her.

"Okay," I said. "If you make them your responsibility. I don't expect any angry communications from your family members if they do get their little bodies mangled in the course of events."

"You won't. And they won't. It'll have been all my fault."

"Sure?"

"Yeah."

I gently nudged the control stick, taking us back on course for the destination of our delivery: Drokul-15. It sounded like a foreboding place, but, from what I've learnt after all my years on the job, a name can mean just about anything. It almost never has a correlation with the actual place.

———

There you go, what did I say? Despite its doom-laden nomenclature, Drokul-15 was a light-pink in colour and, as we descended through the atmosphere, I made out crystal forests sparkling below us. I could tell that Fonch would certainly do a quick trade in a place like this. Lots of safe suburbs, kids wanting to spend their money on the latest tooth-rotter. What I was more interested in, however, was who exactly would pop out of the woodwork to retrieve the weapons we were packing.

A man called Drok, perhaps named after the planet—just as I was most likely named after mine—accepted the consignment. He had a large shop with several sweets on offer around the place. After seeing the kids trailing after me, he dished out a sweet to them each. All the confirmation was worked out in a matter of minutes, with Fonch Confectionaries sending us a receipt with a smiley faced, congratulating us on a successful delivery—condescending bastards.

Drok shook all our hands, thanked us about a thousand times for the delivery. I thought about how he might do better to stay on the subtle side, be a little more guarded about how he treated our interaction considering he knew that he was in fact receiving a massive space gun. Then again, I guess some people get nervous easily when they're doing illegal things. Luckily some of us are professionals.

I ordered everyone back into the ship except for Wodd, who I kept alongside me. After I'd taken proper stock of the *Nava*, for the first time since the *FSA-01061* crew had violated her, I'd discovered all my blasters gone. Everything I'd hidden. And they were all registered too. Perhaps Reynolds wasn't as straight-laced as I'd imagined. So, although I would've liked Foy's quick thinking and steady aim, the fact that I didn't currently have a gun and that she was supposed to be in charge of the kids, made that tricky. Better to have them all back home in the *Nava*. I had her pilot the ship back to the terminal so that whoever came for the guns wouldn't see the tell-tale sign of my ship parked out back.

As it happened, there was a café just across the street from Drok's sweet shop, so that was where me and Wodd took up our seats. I ordered a heavily caffeinated moiser, while Wodd—who claimed that he didn't drink—ordered some standard moisture pack. The bill was pretty eye-watering, looking back on it, and I would've put up more of a stink if we hadn't been trying to keep a low profile.

Nothing happened at Drok's for quite a while. We watched on as the cleaning droids buzzed about the storefront, cleaning up the windows, polishing the brass doorknob, sweeping the front step—if Milky had been with us he would've been having a fit.

A while later, just after I'd polished off my third moiser, a large ship, painted in black drifted through the air, sending loose bits of paper and plastic wrappers scattering over the road. It droned down behind Drok's shop. I watched on as Drok approached the front door and turned the sign around so that it read 'Closed.'

Wodd slept on the table with his head resting on his folded up arms.

I gave him a nudge and he stirred. "We're on," I said.

He looked at me with bleary eyes and then gazed out through the window. "Wha—?"

"A ship, it just landed around back. Completely black. Come on," I said, pressing my hand to the table scanner to pay for our drinks, taking it off the Fonch Confectionaries' expense account of course, "let's go take a look."

We went out the back of the café in an attempt to avoid detection. I was worried that Drok might recognise us if we emerged from the front. We snuck our way along the street, crossed over and then made our way along a narrow side alley in the hope of getting a look at the ship that had just landed. I glanced around the corner right in time to get a face full of blaster.

As they usually do when put into a situation such as that, my hands reached for the sky pretty sharpish, and I sensed Wodd doing the same—bright boy that one, fast learner.

I examined the guy with the gun. Emerald green eyes. Black hair. Leathery wrinkles. It was Gus.

"All right," Gus said. "You boys packing anything I should know about?"

"Nope," I said.

"No," Wodd said, sounding somewhat weedy.

"Fine. My boy right here's going to check you both out just the same, okay? It's not like I'm not trusting, but I always get this gut-feeling right here"—he indicated his upper abdomen —"whenever I find people hanging about looking suspicious that they might not be quite telling the whole truth."

Another man appeared at his side. I recognised him as one of the goons from *The Bitch's*. He was a head and shoulders taller than Gus and about twice as wide. I have to admit that I really didn't relish picking any fight with him. Hell, my coopera-tion was all his. He had a head of lush hair—which I recall being a touch jealous of—and it shuffled around his shoulders as he went through the routine of padding both me and Wodd down. He returned to Gus's side and nodded to him.

Gus allowed himself a sly grin. "So, you gonna regale me with some sort of a story about how you don't know what you're doing around here?"

I decided this was my opportunity to, somehow, get us off the hook here. It wasn't going to be easy—I saw that. "We brought the shipment here, the Fonch to Drok. It's just we got back to the terminal and realised that we'd forgotten to get

Drok's authorisation on the shipment. Without the authorisation Fonch Confectionaries won't believe that we didn't just sell the product off for ourselves."

"'Product,' eh?" Gus said, gun jiggling a little in his hand. "You speak like a smuggler. And those clothes you two are wearing doesn't look anything like that of these Fonch nerds. They're always wearing overalls and shit."

"Maybe you don't know the Fonch deliverymen that well."

"Oh," he said, breaking into a smile and shooting the big guy a glance, "believe me I know what these Fonch deliverymen look like, and I'm one hundred per cent certain you ain't them."

"Why don't you just speak to Drok? He'll be able to clear this up."

"Nah," he said, smile widening. "I'll trust my judgement."

Damn, this was a guy after my own heart.

He shot at our feet, leaving a smoking gash in the ground. "Now move it, will you?"

As we passed by Gus, both me and Wodd with our hands still sticking right up in the air, I shook my head and said, "You're making a big mistake. If only you'd get Drok out here, he'd be able to clear all this up."

"Drok ain't in any state to clear anything up."

My blood ran cold and, as the men marched us around the back of the sweet shop, I managed to get a glance in through a back room window, where I saw Drok lying spread-eagled, mouth wide open. They'd shot him. I guessed it might be time for me to revise my previous judgement that Drok was in on what exactly he was receiving from Fonch—he had just been an honest sweet salesman. And now he was dead.

"Hurry up!" Gus said. "You're lucky. If I didn't twig it was you right away, if I hadn't identified your ship leaving Tetrahedron you'd have been dead, Captain Wright. Still prepared to kill your friend here, though, if it'll get those chubby legs working faster."

"He's not my friend."

"Oh?"

"He's my engineer."

Gus smirked. "Glad your sense of humour's still intact. You're going to need it when you speak to Radley."

If my blood had run cold before, right then and there it froze right up. I actually stopped moving. "You mean, you're taking me to him?"

"Less questions, more movement, fatso."

I stared up the ship's walkway, leading up into darkness. I knew that the minute I stepped up there I would be handing my life over to these two reprobates—and I'd been so sure that Radley had been the one behind wanting me dead before. Were these to be my last steps on the face of the universe? Once they got me up there would they just plug me, then flush me out into space when they broke the atmosphere? There wasn't much I could do. If I hadn't gone up that slope right then he would've shot me for not doing so. There wouldn't have been any speculation about it.

I reached my conclusion, deciding that if they'd wanted me dead they would've shot me by now. Last time Radley's men had got me cornered, back in *The Bitch's*, all hell had broken loose, them firing off around at me and Foy. This time, though, they'd already had the opportunity to shoot me between the eyes. I was quite sure they wanted me alive—for whatever reason—and if I resisted they wouldn't bat an eye to use Wodd as leverage. Foy had already testified as to Gus's bloodthirstiness. Just as my life was in their hands, Wodd's life was in mine, and I had to cooperate. Still, the whole situation burnt me up inside, and I rued not having taken the opportunity to replace my blaster. If only I'd had one when they pulled the gun on me I might've been able to take them both down. Yeah right . . . my drawing speed makes hell freezing over look fast.

12: EN ROUTE TO RADLEY'S HIDEOUT AT UNKNOWN LOCATION

THEY TIED both of us up and set us down in the cargo bay, right beside those gigantic space blasters. They set us back to back, probably because they'd seen it in a movie once. I didn't quite see what the purpose of that was, other than for style points. I fiddled about with my bindings for a while but found no purchase in them. These mugs were no mugs.

The vibrations of breaking the atmosphere rattled both our bodies and I decided that this might be a good opportunity to issue something of an apology to Wodd. Once we got ourselves into Radley's hands I was sure that the chances for discourse would be few and far between.

"Look," I said, "like I told you, living the life of the smuggler isn't for everybody. If you want out I'll be more than happy to accept your resignation."

"Captain?"

"Yeah?"

"Is this really the best time to be talking about it?"

"Well, I thought I'd lay things out real honest-like, give you the choice. It's only fair that you get the chance to distance yourself from me before we enter the company of just about the biggest mobster in the known universe."

Wodd did stay silent for a good few seconds, no doubt thinking things through, before saying, "Captain, you stuck up for me back with that FSA fleet, if it weren't for you I'd have been in Radley's hands long ago, or worse, if I hadn't snuck on board your ship, I'd still be stuck on Hortenine-6."

"Yeah," I said, "suppose that's true."

"I owe you, Captain, and I'll stick with you."

"Good man, Wodd, remind me to give you a promotion when we get back on board the *Nava*."

"How would you do that?"

"What?"

"Promote me? There's not really any position open."

"Right, yeah, well, it's the sentiment that counts, isn't it?"

Wodd squirmed a little, apparently still not having quite given up hope on getting his hands free of his bindings, then he said, "Do you think that Foy's getting on all right? You know, alone on the *Nava* piloting it herself?"

I let out an elongated exhale. "Oh, I suppose that she'll just leave her parked in the terminal, not much she can do at this point is there?"

"You do trust her, don't you?"

"Why, just as well as I trust you. She wants to keep those kids safe—like a mother wolf. I don't think she'll do anything to put them in danger, and so, by extension she won't put the *Nava* in danger either."

"You really care about that ship, sir?"

"Of course I do. Every captain cares about his ship."

"I suppose that she's everything to you, really, all the adventures you've flown in it."

"You could put it like that."

"That must be nice."

"'Nice?'"

"Yeah, to have something that really holds that amount of sentimental value for you."

"If you call the *Nava* a 'something' or an 'it' again, I'll find some way to throttle you without using my hands. Maybe I'll butt you to a pulp with the back of my head."

"Understood, sir," he said, promptly shutting up.

The conversation slipped into silence after that brief exchange. If there's one thing about being on the cargo deck of a spaceship it's the realisation of how loud the damn thrusters are. I mean, it's like they pulse right through your eardrums and gnaw away at your brain. You forget all about that when you're up on the bridge, of course—where everything's so smooth and silent you might completely forget that you're whipping through space at ridiculous speeds.

I got a better chance to examine the space lasers. The only look at them I'd had previously was back on Tetrahedron-2 at the Fonch Confectionaries factory. These were big ones and make no mistake. I had a vague memory of seeing similar weapons before, when I was outfitting the *Nava* with her latest arsenal. I had opted against them, both because of FSA regulations and the fact that they'd weigh the *Nava* down, trim her speed down considerably. And, really, how often do you actually wish you had a bigger gun? Freedom of movement, a trim frame and nimble work at the control stick are the best friends of the smuggler.

There not being much else to do, I just closed my eyes and nodded my head down onto my chest, listening to the almost deafening roar of the engines mingle with my mind, turning it in circles and spirals.

———

It was the absence of droning engines which brought me around. I blinked the sleep out of my eyes and gave a large yawn. It felt like, while I'd been sleeping, someone had sawn open my skull, slipped my brain out and smushed it about before, kindly, putting it back. My eyes felt filmy and bulky in their sockets, like a pair of pickled eggs. I craned my neck toward the door to the cargo hold, trying to gain some sort of clue as to our current situation. I recalled all the getting dragged at gunpoint, tied up here in this ship, the two men, and they'd said that I was to be brought to Radley. So that was where I supposed I where I was. Wherever that was.

The door to the cargo hold whirred open on its servo. Light flooded in through the opening, along with a, quite pleasant, scent of flowers. It was weird. For whatever reason, I'd always supposed that Radley holed himself up on some unforgiving planet way out in the middle of nowhere. The two men appeared as silhouettes in the doorway. They approached us at a slow trudge, no doubt weary from their journey.

I spoke quietly over my shoulder to Wodd. "Hey? You awake."

"Just about."

"Leave the talking to me, okay?"

Gus watched over his companion doing the untying. I guessed, as usually works in these brain for brawn scenarios, that Gus always did his best not to get his hands dirty with the grunt work—that grabbing me around the scruff of the shirt back in *The Bitch's* aside. They got us standing there, free as anything. I took a bit of offence at that, that they didn't see either of us as being enough of a threat to so much pull a gun. Then I realised that perhaps it was because Radley's influence roamed this entire planet. That if we *did* try something we would never get away with it. Come to think of it, why wouldn't the universe's most notorious mobster have his own planet?

Those delightful flowery smells I'd picked up on back in the cargo hold turned out to be just as wonderful as I'd imagined. With the two oafs treading on our heels, we arrived at the bottom of the access ramp and emerged into what could only be described as a prim and perky garden.

Birds tweeted in the trees, fruit looked lush hanging off branches and flaxen grass unfurled beneath our feet, extending for stretches as far as the eye could see, up and down rolling hills. The place looked like some sort of paradise.

As the two men marched us on I caught sight of a mansion popping up on the horizon. I supposed that was where Radley called home. It was funny because, despite all that dread I'd felt back on Drokul-15, the fear that Radley's mere name inspired, this whole experience so far had gone a long way to reassuring me. Where I'd been expecting steel-grey walls, towering turrets and gun outposts—maybe a sea of lava, I'd actually been greeted by emerald forests, hopping bunnies and a crisp, clear blue sky. It was tough to be negative in that environment. But I did find a way.

I twirled around to face Gus companion and said, "All this lot's missing is a great, big lake, lovely crystal sparkling thing. Wouldn't that complete this picture?"

"Boss's digging one out," Gus said. "I wouldn't mention it if I were you. Always gets asked about that, only now getting around to doing it."

I thought about another witty remark, something along the lines of 'crime paying after all' but decided to drop the idea—realising that I was supposed to be keeping schtum for the good of Wodd.

They steered us through a pleasant gravelled pathway replete with a fountain and several, what looked like, marble statues. One thing I noticed, a strange feature, was that there wasn't a single droid anywhere in sight. I wondered who did all the maintenance on the gardens. Or perhaps they had them on early-morning programmes. When I couldn't hold myself back any longer I asked Gus the question.

"Boss doesn't trust robots," he replied.

So there was my answer.

The mansion itself smelled clean and an overpowering stench of crushed flowers permeated everything. I brought the collar of my shirt up to cover my mouth and nose.

Gus sneered. "Tell us about it, eh? But that's how the boss likes it. Says it keeps the stench of money at bay."

"I suppose that's a point."

A pair of chunky wooden doors confronted us. Each of them had an elaborate curvy pattern etched into the wood. I guessed that, judging by Gus's comment on the droids outside, these two doors had had no intervention from robots. They were most likely hand-carved. Only a bent president or a mobster general could afford for that to be done.

A man dressed in a white lab coat emerged from between the doors. A scientist, I supposed. He had a look of concern stitched over his face as he looked over us. He turned his attention to Gus. I got the impression that these two went out of their way to avoid one another, just something in the scientist's tone. "This them?" he said.

"What's it to you?" Gus said.

The scientist sighed, gazed back over us and then stomped off into the depths of the mansion.

After a brief pause, while Gus peered in between the doors, he invited us in. I kept my eyes to the floor till I heard the bulky doors slam behind us. Then I peered upward to take in the room spread out before me.

Nothing much remarkable. At least, nothing much at odds with the rest of the mansion—which was to say, gigantic tumbling velvet drapes, windows with a golden sheen and it seemed like that stench of crushed flowers had been cranked up a notch or two. The most surprising aspect of the whole operation was the middle-aged, fairly innocuous-looking lady who sat at the oak desk with her hands firmly clasped before her.

Still reeling from the sensation of being hands-free, I gave my arse a reassuring scratch then said, "Uh, are you Radley's wife or something?"

She wore a business suit with a pair of serious-looking shoulder pads. Her hair puffed up, a little like a cloud and she had an easy smile, which seemed at odds with her focussed gaze. "You must be Captain Arkle Wright."

"That's me."

She got up from her seat, revealing her to be of pretty diminutive stature. She strutted over, looking each of us over in turn.

"Look," I said, "it's all very well having a pair of heavies scare the bejesus out of us, pointing their blasters any which way they like, and then having them drag us all the way out here —wherever *here* is—but when're we going to get to see Radley? You can't put it off forever."

A slight smile tweaked the corner of her mouth. "You know," she said, "even after all my years in the business, one thing I've noticed is that, if anything, space smugglers have got dimmer as a collection of people."

I was almost offended by that, but I knew, deep down, what she was saying was essentially true. Our numbers are pretty much made up by drop-outs: army, school, authorities, you name it, we've got failure in bulk.

"Tell me," she said. "When have you ever seen a picture of this Radley figure?"

That stumped me. "Uh, well, I guess I haven't, ma'am."

"'Ma'am?'" she said. "I think I quite like the sound of that. Your other manners might need a bit of work. All that nagging your mother no doubt gave you to stop scratching your bottom in public has gone missing, I can't help but point out."

"With all due respect, *ma'am*, manners don't much feature in my line of work."

"No, I don't suppose they do."

I was aware of Gus and big guy still standing behind us. I wondered what this meeting might be about, whether it might be some sort of a pre-filter, that this woman would decided whether or not we'd be able to see Radley at all. Maybe she'd simply have us taken outside and shot if we failed to impress her sufficiently. Perhaps I should've been upping my game a little. Those crushed flower petals were really starting to tickle away at my nostril hair—kind of akin to sniffing hydrochloric acid fumes.

The woman returned to her desk where she perched on the arm of her chair and drummed her fingers. A woody *thu-thunk, thu-thunk* resounded through the room. After the first few times she did it, it began to drive me utterly batty. I was on the point of asking her, politely, to stop when she did so herself and said, "My full name is Alis Radley-Hadton."

"Oh," I said, a touch dumbfounded. "So you *are* Radley's wife?"

"No," she said, with a little poison in her tone of voice. "I *am* Radley."

All at once it sunk in. Finally.

Arching her eyebrow, she inspected her fingernails. "Now, Captain Wright, tell me, where is the stone?"

So this seemed the reason why I was still alive, until now. She wanted to get her hands on it. "No idea, sorry," I said.

"You know, it's really been most unfortunate that you've got yourself tangled up in all this business. It would've been much better if you hadn't accepted that offer in the first place."

"What do you mean?"

"Your accepting to run the stone from Kools to Hortenine-6 where my men were instructed to pick it up."

"But you were behind giving me the stone in the first place, weren't you? I mean, all that getting me to take the stone off Kools was a ruse to pin me with the blame for stealing the stone —getting me onto the most-wanted list in the Fritten System— only then to pop me off when I'd handed it over to you."

"I can see that you've given this matter a lot of thought."

"I like to think that I'm thorough."

"Yes, well, I can tell you right now that I wanted you dead, whoever it was that was supposed to drop off the stone— although my men failed to blow you all away, despite blowing apart half of that public house."

"You mean *The Bitch's Leap?*"

She grimaced. "I've always hated that name. Please do not say it in my company."

"Sorry, got a bit of a potty mouth." I jabbed my tongue into my cheek in deep thought. "But, you're saying that you weren't behind giving me the stone in the first place?"

"No, why would I do something as idiotic as that?"

"Like I just said, to pin me with the blame, so the authorities would come after me rather than you."

"Please," she said. "Do you really think that someone like me—someone who is busy stockpiling an army with blaster lasers—is really worried about what the authorities, what those FSA fleets are up to?"

Thinking that this might be a good point to emphasise how little I actually knew of Radley's operation, I said, "Not really, no."

She rose to her feet and stalked back and forth, like a slighted general. "No, I need the Stone of the Angels, and I shall kill whoever I have to in order to get my hands on it. It's the final piece of the puzzle. All that I need to put the plan into action."

Again, I really had no interest in finding out what this 'plan' constituted. I just wanted to get out of that stuffy, flower-smelling room. But, at the same time, I realised that this might be time for me to get answers over my own situation. "Then who gave the stone to Kools? How did he get his hands on it to send it over to you?"

"Kools knew people. He was in the right place at the right time."

"Care to be a bit more specific?"

She smouldered away. "No, not really. You need to learn your place, Captain Wright. I heard that you went on a visit to Fonch Confectionaries, and came away with a contract of employment."

"They were extremely persuasive."

"Tell me, did you have time to study those machines—did Mr Clark take you on the full tour of the place, show you exactly how we make the sweeties?"

"In fact he did. It was a pretty complete tour, actually."

"I am glad," she said, her features darkening. "And did he

show you those conveyor belts, the ones which carry the product through the whole place?"

"Well, yeah."

"And did you notice that the conveyor belts are made up of stitched together fabrics? Fabrics that, for the purpose of this metaphor, might be imagined to be space smugglers carrying products around the galaxy? Now that we're on the same page, would you mind as to speculate on what might happen if one of those fabrics got a tear or somehow wore itself out?"

I shrugged my shoulders. "You'd replace it?"

"Yes, I would, or at least one of the maintenance *droids* would," she said the word 'droids' as if it were contagious. "The whole point of this exercise is that you, Arkle, being a smuggler are infinitely replaceable. There are a dozen lined up waiting to waddle into your place."

Although some of the other things she'd said might've been somewhat melodramatic, she really wasn't exaggerating by saying that we 'waddle,' we really do—there's a whole series of jokes built around how space smugglers have a certain obese waddle.

"And just to track back to your previous question, you have no reason to know about how the rest of the system works—you do your little job and leave the planning to the brainy people. Capish?"

"Listen, sister, all that's fine except when you start sending people after me and my crew, trying to kill us. You hauling us in right now, for example, just to insult me by the face of things."

"I *want* that stone, and I shall have it. I'm afraid that I simply don't believe you when you say that you don't have it."

"Can only tell the truth."

"I'm not talking about exactly where the stone is now—I wouldn't expect you to have it on your person—what I want to know is exactly where in the universe you've deposited it, left it for safe keeping."

Right there she just about blew through all my attempted defences. I have to admit that she knew her adversary in and out. Then again, I don't guess you reach the top of a criminal organisation without being lickety-split smart. Not without being someone's niece or wife, which she'd already made quite plain that she wasn't.

"Well?" she said.

This whole situation, the stone among everything else. I might not have understood much about what was going on, but I knew the stone was important and, what with all those laser blasters being bandied about, it was important to keep that stone away from any questionable influences. Some things are bigger than a paycheque. "Sorry," I said, "you're going to have to trawl around for someone else, because I simply don't have it, and I've got no idea where it might be."

"I have to say that I don't believe you."

"Then it looks like we're in a stalemate."

"Or maybe I just need a touch more leverage." She looked over my head to the larger of the two heavies. "Kev? You want to take the other one and have him put in for the electro circuit?"

Wodd broke from his daze and looked around him with ogling eyes.

"Wait!" I said, "I promise I've told you all I know. Leave him alone. If you're going to torture one of us, pick me."

Radley smirked. "Please," she said, "you don't get anywhere torturing a *captain*, it's all about getting to him through his crewmembers, making him feel so bad that he has no choice but to spill what he knows."

The larger heavy, Kev apparently, took hold of Wodd's wrists and tied them together. He lugged him toward the large wooden doors behind us.

"Just a second!" I said.

Radley tilted her head to one side in expectation.

"I *might* have some ideas on the whereabouts of the stone."

13: RADLEY'S BASE – UNKNOWN LOCATION

RADLEY'S PRISONS put those on board the FSA mother ship to shame. Whereas we'd had a pretty simple, if effective, setup on board the *FSA-01061*—that name's catchier than I gave it credit—what with those laser bars and the windowless room, there at Radley's mansion there weren't any bars at all. In fact, I would go so far as to suggest that we were in nothing less than a guest room.

We didn't get separate quarters, of course, something I could empathise with since that would've meant double the amount of guards. As it was we were quite cosy what with our twin beds and en suite shower. There was a pretty view out over the whole of Radley's mansion grounds. I could make out a few bunny rabbits quite happily hopping along, in and out of holes they'd burrowed through the lawn. I guess that was one problem with Radley not employing droids of any kind—that all the little critters could just about have any sort of paradise they wanted. Lucky bastards.

At least my outburst had saved Wodd from whatever torture they'd wanted to inflict on him for the time being. Now I had some time to think, I could work out how I was going to go through with my promise to give Radley *some* information on the whereabouts of the stone. It was tricky because I didn't want to lead her right to it, to tell her that it was on the *Nava*, for obvious reasons—namely that I didn't want her to have it. And neither did I want to point out some completely ridiculous, implausible location, because she was more than likely to smell it a mile off. Nope, this was what you'd call being stuck up Shit Alley without a blaster.

As I stood there, still looking out the window, trying to think of a plausible place that I, a dirty smuggler, might've hidden the stone, I noticed, in the distance, a series of spaceships rising into the air and taking off. I guessed we must've come from pretty much the same place—when Gus and Kev brought us here. If only we could get over there, with Wodd's brains intact, I was certain we'd be able to hotwire one of them and go on our merry way, back out into space. That was one great, big *if*.

I examined the terrain which led over to the spaceport. It was all much the same as I'd taken in on our trip to the mansion —rolling hills, lush green pastures, no obvious sign of armed gunmen ready to take anyone escaping down. I assumed that, in a place such as this, Radley kept an on-planet force to watch over, and I had no doubt that if we dared to step out onto the that lawn a fleet of security ships would descend on us. And then there was that nagging, reckless voice gnawing at the back of my skull, telling me that we could do it. If we *really* wanted to.

Footsteps in the corridor outside our room drew my attention away from my ponderings. I was quite glad, actually, because I'd been getting a little carried away. This was Radley's headquarters—Radley the most notorious mobster in the universe, woman or no, and I was actually thinking of breaking out, going out of my way to spit in her eye.

The door swung open to reveal Gus, trademark smirk emblazoned onto his lips. "Captain Wright, Radley would like to see you now."

I'm not sure quite what I had in mind at that point, but I was determined all the same. Maybe I'm a subconscious planner, that plans just come to me . . . that's my excuse anyway. And it was with that determination that I decided to put up a fight. "My crewmember stays with me."

Gus shook his head. "Not a chance."

"Look here, this whole business was based on the fact that you wouldn't harm Wodd if I cooperated with your search for the Stone of the Angels. Now, do you want my cooperation or not?"

Gus raised an eyebrow. "Are you seriously saying that we have to take young Wodd here and stick him through an electro circuit?"

"What I'm saying is, how do I know you won't sneak him off behind my back while I'm helping you out?"

"I'd say you have every reason to do exactly what we say, no questions asked."

"Even so," I said. "I'd like to hear what Radley thinks about it. Tell her that I want to take Wodd with me, he's not to stay in the room alone. If she wants my cooperation."

Gus opened then shut his mouth, before stalking off in a huff along the corridor.

Round One to Arkle.

Gus stalked back, fuming, a few minutes later. He looked Wodd in the eye, looking as if he was trying to burn through his sockets using nothing more than his irises, and then he turned to me. "Boss says it's fine. Bring your cabin boy along."

As Gus retreated back along the corridor, Wodd tapped me on the shoulder. "Captain? Wouldn't it be better for me to stay here, in the room. I mean, I don't want to cause any trouble at all. Isn't it better that we just do what they say? Won't there be less of a chance that they'll kill us."

"Kill us, *smill* us. If we don't make any demands then they'll have us just where they want us—a pair of placated space bums ripe for plucking. We've got information they need and we're not willing to part for it. They just need a reminder of which boot's on which foot. That's how negotiation works."

"I learn all sorts with you, Captain."

"Just stick with me and you'll never have any need for education."

––––––––

Maybe I overextended our hand just a touch. Gus led us through several winding corridors, ominously further down into the building, into what I guessed to be a second, or even third, basement. Looking back on things, everything just screamed 'medieval dungeon,' right up to the steel door which guarded our destination. The benefit of hindsight, eh?

While we stood on the hearth, we got decidedly a little wary. At that point Gus whipped out his blaster and waggled it around our faces. "In," he said, as if we were nothing more than a pair of naughty dogs.

As we skirted the rim of the room, pretty much taken up with an electro circuit—a torture device consisting of a wooden chair, an insulator, leather straps for legs and arms, also insulators, and then there's the titular 'circuit,' for want of a better description, a large computer circuit which is pressed to the victim's chest. Very much a conductor that device.

Radley entered from the door on the other side of the room. She removed her suit jacket and hung it off a hook on the opposing wall, very much with a carefree manner which suggested she did this sort of thing rather a lot. Next she rolled up the sleeves of her blouse and looked between me and Wodd. "All right," she said. "Which one of you is going first?"

My brain broke out of its rut. "Wait," I said. "I thought we had a deal?"

"'A deal?' What *deal* was that exactly?"

"That you wouldn't torture us if I were to give you the secret to the stone?"

She frowned, turning her forehead into a mountain range of wrinkles. "Funny, I don't recall saying those exact words."

"Well, it was all kind of implied."

She examined the operation panel on the wall behind the electro circuit. She waved her hand over the central console and a series of options appeared. She tapped through them, bringing it to a screen which said, quite merrily, I thought, 'Ready!'

"No," she said. "You've had time to tell us what you know. I left you to stew in that room for a day and got nothing. Conditions change, and I have a rather urgent need for the stone's whereabouts. No more sweating you, being all polite and patient."

"Ah," I said. "But that's just the thing. Just as your dear henchman came to get me and my crewman, I was just that moment thinking of the best way for you to get the stone—you know, avoiding any congestion, FSA fleet patrols, all that unwanted complication."

"Hmm?"

"In fact, I can tell you right now."

"Can you?"

I racked my brains and opened my mouth. There was that giveaway, slight pause before I said, "It's on Hortenine-6."

"What?" she said.

"That's right. Actually," I said, thinking that I really had a convincing story now, "I dropped it while we were making our escape from *The Bitch's*. Have you thought of retracing that place? I mean, really going over it with a fine-toothed comb?"

"It's not on Hortenine-6."

"You sound awfully convinced."

"That's because we have ways to track the stone. I can conclusively say that it's not there."

"Maybe there's something wrong with whatever equipment you're using."

She shook her head. "No, the equipment's infallible."

"You sound very confident."

"That's because I know my business. In fact, I make it my business to know my business."

"Right," I said, eyeing the electro circuit again. "So, there's nothing I can say that'll change your mind?"

"Look, I've gone to all the trouble of bringing you both down here now, to this room. I might as well give you both a quick fry on the electro circuit. You'd be surprised at what people know once they've got a bit of electricity scrabbling around their veins."

"Uh, uh," I said, really searching for something now, "haven't you read those reports, you know, the ones that state that victims of torture aren't all that likely to divulge the truth? It's really an inefficient way of going about it."

She shrugged. "Maybe it is. What difference does it make, though? You're lying to me now, so I might as well have some fun with the electro circuit, see what lies you can cook up later. Makes things a bit more entertaining."

"That sounds a bit sadistic," I said.

"Yes, well, you don't get on in this business without having a bit of the devil's backbone. But I've got the feeling that you or your crewmember will be one of those that does spill the guts of the matter without too much trouble. Pain has a habit of getting people to tell the truth, whatever your sources might say. The majority, in my humble experience."

I glanced around the room, seeing Gus still standing in the doorway, blaster in his mitt. In that moment I saw that he was a little distracted, examining some detail on the electro circuit and my pre-Neanderthal brain snapped out of neutral.

I flew forward, arms scrabbling all about and caught him off guard.

He shot a beam. Its warmth flourished past my cheek and I listened to the dampened *hiss* as it made contact with the wall behind.

I snatched hold of the blaster and tugged it from his hand.

Gus stumbled backward with the force of my grab, tripped over the electro circuit and landed square in the seat of the chair.

Before I got all big-headed about what I'd just managed to achieve, I pivoted around and pointed the blaster at both Radley and Gus. "Stay where you are," I said.

They both glared at me.

"Actually," I said, allowing a little complacency to creep in. "Put your hands in the air."

Grudgingly, they both did so.

"Good, that's good," I said, then turned my attention to Wodd. "What're you waiting for then, kid? Let's get the hell out of here."

Wodd remained shook up for another few moments. He looked to both Gus and Radley as if asking their permission to leave. Finally, he shipped himself out into the corridor, disappearing from sight.

Radley sneered. "You'll never get away with this. You do realise that I'll make it my number one objective to have you hunted down and killed?"

To be fair, I was already feeling a little queasy about what I was doing—and the way I'd gone about it. But I'd taken the leap now and there really wasn't anyway I was going to be able to worm my way back up. "Yeah," I said. "Well, I'll be ready."

I shot a beam at the floor, sending up a puff of dust and causing a heap of confusion in the room. Keeping my head bowed as I rushed out of the door, I thought over my last words, wondering if, given a little more time, I might've come up with something a little more menacing. Just as with everything else, I admitted to myself that what was done was done. I'd made an enemy for life—however short that was going to be—and now I'd have to live with that choice.

Wodd, obviously not quite used to these daring escapes just yet, lingered about in the corridor, awaiting my cue.

"Go!" I said, ploughing past him and snatching hold of his sleeve.

Together, we bounded back up the stairs into the main hall of the mansion where we were confronted with Kev. Poor Kev, he looked more bemused that an ape having a suit fitted for a wedding as I shot him in the shin. He doubled over crying out in pain, and I murmured a word of insincere apology as we blazed out through the door and into the expansive gardens.

I expected a dirty rain of cruisers to rain down on us, but we had no such welcome. I watched off in the distance as space-ships shuttled upward through the heat haze from the space-port. We would get there soon. We would boost one of them and be away. Geed up by this prospect, I tugged Wodd close, trying to keep him near to me in case anyone saw fit to shoot at us. I felt for the kid, he'd never been on the run from the most successful mobster in the galaxy before.

Dainty leaves and prickly branches brushed our clothing as

we sprinted through the gardens and onward, toward our destination. I saw off the urge to glance back over my shoulder,
telling myself that it would only slow us down. I was almost
certain that Radley and Gus would only just be leaving the
basement—and they'd be more occupied with getting their
lungs clean of that dust than chasing after us.

Perhaps I should've be a little more measured in my
thinking because, when I inevitably did turn, I caught sight of
Radley and Gus bobbing down the front steps of the mansion,
apparently both now with a laser blaster apiece. That was also
about the time when I heard the tell-tale *whine* of the security
ships making their way in our direction. Thankfully we were
already nearing the spaceport. In fact, I could make out the ship
which Gus and Kev had brought us in on. It was just standing
there, parked up, walkway still down—they had the audacity to
assume that no one would try and boost a ship here, not on
Radley's planet. But, then again, me and Radley were just
getting to know one another.

We panted our way up to the spaceport, through the unat-
tended gate. I risked another look back to see, on one side,
Radley and Gus drawing closer by the second—but still a good
four or five hundred metres away—and, more worryingly, on the
other side, I spotted a security ship, two actually, making in our
direction. The ships were hoverbikes, just one occupant on
each, but both of them had a nasty-looking blaster that was just
crying out for a little usage.

I checked out our options and decided that the ship Gus
and Kev had brought us on looked the best bet, so I snatched
hold of the gaping Wodd yet again and dragged him in the

direction of the walkway. We jogged up into the ship and I flipped the switch to shut the door behind us. I watched as it cranked upward, impossibly slowly, seemingly too slow for us to see off the dual threat of the security ships and our pursuers on foot. I knew better than to wait around and I bolted—well, my body doesn't allow me much in the way of 'bolting' *per se*, but I did get up a half-decent jiggle. The upshot of all the rushing about was that I got to the controls of the ship and sank down in the captain's chair, marvelling about how things had reversed so delightfully—that mere minutes ago Radley had been on the point of torturing me and my good ship's engineer, and now I sat at the controls of one of the more menacing members of her fleet.

I ditched the blaster, not having any use for it here, and wasted no more time as I set the ship up along the take off routine, putting up the shields while I got my bearings. I listened as the blaster beams bounced off the protective shell and watched as the security ships buzzed past the main windscreen several times. I swore to myself more than once as I wrestled with this unfamiliar interface. Once you're used to flying one ship, and you don't have much variation, flying just feels downright strange in anything else.

As I scrabbled to get the thing off the ground, Wodd said helpful things like, "Sir, I think they've penetrated the blast shield!" and "Captain, I'm sure I just heard the walkway crank open," then "They're inside, sir! They must be by now!"

I flipped the ground thruster switch, leant over, looked Wodd right in the eye and said, "Shut up!"

I grasped the control stick as I felt the ship leaving the

ground below us. It felt much bulkier than the *Nava*, it should've done being at least four times her size. As I wrestled with the controls I had to keep reminding myself that big girls need love too—it became something of a mantra for me as I lifted her upward, pointed her to the sky. But, as much as I tried to fire the thrusters, they remained deafeningly quiet. The ship hung about ten or twenty metres off the ground, and we weren't going anywhere. For the first time during our daring escape, Wodd contributed something useful.

"Sir!" he said. "We're still locked into the port."

Now, every spaceport in the universe has such a system. It's generally controlled by whoever staffs the control tower at the terminal. The system consists of an invisible chainlike construction which holds the ship in place to its launching pad, and will not be released without appropriate permission being granted by the land authority. This isn't merely a physical restraint, it actually exercises control over the ship's computers, overriding the native controls. This was Wodd's time to shine, if ever he'd have one.

I turned to him. "Don't just sit there gawking like you've seen a *nekid* lady sitting on the nose of ship, talk to this beauty's soul, will ya?"

Wodd shifted out of his seat, wide-eyed. He popped the panel off the electronics system in a matter of seconds. God, sometimes I love that boy.

Contrary to Wodd's earlier paranoiac outbursts concerning the progress of our adversaries, I caught a gander of the damage meters and saw, with no little horror, that they'd more or less expended our blast shield at the rear. I pictured us from their perspective, floating above the deck, like a helium balloon. I thought of them as being little kids taking pot-shots at us with their slingshots, except instead of sling-shots they had high-powered, army-issued blasters. And I reached the conclusion that Radley had given up on what she considered diplomacy, and considered me more than a fair target at present, whether or not she shot her own ship out of the sky.

Wodd muttered to himself as he worked and I resisted the urge to give him a good cuff around the ear to speed him up, just like a good captain should do from time to time.

Hopelessly, I tried the thrusters again and again, to no avail, and I watched as the happy green colour flushed out of the damage meter, bringing us into orange, and then red. Seeing this, I said, "Kid? It's too late. We're going to have to bail out. They're going to be melding us into the ship's body before too long."

On his hands and knees, head stuck into that electronics unit, like a pig in a trough, Wodd waggled his finger at me and called back. "I've almost got it, sir! We'll be out of here in seconds."

"Seconds we don't have," I said.

The ship lurched and I heard the unmistakable, infinitely melancholic downbeat *moan* of the blaster shields retreating. I leapt from my seat and jerked Wodd to his feet. I shoved him up the ladder leading to the upper deck of the ship. A transparent ceiling revealed the sky above us and, further up, space. But we weren't going up there any time soon. Our first priority was to get out of this soon-to-be, melted hunk of metal. I located the escape pod and jabbed the red button to open its lock. No response. I jabbed it again.

"Shit," I said.

"Is something the matter?"

"What do you think?"

The ship lurched again, and I lost my footing, tumbling all the way along the now-slippery floor and landing with a *thunk* against the opposing wall. They'd damaged the stabilisers. Before too long the thing would be spinning around like a moiserhead after tenth hour. I held onto a pipe which jutted out of the wall, and caught Wodd as he tumbled down to join me. "Looks like this is a pretty thorough mess, kid."

"What're we going to do?"

"Dying might well be the easiest option right about now."

And then, in the middle distance, beyond the steaming sounds of blasters, I heard a familiar *hum*, a divine *hum*. Why, I'd know that *hum* just about anywhere. No, scratch that. I'd know that *hum* anywhere at all. It was her, my girl. The *Navaplastas!*

———

I got over my jubilation pretty fast. Just about the time the ship jerked beneath our feet for the umpteenth time, I clicked that we were still very much on a sinking ship. And that we would become quite intimate with it in a very molten way within a matter of seconds if we didn't act fast.

I kept my eyes fixed to the transparent ceiling, and I caught sight of the *Nava* just as she buzzed overhead. I watched her blaster firing on those attacking us from the ground and I noticed that the shooting subsided. I had time to speculate who might be at the blaster: Milky, while Foy's cousins watched on, just as the ship swung around and sent us flying to the other side.

As we lay there in a heap, feeling the ship gyrating over and over again, Wodd said, "Captain? How're we going to get out?"

"I don't kno—"

In a flash of light the ceiling above our heads smashed wide open. A direct hit from the *Nava's* cannons. I stood stunned, thinking about how close that shot could've come to killing both me and Wodd, but not too long, seeing our chance to dash over to the newly opened escape route.

The ship got caught in a gentle flat spin. I felt my stomach crunch in on itself and nausea seep through me, but I held back my vomit. There're times for vomiting and times for action. And this was a time for action.

Obviously several steps ahead of my thinking, Foy hovered the *Nava* right overhead, and I watched as the familiar collection tube dangled down, ready to suck us up. At that point I recalled that I hadn't had the damn thing looked at for ages—not bothered to service it. The reason? I had difficulty getting my wide gut through its not-so-ample girth, okay? And being, until recently, a solo pilot I had never really had reason to use it. Never having had to pick anyone up.

I'd like to say that the reason I allowed Wodd to step on my shoulders and be the first up the pipe was because I'm a noble and clear thinking person, a true captain. But, it was more likely for one of those reasons I've mentioned above. Those, and I wanted to see whether it might chew up Wodd. He was the guinea pig.

The tube did its work on Wodd, sucking him right up into the *Nava*. I watched on as the tube dangled lower, getting closer to me. The ship below my feet sped up its revolutions and I knew that I'd have to take the leap sooner rather than later, or I really would be done for. And so I did jump upward, feeling the suction struggling to drag my flab kicking and screaming into the belly of the *Nava*.

I didn't get stuck. Not quite. There were a few moments where I was close, where I thought that I would never ever get any further along. But just as I thought I'd got stuck for good the suction would find its second wind and gargle me along the pipe. Before I knew it I was lying crumpled up in the cargo bay of the *Nava*, safe if a little perturbed.

There was no time to waste as I scrabbled onto my hands and knees before breaking from a crawl to an upright position. I arrived in the cockpit just in time to see, through the windscreen, the ship spiralling downward, into the spaceport and then, with a final flourish of the tail, plunge headfirst into the hard, hard ground.

Boom!

14: RENDEZVOUS WITH FSA-01061

GENERALLY SPEAKING I am not an emotional person. However, there are certain circumstances when I'll quite gladly let go of my otherwise stiff, unforgiving space smuggler persona. That was why, as Foy steered the *Nava* upward, toward the stars, I couldn't help but let out a sound, something approaching, *"Ta-wee!"* and clasping her tight. I only let go when she told me that she needed her arm, and air in her lungs, to snap on the thrusters. I let her loose but stopped short of allowing her to leave my grateful gaze.

This woman and these kids had saved our bacon. And they'd done it in our greatest hour of need. I knew, without a doubt, that if they hadn't turned up right when they had, then we'd have been done for—a pair of deceased cyborgs. Of course, they might've turned up when we'd been at the mansion, swept us off the front steps. But not everything in life goes completely to plan. I told myself that from then on I'd make an extra special effort to go out of my way not to be *so* sexist in future. And whenever I complained inwardly about a mewling brat while I sat in a diner taking in a late, late breakfast following a hectic job, I would remember that moment. And I'd further say that all those sentiments lasted a good few minutes before my darkened, decrepit soul ate them up.

Only when we'd got ourselves a good stretch away from Radley's planet did Foy turn around in the captain's seat—a seat which I had to say suited her quite nicely—and ask me where to next.

"You know," I said, trying to wriggle the pent up tension out of my neck and back, "there're times when calling the police is just a good idea."

"And this is one of those times?"

"I think so, my dear."

No matter how good Foy did look in that captain's seat, I soon had it back for my own sizable behind. I found that her rather skinny backside had cut into the groove I'd etched into the chair. But not to worry, I thought to myself, I'd soon get things back to normal. They wouldn't separate me and the *Nava* so easily next time. More easily said than done, I suspected.

We called up the good old *FSA-01061* on our communications screen and I had an efficient, if frosty, conversation with Captain Reynolds. We gave him our coordinates and he agreed to meet us at the designated point. I'm not sure what quite got his attention more—the part about Radley's base or the part about a sweet factory pumping out military-standard blasters. Either way, he was setting himself up for a nice, fat promotion. I just hoped he would remember me when all the dust settled. If there's anything a smuggler can do with more of it's friends within the Fritten System Authorities, or if not friends then I'd settle for an acquaintance, and I was sure Reynolds would make a good one of those.

As we sat there, bobbing about space, waiting for the give-away snaps of light as the fleet entered our vision, I remembered the Stone of the Angels and confronted Foy over it.

"Where is it?" I said.

She grinned at me.

"Safe then?" I said, pressing her.

She gave me a nod.

Better not to ask too many questions. I was sure that wherever she'd thought to stow it, it would be safe. And, following that brush with torture and the like, it was probably best that I knew as little as possible of the exact whereabouts of the stone. Despite my hardiness, the arguments I'd put up in an attempt to stop Radley using the electro circuit, I knew that I would've caved into pain pretty soon. I have no problem admitting it straight out. I'm a cry baby. Yeah? So what?

This time things were quite different. For a start the *FSA-01061* sent *us* approach permission and I angled the *Nava* so that we drew up alongside the mother ship. I watched in wonder, this time able to fully appreciate the quantity of smaller ships which accompanied the *FSA-01061*. Just like lion cubs. Lion cubs with laser blasters.

All things considered I think I prefer being an informer to being a suspect. Both are pretty dire, but the former at least means you're treated with a little respect.

Reynolds was just as unsmiling and business-like as I

remembered him. However it appeared that in the course of our separation he'd gone and acquired himself a sense of humour. "I see you've picked up a few runaways. You'll be opening an orphanage soon."

I didn't say it was a good sense of humour.

He instructed for my crew to be taken care of, for an officer to show them to the cafeteria and to allow them to have their fill. If truth be told, I was a little anxious to get off there with them, but I guessed that, what with all the tantalising titbits I'd just dropped into Reynolds's lap, I had quite a bit of explaining to do. And so he led me off to his office which was located in, what I like to fondly refer to as: the forehead of the ship.

The office afforded a view of the blackness of space unfolding before us. Often I think about it, just leaping into it and forever falling back. At the same time I know that's impossible. My head would pop like a balloon after a few seconds of exposure. But I can still dream.

Reynolds sat me down at the table, covered with document readers with various unconceivable FSA language scrolling across them—one of the reasons the tug to become an FSA captain was never that strong for me. He asked me to reel through all that had happened, why I'd called his fleet out here. And so I did.

During my explanation I took pains to avoid the real reason why Radley had taken me in, swept me off to her hideout, but I had to give him something. So I claimed that it had been because she'd believed, as had Reynolds and the FSA, that I was in possession of the stone. And that was when I had uncovered the extent of the scheme. Somehow I wasn't convinced that I'd done a perfect job on my reasoning—Reynolds had a pretty sharp nose for truth and lies. However, he didn't seem all that bothered for the moment.

"And those guns you saw," he said. "You're sure that they're military grade and that they're producing them in bulk. It might not just have been that one shipment they sent with you?"

"Well," I said, a little knocked back by the question, "I can't say that I saw many others getting packaged, but just the whole setup, Fonch Confectionaries—that sneak peak I got of the gun being loaded into the crate of sweets—it all looked so automated. I have no reason to believe that they weren't doing it on a mass scale, or that they were only loading up that pair of guns for our benefit."

Reynolds steepled his fingers. "Hmm, and could you garner anything on the distribution network? How's she actually getting these guns spread out throughout the universe?"

"Like I said, Fonch delivers the sweets to certain points and it appears that her boys go out to collect them where they shoot whoever receives the shipment before flying off with the guns. The two we happened to stumble upon were Radley's gangsters, but who knows who else might be getting their hands on them?"

Reynolds slipped into a pensive stupor, looking out into the midnight blue of space. As he thought to himself he twirled his thumbs, the only display of nervous tension I had ever picked up from him. This whole situation had certainly driven him to distraction. Here he was sitting right on the edge of what might be a bumper case—no less than busting the universe's greatest mobster. If only he could fit the pieces together.

All of a sudden, he broke from his internal deliberation and fixed me with his stare. "Captain Wright, you have to answer me this honestly. Do you have any idea of the whereabouts of the stone? It's of utmost importance that we get our hands on it. Do you have any inkling that Radley might have it?"

"What's so great about that stone? I thought it was all just a bunch of superstitious mumbo-jumbo."

Reynolds smiled weakly. "If that were true, do you really think we'd be bending over backwards, that Radley would be bending over backwards, to get her hands on it?"

"Well, why's it so important, then?"

Reynolds pulled his hands apart, ceasing his incessant thumb-twirling and he stood up. He approached the large window looking out into space and, with his back to me, he began. "The Stone of the Angels, as it's now known, was first discovered by a deep space probe known as W-9841."

There the FSA go again with those catchy names.

"As you well know, the Fritten System spared no expense in gauging the size and scope of the universe in the early days of exploration. We wanted to know it all, have an idea of the task that was standing before us. Just as we'd completely mapped out the Earth, we wanted to know space just as well—humanity's new domain."

Despite everything, if there's one thing that every good captain can be counted on for, it's layering on the melodrama whenever they get the opportunity. I was glad that, despite being an FSA softie, Reynolds still retained that raconteureal spark. And, to be honest, I was quite glad that Reynolds was giving me a bit of a reminder. I have to admit that, back at

school, history wasn't my strongest subject—but I could probably say that about all my subjects.

"It was in the course of W-9841's search that it discovered,
in a far off section of the universe, at least from the perspective
of the Fritten System, a series of three dying stars. W-9841
parked itself right on the frontier of that system and observed
the end of their lifecycle. Apart from anything else, it was the
first time that we'd really been able to witness the natural end of
one star—let alone three. Needless to say our scientists and
politicians were delighted by the prospect, that the costly
programme was at last bearing fruit. Soon, though, it transpired
that all might not quite be well with this situation. That there
might be more to things than met the eye.

"It was a junior scientist of Pearl Corp—Kray Miller—who
first floated the possibility that these three star deaths might be
brought about by other forces, forces which were not understood by any scientist. Of course, at first, his ideas were laughed
out of the room. I suppose him being junior in Pearl Corp had
something to do with that. But, as W-9841 piped back more and
more information, more images and analysis of these dying stars,
Miller's fears seemed to gain more and more justification. It was
really a sample received around a year later, in Earth time, that
changed everything.

"Pol Narmit, the scientist who built Pearl Corp from the
ground up, declared to the Earth's media that, following analysis
of a sample taken from one of the three stars, these stars had
reached a premature end to their lifecycle, and that there was
no known scientific explanation he could reach to reason why
this was. What's more, the stars were dying at an astonishing

rate. Much faster than had ever been observed before. Of course, the entire Earth's media leapt right on this and immediately declared this the work of a higher being—some sort of 'god' who had intervened in this system, and decided to terminate these three stars prematurely and quickly as some sort of 'sign.' As I'm sure you're aware, the scientists didn't act quite so foolhardily, wanting to wait for more evidence to come through. Because they were sure there would be a far more satisfying explanation to all this. Some facet of science that they had totally overlooked until that point. Some argued that if this were some 'god' flexing his muscles then surely he would've done something a little more dramatic, not left us one solitary clue at the very edge of our existence. Others argued that the very nature of it being difficult to find was merely a test. And so the world waited, holding its breath, wanting to know more about this phenomenon.

"The stars expired within a period of ten Earth years, their glow disappearing completely into the gloom of space. Pearl Corp decided to take a big risk, sending in W-9841 to further investigate the scene. It was Pol Narmit who gave the mission the go-ahead, content to risk losing the probe—and all the physical samples it had gathered thus far—in the pursuit of more information. Well, as it tracked through the space where the stars had once been, not only did it find the area to be utterly unremarkable, filled as it was with just uneventful nothingness, and easily tolerable for even the flimsiest ship, it also found only a single souvenir of that incredible demise of the stars—a tiny fragment. What is known as the 'Stone of the Angels.'"

I sat there in impressed silence. If I'd had teachers like

Reynolds back at school maybe I might've learnt something. As it was, though, I had Mr Fennink and Ms Rodgers, a pair of droids who would simply stand at the front of the class and drawl their way through whatever real-life irrelevant titbit their programmers thought to throw us that day.

Feeling a bit of strain in my shoulders, my body was still feeling the effects of that daring escape from Radley, I flexed my arms upward and fluttered my fingers. When I'd got my blood flowing again, I looked to Reynolds and said, "That's all well and good, but you still haven't told me what's up with the stone. I mean, what's so special about it?"

Reynolds gazed at me, as a teacher might gaze with pity at the dunce of the class. "They brought that little fragment of rock, the rock which the media had been so content to brand 'The Stone of the Angels,' a little miracle out there in the big, bad universe. Of course it was Pol Narmit and Pearl Corp who got their hands on it, being that W-9841 was their probe. However there were frequent mutterings that the stone would really be better served in communal hands, and that Pearl Corp really had no claim on a natural piece of the universe—especially such a fascinating one. And all this fuss over a piece of rock no larger than a fingernail.

"Anyway, whatever the arguments were, Pearl Corp got to work analysing this Stone of the Angels and what they found was what could only be described as an untapped, almighty energy source. Scientists working on the stone calculated that this one piece of rock had more power than the entire human race could produce in hundreds of millions, if not thousands of millions, of years. Many speculated that this was nothing less than those three stars joined together, 'bottled' into a single substance. Extracting whatever this essence was would be a different matter altogether.

"They worked for years and years trying tap the energy source beating away inside. Pearl Corp kept the stone under wraps for decades, scientists passed their struggle onto the next generation and then onto the next. Each time there seemed to be a breakthrough it turned out to be a red herring and the Stone of the Angels defied solving. As Pearl Corp's financial situation worsened, partially because of off-planet expansion, the death of their visionary leader Pol Narmit had been a massive setback to their capacity to keep up with progress, they sold the stone off to the State, so that it might be put in a museum. And it remained an enigma for many years, behind glass. People forgot about it. Sometimes it was talked of as a sort of Pandora's Box, that it might be better left unexplored, and it seemed that human development seemed to agree as it gathered dust. All this remained the state of affairs until recently when the stone was reported missing.

"Now, although the stone was more or less forgotten by our collective consciousness, that doesn't mean that it wasn't held under tight security. I read the reports on the robbery, an incredible case—it must've been an inside job—with no clue as to who might've been behind it. The stone one day just disappeared from its case. As if it slipped right off the plane of reality. It only showed up again when it was reported to be in your possession, on its way into the hands of Radley's thugs."

I worked another crick from my neck. All this listening had made me a little antsy. "So, you really think that Radley wanted that stone badly—that I was genuinely supposed to be the messenger boy, the one to deliver the stone to her?"

"That's correct. The way I see it, from her perspective, is that she had a dilemma. If she got her hands on the stone then the FSA would be on her case faster than anything. I mean we know just where she hides out. We operate on something of a standoffish policy. The way the FSA sees it, organised crime is something of a given in human nature. As long as it's kept an eye on, not allowed to get out of hand, it should be okay. That said, Radley let just about everyone know that you had your hands on the stone, and made you number-one public enemy. Her intention, all along, was to rely on your competence"—

I quite liked that. I couldn't remember the last time someone had called me 'competent'

—"that you would avoid whatever it was that we threw at you, attempting to get back the stone, and that you'd safely deliver the stone to Hortenine-6, where you'd promptly die in a fire fight. I guess she picked someone who was a little *too* competent."

"Yeah," I said, thinking about how Foy had saved my life, "I guess she did." I traced my mind back along the process. "So, just let me get this straight. When Kools—Lionel Fox—got his hands on the stone, he got in touch with Radley."

"Of course," Reynolds said, "she'd pay a damn sight more than FSA—which is to say that she'd pay him something."

"But, then, how did Kools get his hands on the stone in the first place? Do you think he might've been the robber or known the guy who lifted it from the museum?"

"Who knows?" Reynolds said. "Is that really important?"

"No, I suppose not," I said. "I guess the thing now is to think about what Radley wants to do with the stone. You said that no scientists actually worked out how to extract the energy source form the stone, so what do you think Radley's got in mind to do with it?"

"Well, it'd be safe to assume that she's got a good idea of how she might go about that. When you were there, at her mansion, did you see any scientists bobbing around? Anyone who looked out of place?"

I racked my brains again—it was becoming something of a habit now—and then said, "Yeah, I did actually. A guy in white lab coat, anyway."

"Right," Reynolds said, "then it's imperative that we track down that stone as quickly as possible."

"Wait," I said, putting the pieces of puzzles together, "you think that her having those guns, getting them together on the sly might have something to do with the stone? You don't think that she . . . ?"

The room hushed. Both of us were thinking it now. Radley wanted nothing short of an all-out, full-scale, universe-wide war. She wanted the stone to power those weapons she'd fitted out her goons with. That was what this was about. And if we didn't work together to stop her, it would happen. I saw things more clearly now, I knew that this wasn't a simple case of keeping the stone safe— concealing it from both sides till I worked out how I might make a quick buck—I had to get this stone into the FSA's hands as quickly as possible because, of everything else they might've been guilty of, they were the lesser of two evils. At least they wouldn't be planning on waging universe-wide war in *my* lifetime.

"Now, Captain Wright," Reynolds said, "I'm going to ask you again. Do you have any idea where the Stone of the Angels might be located?"

"Follow me, please."

———

Despite all the assurances I'd made myself that I wouldn't so much as break a sweat following the narrow escape from Radley, I did find myself then hurrying along the corridor with Captain Reynolds bobbing along behind me. I was following the signs which led to the on board cafeteria, telling myself that it wasn't too late. That I hadn't aided universe-wide war by failing to hand over the stone when I'd had the chance.

The cafeteria was pretty expansive, easily enough room to accommodate an entire shift of the *FSA-01061*—which was to say, space for several hundred. I spotted Foy, Wodd and the kids on the other side of the hall and rushed between the tables, knocking a couple of beleaguered FSA officers out of the way as I did so. When I got to their table I could hardly summon the breath from my lungs to speak. "Please . . . Foy . . . the stone."

Foy glared at me, as if she'd just seen a ghost before shifting her gaze to Captain Reynolds. A slight smile twisted her lips. "Captain," she said. "I really have no idea—"

"Look," I said, "I appreciate the sentiment, but this isn't a routine, I promise you. We need the stone and we need it, *right now.*"

Foy's expression transformed to fear. Her eyes darted about. "I . . . I don't have it here."

"What're you talking about?" I said, feeling my eyes bulging from their sockets.

"I left it somewhere else. Where it would be safe. I didn't want to bring it with us when we came to save you, that would've been too risky, what if they'd shot the *Nava* down?"

"Yes, yes, okay," I said, adapting to the situation. "Come on, tell us, where's the stone now?"

She looked the both of us square in the eye and then said, "Trivus-3. Corfian System."

———

Reynolds needed no telling twice. He hurled orders this way and that, rattling off a thousand words a minute.

We bucked off to the *Nava* where Wodd patched us into the navigational arc of the FSA fleet. I sat at the controls, trying to think through what might have happened—how we'd ended up in this wild chase.

Sitting at the weapons screen, Foy touched me on the arm. "You don't think that Radley's been able to track the Stone of the Angels, do you?"

"How else did they follow us for so long, onto Yightly-21? They must have a means of tracking the stone."

"Do you think my people are in danger?"

"Not if we get there first."

Reynolds's face flashed up on the communications screen, outlining our route and telling us to keep up. I informed him that if anyone would be doing the keeping up if would be the FSA fleet—I was one hundred per cent convinced of the *Nava's* capabilities to get us to Trivus-3 in record time. When Reynolds gave the order, I pulled back the thrusters and then let them go, feeling the force of the thrust ramming me back in my seat.

We soared through space, stars little more than fluorescent flecks dashing by. I gripped the control stick tight, knowing that even if we did arrive in time to Trivus-3, how would we be able to compete with those blasters? Sure, they hadn't been super-powered with the stone yet, but if Radley had been stockpiling those blasters she would have a huge reserve to call on. We wouldn't stand a chance. Not even the *Nava*.

We entered the Corfian System and right away the damage was apparent. As we shot past Trivus-1 and -2, I brought up the surface scanner, a high-focus camera to show what's happening down at planet level. The whole place had been torched. It was reduced to smoking craters. What had once been houses were now smouldering wrecks, burnt-out wooden and canvas frames. I noticed Foy at my shoulder, watching all this. I told her to turn away, but she kept on staring. I couldn't blame her really. If this had been Arkle-4 I would've wanted to see its demise.

The atmosphere in the cockpit deadened as we drew closer to Trivus-3, but I was already sure what we would find. We steamed onward, down through the atmosphere with a couple of FSA scout ships for company. I signalled for them to follow my lead, for them to cover us as we explored, but already I knew that it would be unnecessary. Radley's forces had been here, and departed, long ago. We had arrived too late.

I guess I expected the worst of Foy, that she would break

into loud sobs, perhaps attack me, beat me with her fists, but she did none of that. What she did do was, calmly, get to her feet and venture off into the aft of the ship. I heard her muffled voice back there, speaking with her cousins.

After giving Milky and Wodd a knowing glance, I brought the *Nava* down into what had once been the terminal. The ships, military ones among them—the Corfus Protectors—had all been blown to pieces while they'd still been parked on the ground. They had never had a chance. No one would've anticipated this attack—realised the significance that tiny, dull stone represented.

I waited for a long time at the controls, answering when I got the call from Reynolds circling in the mother ship. I informed him that there was nothing else, that the planet had been reduced to a smouldering wreck. He just nodded and clicked off the transmission. Maybe that seemed insensitive, that he had no words of reconciliation for what had gone on here, but, thinking about it, there was really nothing to say. What was done was done. There was no fixing it. Only possibilities, moving forward, to save the rest of the universe. In times to come Trivus-3 would be thought of as no more than collateral damage. The universe is a big place.

Foy appeared in the doorway to the cockpit. Her eyes looked dug out of their sockets and her complexion had paled beyond all recognition. Her clothes seemed to hang off her as if she'd had all the flesh stripped from her bones. "Captain?"

"Yes."

"May I be granted leave?"

I swallowed hard. "Sure."

She inclined her head and left the cockpit. I heard her foot-steps coupled with those of her cousins, all of them heading for the walkway, leaving the *Nava*, venturing out onto their doomed, little planet, no doubt looking for something that could be salvaged.

While Foy and the kids were gone, I got several calls from Reynolds, who seemed keen to pick my brains on what to do next. Seeing as me and Wodd were two of the few to have visited Radley's headquarters, and survived, we were treated as something like authorities, intelligence, on what they were up against. It would be much tougher now that Radley held the trump card—the stone. But what could the FSA do but fight? If they put up no resistance then the war would be over before it had begun.

When Reynolds asked me, straight out, whose side I was on, I hesitated, not because I was considering whether or not I might be on Radley's side, but more because, deep down, I had never felt a true part of the Fritten System. Sure, I'd done my service in the FSA just like everyone else, but I'd always consid-ered myself an individual, not part of any one organism. I was a smuggler, and it was a lonely occupation. I expected to stick up for no one, just as I expected no one to stick up for me. It sounds sad, but that's the truth. I deferred my decision.

Foy and the kids returned to the ship around nightfall. I watched their grey faces as they bobbed up the walkway, back into the underbelly of the ship. Just as it was to me, the *Nava* was their home now, and the crew their family. And through all that sadness, that deep melancholy passing via osmosis into me, I felt a spark of hope and of happiness, because no longer would

I have to be alone. I truly had a family now. These people needed me. And, I guess, I needed them.

I listened as their muted footsteps passed along the ship's corridors and then, like a returning phantom, Foy lingered at the back of the cockpit once more. She held her fists clenched, down by her sides. Her eyes found mine and I saw they were saturated with tears.

I had no idea what to say at that point. What could I say?

Then she shimmied toward me.

I got an appalling thought in my mind, and convinced myself of it—that she was going to whip out a gun and shoot me right between the eyes. Remember what I said about never being able to shake that impression of someone who's tried to kill you? . . . Or who you think's tried to kill you?

I rested my hand at the spot on my thigh where I'd been accustomed to finding my blaster, but, not finding it there, I had no defence. I was totally at her mercy.

She stopped a few inches away and then brought her arm upward. Slowly, she overturned her hand and peeled back her fingers to reveal her bare palm. Except it wasn't bare. Not quite. Because, right there, in the centre, was nestled the Stone of the Angels.

15: BACK ABOARD THE FSA-01061

W E WERE BACK in Reynolds's office, all of us, standing around his table, the stone sitting atop all the document readers, all the paperwork he had to complete and submit. It was so strange that it was there with us, that we'd believed it lost to Radley—that she had completed the final piece of the puzzle and soon something approaching apocalypse would be upon us. And now we saw that that wasn't the case, we still held something on her.

All throughout this excitement, Foy had remained withdrawn, unmoved by the spectacle or importance of her discovery. She just stood and stared at the stone. I could only imagine what she was thinking, that this innocuous piece of rock had brought unimagined sorrow upon here—destroyed her world. I knew that she wanted to pick it up and hurl it into space, forget about it forever. If we could've that would've been a fine thing to do. But I was sure it would find its way back into Radley's hands. For better or worse we had to protect the cursed thing with our lives. The whole universe depended on it.

When the buzz had died down we decided to stay over on the mother ship for the night, it being roomier than the *Nava*, and the *FSA-01061* mechanics could see to the *Nava's* various ailments in the meantime. We decided to set up camp in the Corfian System because if Radley's lot wanted to come back and take another look around the Trivus planets for the stone then they could contend with us, big guns or no. They would show respect for a crewmember's home world. No more dese-cration on our watch. As we headed off to our quarters, I took Foy to one side, reached out and touched her on the upper arm. She raised a slight smile, but the distance in her eyes remained.

"Just want to know one thing," I said. "The stone, where did you hide it?"

Her smile vanished. "Do you remember my story? About my life back on Trivus-3."

'Vaguely,' I wanted to reply, but decided, this being an emotionally charged moment that it wasn't quite a time for botched jokes. "Uh, refresh my memory," I said.

"I never told anyone about it, where I kept my things—my secret things, everything I ever cared about."

And it was just then that I noticed the box which she'd been carrying beneath her arm the entire time. It was made of sturdy steel and had a chunky lock on it. My brain retraced its steps and the answer appeared at the forefront of my mind. "Under the apple tree. You hid it under the apple tree."

Another faint smile tweaked her lips. "Yeah," she said. "They never thought to look there. No one knew about that place. Not my mum, not my dad, not—" and then her sobbing cut off her words and the rest was lost to garbled cries.

I did my best to comfort her, I mean she'd just had a hell of a day, losing everyone she knew in this world, and I wanted to be able to tell her something to make her feel better, but there was really nothing at all forthcoming. What *was* there to feel positive about? So I just squeezed her tighter, let her head rest against my man boobs, her tears seep right through my shirt and onto my skin. It felt like we'd been there hours before I felt her draw away from me, head bowed, and venture off to her quarters.

I stood there, biting my lip, trying to work out what happened next. Whether what might be best for all of us was to simply slip away into a darkened part of the universe and wait for all this war to blow over. Hell, what sort of aid could I give to the FSA, being a simple smuggler with a bent and battered ship?

. . . Don't tell the *Navaplastas* I said that, she'd just get cross.

———

If Foy weren't enough to content with, after I'd only just got back to my room, stretched out on the bed with the happy thought that when I woke the next day the *Nava* would be all patched up and purring like tabby cat, there was a metallic *knock* at my door, and Wodd rounded the frame and stepped inside. His sombre expression was in keeping with the day's events, so I couldn't much blame him for that. But he did nothing to improve my mood. As he spoke, he refused to meet my eye. "Captain?" he said.

"You're best off getting some rest, son, tomorrow's another big day."

"Where're we going next?"

Although I hadn't totally resolved till that second, I had never felt surer about anything. "We're going to get away," I said, "leave all this behind. This isn't our fight. What could we possibly contribute to an all-out galactic war? Damn, I mean the *Nava* wouldn't hardly lift off with one of those large cannons stuck on her underbelly." I managed to raise a chuckle, but it sounded raw and forced in my throat. "Nah, kid, this is just a case of wiping the slate clean and starting over again. We'll be fine, you'll be fine under my command, you mark my words."

"We're not staying to fight?"

"Hell no."

Wodd hesitated and then raised his head, looked me in the eye. "In that case then, Captain, I'd like to tender my resignation."

"What're you talking about?"

He shrugged. "The reason I wanted to get away from Horte-nine was so I could get help, come back and save them all. I have to fight against Radley, whatever your agenda is, I know that if I don't stand and fight—even if it's just to die—then it'll haunt me for the rest of my life."

"Now that's some pretty strong talk. Death's fairly perma-nent, young one, you know that?"

He nodded.

"What's happened?" I said. "Have they made you some sort of an offer? Some kind of irresistible proposal? Why don't you tell me it so that we're on the same page here?"

"Captain, I've always been honest with you. You know that it was my dream to get into the FSA, to become an officer here. That's the only way I've ever thought I can *really* help my people, find a way to liberate Hortenine. And if you're planning on leaving this all behind then I fear we have to go our separate ways. It wouldn't be fair that I'd be on the ship, thinking of other things, regretting what I should be doing with my life. I couldn't be a professional."

"Right," I said, feeling a little taken back by this sudden rush of passion. Never thought Wodd had it in him. "I see what you're saying, and I respect you for it. My decision's made, though, I fear. I turned my back on Fritten a long time ago and I've never seen reason to come back, not even now. Look at it this way, they've got the damn rock now, that stone, they'll be fine. They've got all the firepower they need to see off these mobsters. But I just don't see how it's my fight. You see what I'm saying, kid?"

"Yes, sir, I do."

"Then you understand how I can't stand shoulder to shoulder with the FSA and help them fight off these mobsters." I grabbed hold of a few folds of my gut. "Here," I said, "war's a young man's game. Does it look like I'd be much good down there on some Godforsaken planet fighting my way through the trenches with a blaster?"

"You might be an important leader."

"'Leader!'" I said, almost choking on laughter. "Nah, boy, you've got the wrong man. Haven't you been paying attention during your time with me? I ain't nothing but a no-good smuggler, I sneak around the universe like a snake slithers through the tall grass, always on the periphery, calculating my profit. And those ain't no qualities for a good leader, let me tell you that."

"We need people like you."

"'We?' What's that supposed to mean, now? That you've already signed the papers, that you're already one of them?"

He nodded solemnly.

"That's how it stands, then? I see what this is. You've not come here requesting permission for your resignation, you've come to tell me you're deserting, that's it, isn't it?"

"Sorry, sir, I've got to do what I've got—"

"Bullshit. You get out of my quarters and I'll thank you not to let the door hit you on the way out. Go on, *get!*"

Wodd hung back, goggle-eyed for a few moments before he turned on his heel and, with a final glance back at me, left me in peace.

I lay back on my bed, staring at the impossibly white ceiling. I always wondered about the poor saps who got stuck with programming those maintenance droids—had to ensure that every last inch of the damn FSA ship was kept spotless. I wondered what the punishment would be for a fleck of dirt—probably discharge them for it, knowing the FSA. I tried to get to sleep for a long time but Wodd's desertion played on my mind. I knew that I had lost a great man, a truly great man. Had he been too good for my crew all along? Perhaps. What chance does an engineer of his quality have to flex his wings on a smuggler's wreck?

———————

It took a little while to convince Foy that we *really* didn't want to get ourselves involved with this war that was about to happen. I told her that her duty now was to look after her two cousins, now that their mother and father had gone, and of course Milky needed taking care of too. What good would it do for her to get herself involved with a war? She'd just end up dead like the rest of her folks, and there's not much you can do dead.

We packed up the *Nava*, all fresh from repairs, when I noticed Reynolds's shadow cast itself over us. When I looked back I saw him standing there, staring at us with his arms crossed over his chest. "Captain? Can I have a quick word?"

I flashed my eyebrows at Foy and the kids, then said to them, "Get on board. I won't be too long. We're all ready to go."

Reynolds sidled up alongside me while Foy and the kids loaded themselves onto the *Nava*. He only broke the heavy silence once they'd slipped out of sight inside. "Captain, I'd like you to reconsider your decision."

"Not happening."

"Look, I checked back over your record again, and I saw that only five years into your service you had a whole crew beneath you, you worked yourself up to captain in that time. Don't go telling me that that happens every day. Obviously I haven't checked out every person ever to join the FSA, but I'd take a good guess that no officer has ever made captain that quickly—at that age."

"Well, Captain, I think I can clear one thing up for you. It's true that I was the youngest ever FSA captain appointed and that I was given a whole bunch of men to order about." I paused, trying to work out the most tactful way of putting my next point. "Did you read any further into my history? My discharge summary?"

"Honourable discharge, no exceptional circumstances. From all I can make out from the official report, you were lined up for a big promotion—hell you probably would've been captaining a mother ship before your thirtieth birthday."

"Nah, that's not the whole story, and you know it."

"What do you mean?"

"You saw the black mark, the confidential file?"

Reynolds flushed slightly.

"It's okay," I said, "I'm not embarrassed about it or nothing. It's how it is. It's my history. There's nothing that can be changed about it."

"Forgive me, Captain, it's well above my clearance code to pry into those sorts of matters. I really didn't want to bring it up, you see—"

I waved him away and then set about unbuttoning my shirt.

"What, what is this?"

Yanking my shirt to one side, to expose my left pectoral, I said, "Please, Captain, don't worry I'm not of that persuasion, and if I were, you're just not my type. No offence." I stretched the skin around the scar on my pectoral and then eyed Reynolds. "You see that, right there?"

"Yeah."

"Know how I got that?"

Reynolds shook his head.

"All right, I'll tell you just what it says in that confidential file—except I'm sure my account's a bit more exciting, probably more detailed too, than that damn official report. Those things ain't no better than a bunch of lies for all they leave out."

Reynolds pressed his lips together and looked away from the scar.

I didn't move to button up my shirt. It felt good to have the scar out open to the air. Most of the time I was the only one who got to see it—when I took a shower or got undressed to go to bed. In a way I wish I'd got it on my face, blazoned right across my cheek, my shame there for the whole world to see. Not lurking in the shadows like some slimy, broken old man.

"I was pretty happy in the FSA," I said, "all things considered. Hell, they were pretty strict on drinking and the like, but, you know what, after a few months in there, going through the training I just about kicked all that stuff I found so fun as a kid. Truth be told, nowadays I don't have much of an appetite for more than the odd moiser, just now and again. Where I grew up there weren't much hope, not on Arkle-4. You see, I grew up in a large city, Bomberlee City. There wasn't nothing there—every morning when I'd go to school there'd be addicts on our doorstep, trying to swindle me out of my lunch money, some were more direct. But that's not how I got this scar.

"Point is, when those FSA recruiters showed up on Arkle-4,

my last year of school, there to hand us our uniforms for mandatory service, I remember thinking that I'd just slip away, I'd disappear into the woodwork of Arkle, just forget about my friends, my family, all that stupid shit. I had no illusions about that service. I'd seen the kids serving for the FSA on Arkle, working as authorities, kicking addicts into holding cells for the night or stopping husbands breaking their wives' noses—not that that ain't noble, but it was just so *small town*. I guess I'm a little like Clive Wodd, that fella you poached, in that all I ever wanted was to get off Arkle-4. And there was just no hope of doing that.

"I tried my best to sneak out of that hall, to dodge the recruiters, but they were persistent bastards and even though I managed to skip them at school they came a knocking at my front door. Pair of them, both with silver hair, big muscles, straight faces. They asked me the usual questions and I thought I'd be set right up for a dressing down. But they were pretty nonchalant about the whole thing. Didn't really seem to care that I didn't want to join the service or that I'd skipped school, like they wanted to just tick off all the boxes on their forms. And then, just as they were readying to go, and I was praising my lucky stars that I weren't getting into any big trouble over missing the official signups, and telling myself I'd just not turn up anyway, one of them officers turned on me and said that there was coming chances to get on spaceships, that they was looking for crews for these big missions, and if I'd be at all interested in that. I guess my eyes just about bulged right out of their sockets. He told me the only provision was that I'd have to sign a proper contract, give them five years of my time, and they'd make sure I'd get up on one of those ships—if I passed training, got through all them tests, of course. Well, I just signed up right there and then. Those men sure as shit knew their way around us Arkle-4 folk. Knew what we wanted.

"Needless to say, I had no problems at all leaving it all behind. Sure I was a bit upset to leave my mum and dad there, all alone, but what could I do? My younger brother would look after them anyway. Apart from them three there was nothing tying me down to Arkle, so I was ready for my adventure, to jet up into the stars and make something of myself.

"Training and all that, no problem whatsoever. For the first time in my life, going through all those physical tests, having to survive down on those desert planets was way more than I'd ever thought possible—much different from watching some teaching droid stand at the front of class and get ignored the whole hour through, sprouting off whatever garbage it'd been programmed with. After I finished up the advanced programme, in what'd be about my fourth year, those trainers in charge of us were so impressed with my performance that they asked me right out if I'd like to work under a captain on one of them Pelters, as we called them back then, the fighters charged with protecting the rest of the fleet. They told me it was dangerous work but they said they thought I had all the capacities, that I was hard enough to be able to manage, and so I accepted. Of course I did. I was making something of myself at last.

"We were posted to protect the good old *FSA-0100T*, couple of generations before this old gal," I said, slapping one of the steel pillars of the *FSA-0106I* beside me. "And we did a good job too. Bet it says that in the file, don't it?"

Reynolds nodded.

"Yup, you really can't believe everything you read. Never tells the whole story." I let out a long-strangulated sigh then continued. "We got put on this one mission, where we were seeing off some rebel sect near the rim of the Fritten—you see, they'd been raiding a nearby planet, terrorising the people, using their resources and building up their forces. FSA decided that enough was enough and they'd stuck a toe over that thin line between annoyance and threat, that they needed taking down. Our job was to go up ahead and scout out the terrain, make sure it was safe for the mother ship to rock in and zap them all to hell. Thing is intelligence had no real idea what kind of hardware they were packing—what kind of blasters they might've had set up, ready to, if not take a mother ship down, deal her some serious damage, maybe kill as many FSA men as they could. So that was our job. To see what we were up against.

"Now, as the lieutenant on this Pelter I had the job of keeping everybody in order, holding the stitching together so that our captain—Hughes—could direct us with a clear head. Well, my job wasn't too tough. They were good boys and girls, every last one of them. Didn't matter that I was several years younger than some—they knew the brass had seen something in me, and that they'd seen to putting their trust in me, so I must've been someone worth respecting.

"I got the bad feeling when we were just coming in through the atmosphere of what was supposed to be the rebel base. This might've been a little before your time, but cloaking devices were all the rage back then—and they were pretty much undetectable. That's all different now, of course. But, back then it was perfectly fine to assume you could drift down to planetside without too much trouble. It was that assumption that sank us.

"I have no idea where they came from, but all of a sudden we were just surrounded by rebel ships, blasting us from all angles. Now those cloakers, they burnt through energy like nothing else, and so, pretty soon after coming under attack, we had no choice but to switch it off—switch power to our shields. And you would not believe how quickly those lasers burst through those shields. It was like they almost weren't there at all. The way they'd taken us off guard, snuck up on us and just about pummelled us with everything they'd got. Real, true guerrilla warfare.

"We didn't last long before they hit some of our damn fundamental systems. They just took them right out. I remember sitting at the captain's side, watching on as the damage meters drained away. We were going down, that was a sure thing, not that the men could nothing. First we knew that we were losing that battle badly was when we started plummeting down, right into the forest below.

"At that point the captain told me, quite distinctive, to head around back of the ship, to go and see to the weapons systems and see if there wasn't something that couldn't be done. And that was when I just froze up, got myself stuck into the seat, staring out through them windows at the approaching ground. He shouted at me several times, but nothing could get me to move. I know this sounds a mite cliché, but that was it, I was frozen out of fear. Just couldn't move so much as a muscle. And then we hit.

"Now, I know you'll be telling me that what the captain told me, to go check on the weapons, that it wasn't gonna save nobody. But, for me, it was all about the order. I knew that I'd been staring death right in the face and failed to follow what my superior had to say.

I paused, feeling a lump forming in my throat. This part has a habit of choking me up every time. "I was the only one who survived the crash. Oh, the captain, he lived on for about five, ten minutes after we hit. But the whole damn Pelter was reduced to smoke and white heat. I did what I could for everybody—which was a lot like nothing—before I had to give up and I crawled out through the roof escape hatch, and that was how I got this scar right here, gummied myself up on a bit of debris sticking out of the hatch. Cut me right through."

"Did the rebels pick you up?" Reynolds said.

"Yeah, 'course they did. Not everyday you get so lucky as an FSA craft being so good as to smash itself into your territory, is it? Oh, I tried to keep myself hidden but their scanners picked me up in next to no time—and they brought me in to their commander. After they'd bargained away with the *FSA-0100T*, they managed to strike a deal—got me out of there in exchange for some armistice time. From what I heard they went back there and annihilated the whole damn bunch of sons of bitches."

"And you left the service soon after?"

"Goddamned right I did."

"But they wanted to make you captain of your own ship."

I shook my head. "Exactly. How could I trust myself to keep a level head if while I was staring death right between the eyes I just froze up? What would happen if those men's lives depended on my judgement, my clear thinking, and I just ended up letting them down?"

"You were young. Now you're much older. I'm sure you're used to making tough calls under fire."

"Nah, couldn't trust myself. Wouldn't be fair to nobody. Better for everyone that I just try and keep myself away from those sorts of situations. I found that what I'm best at is looking after myself."

"You got commended for just about every award going: all that surviving enemy capture, refusing to spill information, doing what you could to aid those on the ship. They all agreed that there was nothing you could do, and you were recommended right away for promotion for outstanding bravery."

"Yeah, well," I said, just about meeting his eye, "I think they knew deep down that my nerves were shot too. At least they never put up too much of a fight against my resignation, didn't have any problem with an honourable discharge." I stepped back and rested my hand up against the outer shell of the *Nava*, feeling better already to be close to her, brushing my fingertips against her hard exterior. "And now, young man, I think it's time that I leave, before I start bawling my eyes out. That wouldn't be too honourable now, would it?"

"I don't mind."

"Sure you don't," I said, taking a step onto the walkway, looking forward to putting a great deal of distance between the *Nava* and the *FSA-01061*, along with this brewing war. I wagered that I already smelled those brutal scents: the blood, the sweat, the anger, and it just about turned my stomach.

Reynolds followed me. "But, don't you see? This is your chance for redemption. You can make up for all that, use your experience to lead men to victory—you'd be saving so many innocent lives, all those in the Fritten, civilians, who have no idea what fate's awaiting them, the evil that these mobsters can pack into a punch, those missiles and lasers."

"But they don't have the stone. You'll beat them easy. I'll be rooting for you, don't you worry." I took another step inside the *Nava*. "The good vibes might be a while in coming, though, have to travel quite a way for where I'm planning to sit this fight out."

Reynolds suddenly lurched forward and clasped hold of my forearm. "Captain! You've got to stay. Don't you see? This is your destiny. You're wrapped up in this right from the start."

Now, whenever anyone starts to talking about 'destiny' or 'fate' my horseshit alarm just gets to jangling in my ears. So it was with a bit too much force that I shook his relentless grip from me and beat a retreat into the *Nava*. When I reached the cockpit, where Foy and the boys all sat around, still moping over the situation, I listened in for any sound of Reynolds following after, but there was nothing. He had given up on me. Just like I gave up on myself all those years back.

As I slumped down in the captain's chair, hand reaching for the thrusters, a wave of remembrance just beat right over me. I was back there, in that ship, among the wreckage. I remembered the screams piercing through my brain, that rusty stench of blood. Someone had grabbed hold of my trouser leg as I made for the emergency hatch. When I'd tried to help him up I saw he was dead, eyes glossed over and lips parted with a final breath. That had been his final grasp for life, and it had been toward me. And then the smoke had just poured out over the whole scene, sending me coughing and spluttering, and it was all I could do to drag myself out of that hatch and tumble down through the foliage to the floor of the forest.

16: QUAIL SYSTEM

I DID a lot of forgetting on the way to the Quail System. All those images, those thoughts and feelings just flooded back. I wished I'd never thought to open up, to fill Reynolds in with my past. Some things are just better left alone to rot in peace. Memory's never a nice place to tread.

I decided on the Quail System simply because it was the furthest job that appeared on the job offers pool—right on the outer fringe of the Fritten, somewhere that would be left entirely unperturbed by the impending war. I hoped that I'd be able to patch things together so that we'd just go from one far-flung job to the next while the war petered itself out. Once all the madness was over, we could all go back to being normal again.

Throughout the trip I found myself growing increasingly infuriated by the droids buzzing around my feet, programmed by Milky. They just about scurried into every crevice they could find. One of them burnt off a good portion of my ankle hair with some sort of blowtorch. I had no choice but to get shirty with Milky and shout him back into his place at the electronics board, where he was supposed to be all along—stepping into those big boots Wodd had left behind. Reluctantly, he replaced the remote control in his pocket and took up his post. All this disciplining was beginning to make me feel like the daddy I'd never wanted to become.

As I brought the *Nava* down in the terminal on Wedawon-36, I noted that the place had a rundown feel to it. There was only a droid running the approach control, while the buildings in the distance looked beaten down, most of them with broken windows or with bricks piled up at their sides. In a lot of ways it reminded me of Arkle-4.

It was a simple job, one which is known—in the trade—as a smash-and-grab. All that was involved was picking up a package from the contact and delivering it through to Wedawon-6. Although the contact could've easily put the item in the standard postal service, I guessed that there were somewhat stringent controls on Wedawon-6, and so they wanted, whatever illicit item it was we were to carry, to arrive there safely. Hey, that's what smugglers are for.

I thought back over all the things that had happened to me recently and, watching Foy help the kids down off the walkway, I thought about how the *Nava* had become more like a nursery than a smuggler's ship. But I was saddled with all these people—a family—for better or worse. And with each step through the tumbledown city I knew that I'd made the right decision in getting us away from that war. These kids had seen enough tragedy and trauma to last a lifetime. I mean, damn, how many kids have watched their parents die before their eyes? That's got the capacity to fuck just about anyone up, and so why should these kids be any different? I did consider picking them out a planet somewhere, a planet for the kids and Foy, somewhere nice they could all grow up in peace, not living this smuggler's half life, bombing around the universe, ducking the law and smelling bad, but Foy put paid to that idea, telling me that these kids were just as much my responsibility as hers. And I guess, although I felt a little different, I didn't put up a fight. In truth, I kinda liked have the kids around. Made me feel like less of an elderly wretch.

The addresses in the city were all screwed up. I kept my hand communicator out, guiding us on the way, but it kept flipping out every hundred metres or so—it just couldn't get a lock on the location. After we'd gone up, then down again, the same side street for the fifth time, I shoved it into my jacket pocket, eyed a café across the street and led my crew inside.

The café itself was somewhat of a bright spark on this otherwise dilapidated street. It was nestled beside two burnt-out buildings, both of them leaning into the café as if threatening to crush it between their dual might. The windows of the café shone in the late-afternoon light and the heavy wooden door suggested something rustic about the place, something a little bit country in this otherwise urban wasteland.

We stepped inside and I heard a bell jingle above our heads. That was just about the jolliest thing I'd heard for about a week and I'm not ashamed to say that it put the suggestion of a smile on my lips. I actually felt my step lighten a little, some heaviness lift off my heart. An old man stood at the counter. He wore a sleeveless jacket and, beneath that, a checked shirt. He had lost his teeth long ago and his smile was more than a little gummy. But at least he *did* smile. "What can I get you folks?" he said.

I perused the menu behind his head, which consisted of no more than a blackboard with scrawled chalk—half-legible prices and items written across it. The kids all fed their order to the man before rushing off to nab a window booth, one looking out into the street where a beaten up maintenance droid was hobbling by, seemingly suffering a bout of functional Tourette's —pausing every couple of seconds to manically wipe an impossibly dirty patch of ground or, as it did at that moment, scrub at a hopelessly dirty patch of window.

"And for you, sir?" the man said.

That old person smell, those dual odours of soap and urine mingled, at the same time bringing back those sad thoughts and putting paid to my appetite. I say it put paid to my appetite, but I still summoned the courage to belt out an order for a full breakfast, side-lined with a daily ration of vitamins, with an apple tart to follow it up. Getting all emotional is hungry work.

A cranky droid brought our order around to the table, telling us to "shave a nise meals" before wheeling back off through the kitchen entrance. We all dug in and just got ourselves equally lost in food. I didn't think about anything else till I saw my moiser had run itself dry—funny how they always manage to do that, eh?—and I hefted myself up and headed over to the counter where I waited patiently for the man or the droid to return to fulfil my requirement. There it is again. Me and patience. Always seems to crop up somewhere along the way, and it almost always leads to disaster. Well, this time was no exception.

The course of events went something like this: I waited at the counter, *patiently*, for around a second, maybe two, and then I bellowed out into the back room for service. There being no response, I bellowed louder, let's say twice as loud as before. Still not hearing a response I rounded the counter, approached the kitchen door—waited a second in consideration that this area might be off limits to customers—and then I just ploughed on through.

The kitchen was a great big mess. Unsurprising given that the old man and the droid seemed the only ones looking the place over. I searched through the piled-high dirty plates and pans, but could find neither man nor droid. After I'd swept through the whole kitchen and come up empty handed, I decided to give up my quest for service and returned to the front of the café once more. I eyed the moiser dispenser, shrugged and then poured myself out another cold one. It just goes to show how much concentration I expend in the pursuit of moiser that it took me so long to notice the overcoated man with the hat brim pulled low to cover his features pointing a blaster at my crew, all of them with their hands in the air. Not having a blaster myself, and having gone to such lengths to get my hands on a nice, cold moiser, I took a sip then said, "All right, why're you waving that thing around here?"

The man kept the blaster pointed at my crew, while he kept his other hand in his pocket. I couldn't see his face at all because of the brim of the hat. I hate it when people don't look you in the eye when they're talking to you, gives them a wild edge, like they're playing you in some way. So *without* looking at me he replied, "You're Arkle Wright." The way he said it wasn't a question, I guessed he must've seen my photo around, like everyone else, on those wanted announcements. "I have something for you."

"You do, do you?" I said, thinking that this was an especially poor line into giving me some sort of a nasty surprise. I don't know what I thought it would be exactly, although I speculated that he might have some sort of detonator in his pocket, and that he was ready to blow us all away.

The guy just stood there, totally unmoved, and then he removed his hand from his pocket. He held a small package. It was wrapped in old-style brown paper with a piece of twine tying it together. This guy certainly had a sense of retro. He seemed to move his gaze in my direction. "Take it," he said.

"What?"

"I'm your contact. Take the package."

"Wait a minute. Listen here, buddy, I might be a smuggler but that doesn't mean you can simply hop on in here, threaten my crew at gunpoint and then *demand* I do you a favour. What if I say deal's off, eh? Why in hell's name should I even think about delivering your package?"

"The destination's not important."

"Huh?" I said.

"Just take the package. If you don't take it I'll shoot one of the members of your crew. It's imperative that you take the package from me."

I looked over my crew, the fright sketched on their faces. I knew that they wanted this over as fast as possible—to be out of danger. It would be all on me if one of them got hurt. That thing I'd seemingly wanted all these years would come true—my attempts to stay flying solo, to not make connections with people.

I took another sip of my moiser, knowing the trick with these standoff situations was to remain calm, give the impression of being unruffled. "What did you mean when you said the destination's not important?"

He shot a beam into the roof. Plaster chips floated down and the newly opened hole spewed smoke. He inclined his head back in my direction. "Take it, now."

I put the moiser down on the counter and stepped toward the guy. "All right, all right. There's no reason to get your knickers in a twist about it. You're a jumpy lot out here, ain't you? And to think I came out all this way to escape the madness. Looks like I might've just stepped on a landmine."

As I drew closer to him, I made a grab for the guy's blaster. He side-stepped me with nimbleness I'd not anticipated and I ended up on my arse, on the hard tiled floor—somehow with the package clutched to my chest. I could only watch on, bemused, as the guy holstered his blaster, turned his back to me and then wandered out of the café, back into the street, as if nothing had happened at all.

After I got my thoughts back together and managed to collect myself following that utterly bizarre encounter, I helped myself back up into the window booth, perching on the edge of the foamy-cushioned bench. I set the package down on the table and eyed it.

"What do you reckon it is?" Foy said.

Who the hell called a smuggler out to pick up a package that wasn't to be delivered? I glared at the brown paper, as if the package itself was to blame. I snatched it up and gave it an angry shake. Something inside rattled. I looked over the others, all with their eyes fixed on me, looking for my prompt on what was to happen next.

The old man reappeared from within the kitchen and the service droid soon after. While the service droid took our soiled plates away, the old man pressed us for anything else. I told him about the moiser and he rang that up on our bill, apparently not all that bothered I'd decided to turn his café into a self-service buffet. Just as he made to retreat, having accepted my payment through an aged fingerprint scanning mechanism, I snatched hold of his arm and said, "Did you see him? That guy who came in here and threatened my crew?"

The man shook his head.

Something wasn't right about the old man. It just seemed too much of a coincidence that just as he had disappeared that weirdo with the wide-brimmed hat and long coat had shown up. I gripped his hand tighter and said, through gritted teeth, "Who are you?"

The old man tried to back away. Although he looked perplexed as to what was going on I was sure there was something else there, that there was something of a bad actor about the way he was putting us all on. And then I caught it. Just a second but I saw it plain as day. As he craned his neck to look over his shoulder, his whole complexion shifted—turned a light purple colour—and, I swear, I saw the whole fabric of his skin change to fish scales. Out of shock at witnessing this bizarre event, I let go of the old man and he shuffled backward, recomposing himself, taking on his previous beleaguered expression.

I looked to Foy and the kids for confirmation—that they had seen what I'd seen. Their faces, the open mouths, the glazed-over eyes, told me they had. But, just like me, they had no means of explaining it. As I turned back to see the old man I saw that service droid, the one which had so innocently taken our dishes away, had transformed itself. For a start it had shot up to being more than three times its previous height, so that its head now scraped the low-hung ceiling. Gun turrets had sprung up and gave it the appearance of a frightened cat—all its fur standing on end, teeth and claws bared. When I sensed movement out of the corner of my eye I noticed the robot—the apparently mad one which had passed by the window earlier in our meal—now stood in the doorway, similarly kitted out with offensive-looking weapons. Back at the counter, the old man stood at the service robot's side looking nonplussed. What the hell was all this about? Was it some sort of ambush? Before I got the chance to speak up, the old man's frail whine cut me off. "Arkle. Take the package."

"How do you know my name?"

The man simply nodded, as if in acknowledgement of the standoff we were still neck-deep in. The service robot whirred one of its gun turrets and that was just about all the motivation I needed. I crossed the café, back over to our window booth, and I swept the package up in my hand. "Come on," I said to my crew. "Let's get out of here."

The robot which guarded the doorway considered us with its tinted camera-lens eye and then rolled out of the way.

I risked a final look back into the café, only to see the old man busying himself with moping up some mess on the counter, while the service droid had returned to its normal size. I wondered whether it had all been a dream, or if I'd just had some sort of a fit. Outside, standing in the street, I looked at my crew, and that was all the assurance I needed that I wasn't going mad after all.

As we trod the lonely way back to the terminal, to the *Nava*, my curiosity got the better of my stubbornness and I whisked the paper off the package and opened it up.

Right there, in the middle of the package, was the Stone of the Angels.

Of course it was.

17: WEDAWON-36

M Y WHOLE BODY just went totally numb. Despite everything, those droids with the big guns, that weird transforming old man, I bounded back to the café. Only one problem. Couldn't find it anywhere. The street, which had been deserted apart from the solitary café, was now completely empty. I just stood and stared at the vacant, burnt-out building which had been the café only moments before. This was all impossible. Totally impossible.

I checked the place over, of course, but I found nothing of note. The place seemed to have been deserted years, if not decades ago. Just another scene of desolation on Wedawon-36.

Throughout this entire backtrack, I'd kept the Stone of the Angels neatly clasped in my fist, having discarded the brown paper package somewhere along the way. I stared down at the stone and tried to see through it, to its secrets. Why was it that this apparently incredibly important fragment of the universe kept finding its way into my clutches? I guess I could put one thing to bed now—there was no way that Radley had been involved in giving me the stone in the first place, to stir trouble, I could quite happily believe her story now. That would've put my mind to rest if it hadn't raised about a billion other questions. Guess that's just the nature of the universe, ain't it?

Back on the *Nava* I got my head together somewhat, which was to say I stopped shaking all over and my grip on the stone relaxed enough to palm it off to Foy. It felt better to get that thing away from me. Never in my life had I thought an inanimate object would cause me so much grief. I didn't return to feeling normal till we got ourselves out of the atmosphere and bolting through space once more.

I had no destination in mind, and I was wary about going back onto the job pool, trying to find something to distract us from all the weirdness going on. However, it appeared that the universe refused to leave me alone. I checked the mail to find a message from none other than Captain Reynolds, all in a flutter because the stone had gone missing. I was of half a mind to toss the thing out the hatch and let it float off into the evermore, but I hadn't the guts. Deep down I felt that, somehow, it would find its way back to me. Whatever had happened back there on Wedawon had been a tad too weird for my liking. It didn't seem a good idea to piss off that old man, or whatever it had been, it would only mean danger for those close to me.

It was Foy that nudged me from my deliberations. "So," she said, "what's next?"

"Search me, hun."

"I mean with the stone. What're we going to do with it?"

I shook my head. "Honestly I have no idea. You got anything?"

"This thing," she said, eyeing the stone in the palm of her hand, "I don't know. It just seems that destruction follows it everywhere it goes. If only we could find some way to destroy it."

I probably wouldn't have put it in such melodramatic terms, but I said, anyway, "My thoughts exactly. Especially seeing as it's got an unhealthy attraction to me."

"Haven't you ever come across anything in all your travels through the universe? Something that would be able to get rid of it for good?"

I sat there staring into the space opening out before us, trying to think of something. And then, right from the back of my mind something leapt up and nipped me. For the first time in a while I managed a smile. "Actually," I said, "I think I've got an idea."

We left Fritten behind, skirting out into the murky frontiers once more. I felt better out there, knowing that the brewing war was all back in the thick of the Fritten System—if Radley got the bright idea to fire off some of those laser blasters again we wouldn't be around to hear them. We were headed for Dromodis, a star nearby where—about twenty years ago, when I was just starting out in the smuggling game really—I was once given a job of disposing of some sensitive part of a database, charged with tossing the server right into the centre of the star. I recalled my client, a scientist, going into vivid detail about exactly how hot the star was, and how it was really nature's shredder. That idea had stuck in my mind for ages after I'd deposited the server in the star, watched it disappear into the furnace. Only now had I actually been given some reason to use it and, to be honest, I was pretty excited about having a motive to return.

The star glowed a faint pink before us, twinkling in the sky. I was aware of the kids: Milky, Brian and Terry all watching on, extremely eager to see what was going to happen. I guess I hadn't outlined clearly enough that they weren't likely to see much. The stone would just barrel its way toward Dromodis where it would be absorbed by the extreme heat.

We got close enough for the *Nava's* systems to *whine* and *shriek*, dishing out all sorts of warnings as to the extreme heat acting on the shields. Milky pored over the electronic systems, quietening things down—although he wasn't a Wodd, he was much more competent than I would've imagined, he seemed to have a natural talent for it. That or he'd just been especially vigilant in watching Wodd at work, learning his actions and the various functions rote. Whatever it was, he was a superb replacement.

I switched on the reverse thrusters and brought us to a standstill. Dromodis now filled just about the entire front window of the *Nava*. I couldn't quite remember how close I got to it on my last job—the whole database destroying business— but I was reasonably sure that we didn't want to get a whole lot closer than we were now.

I left my seat behind and made my way through the ship to

the disposal hatch, all three boys bouncing on my heels like hopped-up terriers. They wanted to see a big *boom*. I recall holding the stone in my fist, gazing at it for what I knew to be the final time, already feeling a little unsure about going through with this act. What is it about humans that means we just destroy anything before fully understanding it? But I was clear of the lives that were on the line, this galactic war. It would open a whole new battlefield, give a new meaning to weaponry. Until now we'd dealt with thermo nukes, and that seemed about the right measure, just enough to blow a big enough chunk out of a planet to round off whatever discussion had been taking place. This stone that I held in my hand, though, it could change everything—if the information which Reynolds had dished out to me held to be true. And I had no reason to doubt him.

I dragged open the hatch and deposited the stone inside. As I slid it shut, I paused, glaring at that ugly brown piece of rock. Funny how such a tiny little thing, seemingly insignificant, could be the trigger for such drastic and violent action. I looked over the kids and managed a smile. "All right," I said. "If you wanna watch this go off then you'd better get yourselves up to the observation deck. I'll have the navigational computer track it."

The kids all skittered up the ladder, fighting to be the first up to the observation deck. Even through all that gravity, the self-importance I felt at what I was about to do—in destroying one of the great, unknown wonders of the universe—my heart dipped and I felt something along the lines of what I'd describe as fatherly affection. Kind of like that thrill of captaincy, knowing you have people under you trusting you to do right by them, keep them safe from harm. But it's completely different all at the same time, because you know they're more than simply men-at-arms, they're part of you in some way. These kids had no family and I was the only man lying about handy so I might as well forge myself as a father figure to them.

I slowed my breathing and then reached for the bright red lever which flushed the stone into outer space, sending it on a deathly trail right into Dromodis. I waited there for a minute or so, just staring at the hatch where the stone had been only moments ago. It was outside now, being flung at great speed right into the centre of the star. Soon this whole affair would be over and I could get back to my life—or at least get back to rearranging what was swiftly becoming my new life, kids and all.

I joined the kids up on the observation deck. The navigational annotations marked the stone, following it with a green hoop, tracking its path as it rocketed its way to the star. All three of the kids gripped the guardrail, eyes lit up with wonder and lips slightly parted. It reminded me of a time when I'd been much younger—back when Arkle-4 had invested something into its communities—and I'd gone to a firework display. I couldn't remember the reason for it, what the whole celebration was about, but what I do remember is the colours, impossibly bright and the *pops* and *crackles*. I guess it was just about the closest I got to laser beams before I joined the FSA.

The small green hoop wobbled over the glass, getting closer to the star by the second. I estimated that it would be gone, at least disappear from the tracker within the minute—the heat would be too much for the sensors. And then it did just that.

The tracker blinked a couple of times and then the green hoop turned to a red cross, informing us that it could no longer get a handle on the stone.

"All right, kids," I said, reaching forward to ruffle Milky's hair. "Show's over. Looks like that's all you're gonna get. Let's get back down to the cockpit and onto the next adventure."

Maybe I was a little too smug and I spoke a little too soon. That seems to happen to me quite a lot. Just as I turned on my heel and made for the ladder, and that proffered 'next adventure' a blaze of light lit up the entire observation deck. It was so bright that it scorched my retinas, a light so painful that I had to fall to the floor and bury my head in my hands. The kids all cried out in, what I presumed to be, a similar pain. I heard Foy call out from the cockpit, clearly wanting to know what the hell had just happened.

I only dared flex my head upward after a long pause. I tested my surroundings, cranking open one eye at a time, to see that the blinding light had dissipated and things, on the face of it, were more or less back to normal. I guess the first thing I noted on getting back to my feet and looking out through the observation deck window was that Dromodis was gone. It just was. Where it had once been in space, that giant pink fireball, it was no more. I took a shaky step up to the window and took a gander out of it. There was nothing there. Zilch. The damn stone, as I read it, had blown up the whole star.

I looked at the kids, all of them standing behind me, gaping on at the sight—or non-sight—of Dromodis. As I spoke my voice felt far off and my retinas still stung from the impossible brightness of that light. "You kids seeing what I'm seeing?"

They all nodded in reply.

Foy appeared at the bottom of the ladder and called up. "Captain? I'm picking up a ship on the navigational computer. It's headed right for us."

Just about the last thing I needed, someone getting on our case. I wondered what the rap was for blowing up a star—was it even a crime? If it was then I was guilty as all hell. I guessed that there was very little to do now but meet this ship, take whatever punishment they deemed suitable to hand out. Had I really just destroyed an entire star?

I returned to the cockpit and got onto the task of identifying the approaching craft. Thing was that the system just couldn't track it—couldn't get a lock on either its form or identification codes. Right then I wished that Wodd hadn't decided to desert us. I was sure he would've found a way to identify that craft so that we might've had some sort of a heads up on what it was we were up against. But, with no other feasible option, I slumped back in the chair and watched it draw closer, coming from the direction of the disappeared star.

As if this was just some known, friendly ship, I authorised the approach and powered up the walkway, sent it out to meet our visitor. Seeing as the identification systems were down the first opportunity I got to ID the ship was when it arrived in visual range. And then it was utterly disturbing, because it was like no other ship I had ever seen.

Whereas most medium-small ships, a ship around the size of *Nava*, have a pretty similar, unvarying shape which consists of a narrow hull, the cockpit vested there, while the ship gets wider as it goes further back, until you reach the rear thrusters, usually the widest part of the ship. Kind of cone-shaped. This ship, however, appeared to have no windows whatsoever, no obvious cockpit, and it had an even shape all the way along, which was to say that it was cigar-shaped. In all my years of smuggling, seeing all kinds of ships, from weird to traditional, I had never seen anything at all approaching this one. And I knew in that instant that whoever this captain was, he wasn't any part of the human expansion into the universe. In short, this was an *alien*.

Now, humanity has spent the best part of the last millennium expanding into the universe, probing its secrets, and colonising wherever it's deemed appropriate. It seems that there's simply nothing which can stop the incessant onward stomp. And I might not be any sort of a history buff, but I know the basics—namely that we'd never come across any other sort of intelligent life. I remember seeing countless scientists, when asked on the subject, claiming that there was quite a high possibility that at least one or two other *alien* races inhabited our own universe, but most likely they would be well behind our own—nothing approaching what we saw as aliens. For this reason, they argued, that we might well have already stomped out some alien life during one of our colonisation missions—in the course of constructing our on atmospheres on these alien planets we had destroyed whatever life might've existed there previously. It sounded sad to me, but it seemed pretty inevitable. Needless to say, after hundreds of years of all this talk by the brightest scientists of our generations we'd got to thinking that indeed we were the only ones in the universe, and that it was ours for the taking. But now, seeing that ship, I knew that I—*we*—had to reconsider everything. This changed everything.

My hand shook as I awaited the walkway, watched it swoop out from the side of the *Nava* and inject itself into this alien ship. It seemed that, whatever the disparity between our technologies, that this alien ship could easily accommodate us. My mouth dried up as I observed the confirmation on the screen, telling us that we'd made contact. I set the atmospheric acclimatiser on, so that we'd make a hospitable environment for our guests. Much to my surprise, however, nothing changed. The temperature remained equal and there was no change to the lighting on the *Nava*. I got the impression right out that these aliens knew their way around our world pretty well. And, to tell the truth, it scared me.

There was a long, impossible wait as I observed the walkway, waiting for something to emerge from that alien ship. In that time I thought back to Wedawon, that café, and re-examined what we'd all witnessed. That man had changed, those droids, and how the whole place had up and disappeared from view when I'd returned. Even before that, how that hand communicator had led us all through Wedawon and then left us stranded, conveniently, at that café. Now I was starting to get the impression that there was a lot more to all this than met the eye.

The walkway windows darkened with shadows, beings making their way along it, approaching the *Nava*. I had a very short time to consider my role here, being the first ambassador for all humankind in welcoming these aliens. And what a guy to choose. Me, a smuggler? I ventured through the ship, kids following behind, Foy too, and I stood at the entrance to the walkway, only then considering my appearance, wondering whether my tubby gut poking out through the burst buttons of my shirt might make a poor impression on these extra-terrestrials—or whatever name I could give them out here in this cold and, apparently, unempty sector of space.

The waiting seemed interminable. I watched those shadows get closer and closer, making their way along the walkway, and then, all of a sudden, they were at the airlock, right before us, ready to break the barrier between our cultures. I took a deep breath and then depressed the button beside the airlock, allowing our guests in.

18: IN THE ASHES OF DROMODIS

THAT DOOR, it swept upward almost too quickly, considering how slowly everything seemed to be moving right then, and the aliens stood before us—a pair of them. Their appearances were in accordance with what we'd witnessed back on Wedawon, which was to say, they had light purple complexions and their skin was like fish scales—sparkling in the florescent light of the *Nava*. After I'd taken in these aliens' appearance I noted, with dismay, the object in one of their hands. The Stone of the Angels, right there, offered to me once more.

I balked at them for a long time, them watching us, us watching them. Then I cleared my throat, telling myself that someone had to take the first step, get this meeting off on the right foot, and so I said, "Hey there, my name's Arkle Wright, Captain of the *Navaplastas*." I paused. "I'm human."

There was a pregnant pause and then one of the aliens spoke. "Yes. We know who you are. We know what you are."

The alien's voice had a floaty vibe to it, it seemed to hang and vibrate in the air, although I must've thought that later on because, at the time, just about the only words my brain could summon were: *Holy fuck!* and *An alien!*

I noted the slight difference between them, that one of them was a couple of inches shorter than the other, and I noticed that the shorter alien had a lighter shade to its skin. I decided to ask the question this observation prompted. "Uh, are you a 'he' or a 'she?'"

The aliens exchanged glances, then the shorter one said, "We are asexual. There is no 'he' or 'she' for us."

"Oh," I said, informed.

"Arkle Wright," the shorter alien continued, "it is your responsibility to keep this." It jiggled the stone in its hand. "You were the one chosen to take care of it."

"Was I really?"

"Yes."

"And just who decided that?"

"We did."

Now this whole encounter was beginning to creep me out quite a bit. I looked between the two of them, doing my best to smile—not to show them that I was at all taken off guard by this meeting, perhaps hinting that I met aliens just about every day. "I think there's been a mix up, you see, I got this stone from someone else, one Lionel Fox—went by the name of Kools—I'm sure he's the one you want. Only"—I scratched the back of my neck, not wanting to inspire any form of ire here—"he's *dead*."

"Yes," the shorter one replied. "We know."

"Well," I said, "guess you two know quite a bit, eh? Probably better that you just tell me what I have to do and we go our separate ways?"

Although neither alien reacted in any way I sensed both of them sighing to themselves. Just something in the air.

"But," I said, "before you go on with your briefing, do you mind telling me what the hell just happened to Dromodis, are you going to tell me that this stone managed to destroy the whole bloody thing?"

"Yes," the shorter one said.

"Ah, pretty potent, then?"

"Yes."

The whole conversation reminded me a bit of talking with my superiors when I'd been in the FSA, which was to say that it was all as sans-humour and emotion as possible. "All right," I said. "What is it that I've got to do?" I paused, somehow managing a grin. "And how much am I going to get paid?"

"'Paid?'" the shorter alien said, cocking its head to one side.

"Yeah, you know, something you do in exchange for goods or a service? This would come under the latter, I guess, although I'm not much of an expert—I'd be the first to admit that I don't really know trade law in and out. Not like you two, who 'know everything.'"

The shorter alien held its ground but something about the way its gemlike, crimson eyes smouldered gave me the impression that I was really getting on its nerves—not that I cared all that much. I mean, there they were, on *my* ship dishing out a bunch of condescending comments in my general direction, and generally making my self-esteem feel all damaged, and stuff. A ripple passed over the shorter alien's scales and it said, "Arkle Wright, your duty in this universe, in your life, is to deliver that stone to Alis Radley-Hadton. That is the purpose for which you've been designed."

I thought they might've jammed some cloth in my ears. "Uh, come again?"

"That stone must be taken to Alis Radley-Hadton, that is your purpose."

"And what was that about 'designed?'"

The shorter alien's patience apparently expired at that moment because it lurched forward and jammed the stone into my chest, forcing me to take it. That would've been enough, but just as I thought we were set to go our separate ways—albeit a little testily—the shorter alien made no motion to leave. It grabbed a sizeable wad of flab, my pectoral muscle, right at my scar, as it happened, and twisted harder than anything I could've previously fathomed.

Pain's an understatement, and, anyway, it didn't seem to be the defining point. It was the images flooding my brain, rushing by, the emotions they elicited that really hurt me. I can still see those pictures now: being a kid, on my first day to school, when an addict had snatched my bag, whipped the shoes off my feet, and then when I'd been a bit older—a teenager—and in a blitz of drink and drugs I'd committed the same act to another unsus-pecting kid, and then the shame and humiliation I'd felt later when I'd been caught by the authorities and put away for a month or so. This alien somehow pulled these memories from somewhere deep within my brain and strangled me with them. I guess the best I can go into describing it is to say it was just about the closest I could ever get to hell.

The alien stepped back from me, releasing me from its clutches. Funny, being that they both kept their faces completely stripped of emotion throughout our encounter, but I swore that a smug grin appeared on its lips. "Now, Arkle Wright, you *will* take that stone to Alis Radley-Hadton. Just like you were supposed to."

I doubled over, hands on knees, panting for breath. Still reeling from those blistering images, those shameful memories, I really had no basis to argue against this. When I did find some space to breathe I looked up at the two aliens. "Who the hell are you and what do you want?"

A slight hop entered the alien's voice. "*We* are the rulers of the universe. *You* are a blind rat in a maze, and you would be well-advised to do what we say."

"Right," I said, feeling my ribs squeezing the air from my lungs, "guess that's a point of view."

————

I'm not quite sure what I'd expected from my first meeting with an alien species—first contact—but I had certainly not believed that it would end with me running some sort of smuggling job for them. Looking back on the exchange, it felt a mite unfair that they'd more or less pressured us into accepting. But then, those images that alien had summoned in my mind returned and I knew that I would do anything for them never to return.

As I sat there in the cockpit of the *Nava*, seeing Foy at the weapons system, I guess I should've thought twice—not have issued the order so readily. But those aliens, their ship, it was so close, just tempting us to take the shot. And so I instructed Foy to fire at will—to blow those bastards out of time and space. Bad idea.

The laser beams we shot bounced right off the shell of the ship, returning to us almost as quickly as Foy fired. The *Nava* absorbed the first few strikes before the beams made inroads into the shields. Milky kept them up as long as he could, but, soon enough, the beams found their way through and started to do damage to the *Nava* herself. There was nothing else to do, so I called off the strike and watched the alien ship—untainted— float away gently from us.

"Bugger," I said.

Still staring down the scope of the cannon, Foy said, "That's one way of putting it."

I slouched in my chair and drummed my fingers against the sides. "Wow, I mean, wow. Did you ever think you'd meet an alien species?"

Foy shrugged. "Don't know. I suppose I always dreamt of it. I have to say it didn't really turn out quite how I imagined."

"No," I said. "They were quite rude, weren't they?"

"Like you're one to talk about manners."

"There are certain things that you just don't do on another captain's ship, and they crossed a bunch of lines. That's why we had to fire on them."

Foy relaxed back in her chair, obviously not seeing much point in filling the *Nava* with more holes from our own laser beams. "What now?" she said.

"Well, I'll tell you one thing right now."

"What's that?"

"No way Radley's getting her slimy hands on this stone. That's settled."

"Uh, Captain?" Milky said, from behind us.

"Yeah, kid?"

"What's that on the fringe of visual range?"

"What're you talking about?"

Milky appeared at my shoulder and pointed out the object —or should I say 'objects'—which sat right on the horizon, coming in from the opposite direction from where we'd just blown up Dromodis.

I got the scanner on the case soon enough. And this time, unlike with the aliens, the identification module did its work sweetly and swiftly—not that I was all that fond of what it showed.

Radley's ships. Every last one of them.

19: DROMODIS CONTINUED

W E GOT THE SHIELDS UP as fast as we could. Those hopeless shots at the alien ship had drained our energy pretty significantly and since we'd destroyed what had been the only star around for hours and hours of travel we had no prospect of a quick recharge. Now, look here, I love the *Nava* more than life itself, but even I had to be realistic— knowing that she had next to no chance of facing up to an entire space fleet. But that doesn't mean we didn't give it a right, old go.

I had Milky fire up the front shields to full strength while having Foy get the guns charging. As we bombed closer to Radley's fleet, and we started to take fire, I spun the *Nava* around and around till we were dizzy as all hell. We near enough blew ourselves up on several of the first ships—the fighters—which approached. I focussed on getting as close as I could to them, the idea being to just totally freak them out, to make them think that we were so crazy as to cause a huge collision in the middle of space. After the first few manoeuvres they seemed to get the picture and kept their distance—preferring to fire their cannons at our now exposed, and unshielded flanks and backside. Probably not the best tactical move in the history of space combat.

Needless to say, they pommelled our backend and I counted to three before Milky read off that our shields had been completely depleted and that we were now taking physical damage. I knew, as far as Radley was concerned, that she had no real concept of how sturdy the stone was—that it had just destroyed an entire star—so I was pretty sure she would want to take us alive. Pretty sure.

After we'd been hammered for a good five or ten minutes by those mighty laser cannons I got to thinking that she really did mean to blow us up. I could hardly bear to imagine the damage being inflicted on the *Nava* and, more to the point, how much it would cost to get it fixed. I just sat there in the captain's chair feeling the vibrations pass through me, the ship shuddering all around us. Before long I had no choice but to have Milky channel all energy into preserving the life support systems. Much as it hurts my heart to say it, the *Nava* was reduced to nothing much more than a floating piece of space junk—a battered tin can floating out to sea.

Only we weren't going anywhere. The mother ship caught us in its tractor beam and I watched as it pulled us into its yawning-open cargo bay. It was dark and looked cold up there, but there was nothing we could do. Radley had won.

I closed my eyes as the *Nava* was pulled up through the

doors, and they were shut behind us, leaving us in pitch black darkness—now that we didn't even have enough power for lights. This was surely the end of it all—I guessed I'd had a good run with the smuggling and I had to be honest with myself, accept that I'd always run the risk of a demise something along these lines. I just would've liked a bit long, considering I'd just sorted myself out with what appeared to be a dependable crew. Things like impending universe-wide war tend to get in the way of even the best-laid plans. And I'm not about to argue that my plans had been laid at all.

All at once the lights blinked on around us. Bright white fluorescents. I shielded my eyes with my forearm and called everyone together close. I resolved one thing—that I would let them kill me before they had any chance to harm Foy or the kids. And, this being the most fearsome mobster in the galaxy, no doubt on a bit of a blood buzz considering she was about to head up one side of a massive galactic war, I had no qualms that she would do *whatever* she needed to get what she wanted.

A bunch of hoods made an appearance from a sliding door from within the cargo bay. They were well-armed, each of them clutching a blaster across their chests. Those looked to be army-issue too—I suppose they had to be if Radley was truly serious about waging war against the FSA.

Since the *Nava's* security systems had no power to draw on, the hoods found their way inside in no time at all. And I listened to their footsteps *thud* their way along the corridors. I refused to turn my head toward them when they called out, and the first I knew of them inside the *Nava* was as a pair of them yanked my arms behind my back and cuffed my wrists. I felt the

Stone of the Angels heavy in my breast pocket. For a funny moment I thought I felt it squirm there. A flush of heat seemed to pass through it. Then, just as soon as I'd noticed it, the sensation was gone again.

I kept my head bowed as the hoods led me through the mother ship. I could hear them hustling Foy and the kids behind me, the sound of Foy protesting at the hoods cuffing the kids. I wanted to help her, but, when I tried to jerk myself around to get a look, the hood assigned to me punched me in the temple, sending me tumbling to the ground.

Only as I sat there in a heap, staring upward with an extremely sore head did I notice that it was the same mobster who had kidnapped myself and Wodd back on Drokul-15, Gus, the bastard.

He jerked me back up, not all that sympathetic to my throbbing brain, then prodded me back along the corridor, in the direction I supposed he intended me to go.

"Careful with him," another of the hoods said. "Boss wants him alive."

Gus sneered. "Don't give a shit. You don't know this one. He just about blew up the entire terminal at headquarters last time I had a run-in with him."

"That was him?" the hood said, somewhat unbelieving.

I have to admit that I quite enjoyed the somewhat-reverential tone being bandied about. But I guess Gus didn't quite share my enjoyment since he promptly delivered a blow to my head with the stock of his blaster, sending me spinning downward into a pool of tar.

———————

When I awoke, I was alone in a white room. I thought that these guys had spent a little too long among their film collection—too much time glued to their vidscreens. It was a pretty standard tactic, a way of intimidating me with all this *whiteness*, this apparently surgical-level of cleanliness. Then again, if there's something a smuggler fears more than anything else, it's a healthy dose of soapsuds. We're a bit like animals in that way—pretty happy to just snuggle down in our own smells and general filth.

My mind still felt a little warped following its brief, but intense, meeting with Gus's blaster stock. As I got up I swayed from side to side, several times, only keeping myself from tumbling to the ground with a little help from the, thankfully, sturdy wall.

Once I got my thoughts together I turned my brainpower to the rest of my crew. Were they being held nearby, perhaps in the next room? Or were they somewhere else entirely, off in some unplumbable depth of the mother ship? It mattered not all that much considering that I had no ability to leave this room for the time being. And, with nothing else to do, I decided on conserving some energy and taking a bit of a kip, on the otherwise not-uncomfortable tiled floor.

Talking brought me around what I supposed to be several hours later—judging by the vividness of my dreaming: the lack of clothes the women wore, and the way that my brain now felt like gloop trapped within my skull. I propped myself up on my elbow, trying to listen in on the conversation taking place just outside my door. Right away I identified two speakers. One of them was Gus and, I realised pretty soon after, the other was Radley. I picked up on the conversation, getting the feeling that it had gone on for several minutes already.

". . . That's too dangerous. I say we kill him already," Gus said.

Can't say that I was all that keen on that course of action.

Radley held back for a few seconds before replying. "No, that would be the brutish thing to do. It's just not right, not right that it's always him that's popping up in all of this. I mean, what's so important about him? Does he look like anything other than a space bum to you?"

"Nope, but I'm the one campaigning for the speedy retraction of his mortal coil."

"I think we need to keep him close. That's the only way we'll have a chance of working this whole thing out—what it is that he's got about him? Did you know that he's got a history with the FSA?"

"What's that got to do with it?"

"Well, it could have everything and nothing. Of course, those records I had pulled on him, about him being honourably discharged years ago might well tell the truth. But, equally, we should examine the possibility that he could be a plant."

"You mean a spy?"

"We've got to be careful. That's all I'm saying."

"What do you want done?"

"I want you to garnish as much information as you can. At this point, realistically, now that we've got our hands on the stone—that Michaels is working on it—there's very little the

FSA could do to stop us. Even without powering up the laser blasters with the stone, I'd wager that we'd outgun anything they could send our way. But, still, 'know your enemy' and all that."

"See?" Gus said. "I don't see why we don't just kill him and be done with all this indecision."

"You might have a point. But we'll keep him alive. For now."

Guessing that the conversation had just reached its natural conclusion, I stopped supporting myself against the wall and allowed myself to flop over onto the floor. If there's one thing I've learnt from being taken prisoner it's to play up your role of being beaten—to show that you're most definitely *their* prisoner. So that's what I did.

The door *swooshed* back as only they do on the most expensive ships—I might invest a lot into the *Nava* but even I can't justify *swishing* doors—and Gus strolled in, looking mighty smug, I noted out of the corner of my eye. As I observed him I also noted that he had a pair of guards waiting by the door, I guess even the most stupid mobsters learn from experience.

Gus crouched down beside me and stuck his bony fingers to the pulse at my neck. I had an urge to lurch up and smack him in the mouth, but those two blaster-bearing guards suggested sudden movement might not be the best course of action at that moment in time. He rose up after a few seconds then turned to the guards. "Pulse is steady. Let's take him."

I kept up my floppy act as the guards dug their hands beneath my armpits—I actually felt a shade of sympathy at them having to go there, granted I probably would've felt more sympathetic had I not been their prisoner.

They dragged me along several corridors. As they took me, I did my best to get a few sneak peaks at my surroundings. I was careful, not wanting to alert Gus to my consciousness, that I'd overheard the conversation between him and Radley. All I got to see, however, was door upon white door blurring past and no sign or clue whatsoever of my crewmembers' whereabouts. Damn.

After the guards had carried me for about five minutes or so I got to wondering why they hadn't just got some droid to do this task—and then I recalled that Radley had some strange revulsion for everything droid-like, and supposed that must be the reason. I guessed that her muscle didn't thank her for all the extra physical work they had to do—although I don't suppose they complained too much, not with their boss possessing easily the mightiest force in all the universe. Mightier than the FSA in any case.

My mission was clear, I needed to somehow shake my escort, get myself free of these two lunkheads, then Gus, and have a look around for this guy Michaels. I got the impression that he might well be the most important part of this whole jigsaw puzzle and, if what Reynolds had relayed to me was true —that scientists had battled for generations in finding the stone's secret—then it could be safely assumed that Michaels was very much in the minority of those 'in the know' as far as the stone was concerned. And then it might simply be a case of dispatching of him and thus ensuring the universe would be safe for several more years to come. That was the theory anyway. Sometimes my generous, unselfish thinking really gives me chills.

Sweating and swearing under their breath, because remember I'm not an unsubstantial load, the guards lugged me on through the ship, out of what I dubbed the 'white zone' and into a zone marked by ultraviolet light. This all did seem quite ominous.

We beat through another of those fetching swishing doors where, I garnered through an eye opened a slither, there was an electro circuit ready and waiting. Torture. Again.

Now, I'm sure as you've worked out from my last encounter with torture, that I'm not really much for tolerating pain, so it was at that point that I gave myself away, a shudder passing through my body, alerting the guards to my conscious state.

"Oi!" one of the guards said. "He's awake!"

Not seeing much point in keeping up the charade now, I blinked my eyes and looked about me—to feign like I'd only just come around.

Gus entered the entirety of my vision. He had a grim smile on his face, his eyebrows just about shooting up and out of his thinning fringe. What struck me soon after was the eye patch covering his left eye. I resisted the urge to smile, knowing that I'd done that. "Well, well, well," he said. "Morning, Captain Wright. You remember me?"

I squinted in a way that could be interpreted as somewhere between struggle for recognition and that bleariness that follows sleep. Then I said, "Never seen you in my life."

Gus's grin disappeared then he turned his attention to the guards. "Strap him up."

The guards shoved me down onto the chair and lashed the leather straps over my wrists and around my ankles. Pretty soon they'd got me restrained pretty nicely—even if I am admiring it from the point of view of the victim—and I found myself sat there without all that much I could do about it. Things looked pretty straightforward this time out. It was three against one, two of them with guns, and if I did manage to escape it would only be out into a mother ship full of other hoods. No, this was all looking pretty foreboding, I had to admit.

The two guards backed up and took up positions at either side of the door, their expressions stoic and blasters pointing to the ceiling. If I'd just taken a momentary glance at them I'm sure I would've thought them to be soldiers. One thing about this whole mess was apparent and it was that Radley had trained up her men to be nothing less than an army. That was the point when I grasped it really was serious.

Gus lingered over me, cracking his knuckles and surely enjoying every thrill he could wring from this sadomasochistic domination he had over me. Maybe he had a thing for fat guys. He strode back and forth, eyes flicking about their sockets, occasionally venturing over to the electro circuit beside the chair, as if he might leap out of inaction and switch it on at any moment. But there was one thing that he hadn't counted on—namely that I had overheard his conversation with Radley and I knew that, for whatever reason, Radley wanted me kept alive, 'for now,' as she'd put it, not a little melodramatically.

"Now," he said, turning his attention to the ceiling, as if he wasn't interested in this exchange at all, "Captain Wright, you've got yourself a nasty little habit of cropping up all around the universe and getting on the nerves of my employer. I've been charged with the task of getting some information from you and, I'll tell you this for nothing, I'm authorised to use whatever force I deem necessary to extract said information."

Liar.

He continued, "The first answer I'd like from you might well be the last, and it is, how in the name of the universe did you think you could get away from us?" He pulled back his eye patch to reveal the blackened crater, all that remained of his left eye. "Did you think you would get away with this?"

"Pardon?"

He smiled to himself, obviously not too bothered by the missing eye for the moment, apparently having greater things in mind. He continued, "We have the greatest fleet ever imagined in the history of the universe—"

"*Human* history," I said, thinking over my recent close encounter.

Gus sniffed a laugh. "I *am* glad that you've clung to a sense of humour throughout all this. It's a good test of character, I'm sure you'd agree?" He stopped his pacing and faced up to me. "That business back at headquarters, your *daring* escape from the mansion. Do you know how many prisoners have entered the mansion and managed to leave alive?"

"Nope. Don't much care either."

"Precisely zero."

"That so? Would've thought it'd be a bit higher than that. No, wouldn't have imagined, what with that particularly slack security protocol."

"And you're one to know about security."

"What's that supposed to mean?"

His slimy grin widened. "You've got some pretty mean security on that ship of yours."

My heart sank. "You better not have got so much as a fingerprint on the *Navaplastas* or I'll cut off your balls."

"You're sounding rather desperate, Captain. I really wouldn't consider yourself to be in any sort of position of power at the present time. Not really in a position to make threats."

"I'll make all the threats I want if you're only going to kill me at the end of it. Maybe one of those bozos"—I nodded in the direction of the two guards—"will snap to their senses at some point, realise that maybe they should take a cue from that smouldering, dead smuggler. I'd watch your balls if I were you."

"Thanks for the advice," he said, ducking down beside the electro circuit.

Maybe I was a little strong with my threats. One thing I've noticed throughout all my journeys is that when someone believes they have the upper-hand over you it'll only infuriate them to make some threat about cutting off their balls. But, knowing that I was relatively safe, what with Radley granting me a stay of execution, I felt like I was treading within my limits, toeing the line but not coming close to stepping over. Yeah, right about then I started to think that maybe I was mistaken.

All I remember of that first shock was Gus tweaking one of those knobs and then the sensation of what felt like a hundred, white hot blades jabbing into my skin like I was some kind of sturdy knife rack. Although I'm generally pretty squeamish about any sort of pain I have to admit that till that point I had reserved a kind of myth that fat guys don't feel electric shocks as bad as the thin folks—working on the theory that my fat would work as some sort of insulator. Not true.

It felt like bones would burn their way right out through my skin and land in a bloody pool at my feet. Luckily that didn't happen. But the pain was damn-near unbearable. As I shuddered my way back into a straight-backed sitting position, I observed the guards at the door—they both looked pretty scared. Nah, I'd say they looked downright terrified that they were about to witness a murder, and don't think the irony's lost on me considering that these were guys who were quite prepared to engage, or a least participate in, a full-scale, universe-wide war. Perhaps they'd been misinformed of the definition of war.

Gus wasn't finished yet, though, as he sparked up the electro circuit again, sending a fresh wave of bolts through my system. I crunched my teeth together. When the current ceased I tasted the familiar rusty tingle of blood in my mouth. And then it came in thick wads. I found myself having to swallow it just to breathe. In all that panic I'd bitten right through my tongue.

This time Gus stepped away from the electro circuit. "Not so tough now, are you, *Captain* Wright?"

Still feeling the reverberations of the bolts bouncing around my skull and the blood congealing in my mouth, I managed to get out, "I . . . never . . . said . . . I . . . was."

Gus scoffed and then tossed me a soiled grey rag, not that I could do much with it, considering that my arms and legs were tied up, so it just draped there on my lap, doing nothing much at all useful.

The two guards had now completely broken out of their

respective dazes and one of them confronted Gus. "Boss said to leave him alive. He won't—"

Gus's eyes flared and he approached the guard with his finger outstretched. "How dare you! How dare you ruin all this!" He glowered over his shoulder at me. "Don't you see what you've done? The whole point of this exercise was to sweat him. Now how am I supposed to do that now that he knows I don't have the authority to kill him?"

The guard seemed to realise his mistake and shirked back, even seeming to give me a look of apology.

I appreciated the sentiment.

Gus continued to stare at the guards and then, clenching and unclenching his fists down at his sides, he said, "All right, you two, you're dismissed. Leave us alone."

The same guard who had spoilt the game said, "But, sir, we've got orders to remain here, the boss said—"

"The *boss* has got far more important things to see to not involving space bums that would do better to die." He paused for effect. "But you're quite welcome to break up whatever meeting she's in the middle of if you have a problem with me exerting my authority." He lingered, waiting for a response. "Well?"

The guards exchanged glances and then made for the exit.

My heart throbbed in my throat. A strange, tickling sensation passed across my skin. I guess it was the anticipation at another shock soon to pass through me, and now I had lost those two witnesses, the guys obviously given the brief by Radley to keep a lid on Gus. If ever there was a time to get down on my knees and beg, that was it. Problem was that I couldn't so much as move a finger, let alone bend a knee.

Gus turned around from the closing door. There was no trace of his smile now, and somehow I saw that as being a bad thing. At least before there had been some sense of joviality in the room, no matter that it had an evil intent. We were getting down to business now and, to stretch a cliché, I was on the business-end of things.

"Any last words?" he said.

My eyes wandered the room, looking for any means of escape, no matter how unlikely. I spotted a communications panel over by the door, but other than the electro circuit that was the only piece of furniture in the place. I turned my attention back to Gus. "How about, 'let's be friends?'"

This time Gus didn't so much as crack a smile. He did, however, cock his head to one side. "Funny that even when you're staring death in the face you see fit for a joke. What do you think that says about you as a person?"

"That I like a bit of a chuckle?"

"Or, perhaps, that you're forever the jester. Even laughing at the end when there's no light for you. Don't you have something serious for me? Some important message for me to pass onto your crew, for instance? What about the girl, Foy? Doesn't she deserve something?"

My throat constricted. I thought of them all, in anonymous rooms throughout this mother ship. I wondered if they'd been kept together. I guessed that the place was big enough to find a room for each of them. But, all the same, I wished they weren't alone. As the case was, I did actually have a message for them, although I was—understandably—somewhat hesitant to pass it on to Gus for him to distort or twist. Then again, did I really have much choice?

"Well?"

"Yeah . . . yes, I do have something."

Gus flexed his eyebrows.

I bowed my head, flipping through their faces in my mind's eye. I remembered Foy's easy smile, her light movements at the cannon, and I thought of her cousins, and how scared they'd looked up on the vidscreen while I'd been ready to blow them out of space. I even recalled Wodd, how he had looked down-trodden, like a betrayer, as he had delivered the news that he would be leaving the crew. And then, finally, I thought up Milky. The kid that I had thought I might be able to act as some father figure for, an inadequate surrogate. Now I wouldn't have the chance to even test that out, see if I could do it. And I thought up all those times when I'd shouted at him for messing about with those droids, when that was the job I'd given him. I was sure he would turn out to be a fine programmer.

"Nothing, then?" Wodd said.

I opened my mouth to speak but my words were curtailed by the sound of scuffling, seemingly coming from all around us. It took me another few moments to realise that it was something in the ventilation tubing, making its way around, getting louder as it came closer. Both of us craned our necks to look above, to the ventilation duct. The noise came to a stop. There was another brief pause, Gus turned around with a light shrug, and then a blaze of light filled the room.

A large, smoking hole blew right through the duct, blowing

it off across the room where it landed with a *clatter* on the floor. And then, what should poke its head out, but a maintenance droid—one I recognised from the *Nava*, one which Milky had spent all his time programming. It had a fairy sizable laser cannon mounted on its otherwise flimsy frame and it whirred its way over to us.

For a few moments Gus was rendered speechless by this sight, until it pointed that cannon in the direction of his shins. Then he snapped to his senses. Just a little too late. The cannon blasted and the laser beam flared up. Gus let out an almighty *yowl* and writhed about on the floor, doubled up in pain. Although I wouldn't go so far as to say I'm an opportunistic masochist, I have to admit that I rather enjoyed seeing him getting a bit back. And I had just enough time to relish it as the droid turned on me. Any sense of victory or justice soon evaporated as it fired again.

Just like a kid, I shut my eyes as that cannon charged up and then released. I only dared open them again when I realised that I wasn't in pain. At first I thought I might be in some sort of heaven, having been put to death by a malfunctioning robot and then, when I opened my eyes, I saw the droid staring back at me, blaster cannon smoking away, and looking extremely satisfied with itself. At least as satisfied as a machine can look.

As I took in my leather straps, I saw that the droid had blown them to shreds. I could stand. And I did so, picking my way over Gus's frenetic wriggling and screeching.

Freedom.

20: FREE ON THE FONCH EXPRESS

AS I SLAPPED THE BUTTON to open the door, I looked back over my shoulder, considering dealing Gus there a brisk kick in the ribs. But I decided against it, not wanting to stoop to his level. Sometimes I get all moral like that. The little droid, bless its rubber tracks, whined its way out behind me. I was pretty glad to have that rotating cannon on my side, at least it would save me having to search for a weapon. And then, from behind me, I heard Gus splutter something.

I turned around to look at him.

Only now did I see that he was in pretty terrible shape. His pupils were dilated and that shot to his shins was bleeding profusely. That kind of blood loss only led to one thing. It stuck a chord, brought back those memories on the FSA ship—so long ago now. I froze in my tracks.

"Arkle?" he said, barely a whisper.

I lingered in the doorway.

"Please, I want to explain. They . . . they . . ." His words seemed to get away from him. His chest shuddered and then he appeared to get his second wind. "I didn't want to do it, Arkle, please believe me. All those people"—he shook his head—out of pain or memory, I couldn't say—"there was no choice. *They made me.*"

"Who's 'they?'"

His eyes bulged. "The . . . the *aliens.*"

Maybe it was the built-up tension or the stress of the droid's appearance, but my whole body just twitched uncontrollably. "What do you mean?" I said.

Gus fought for every breath. "I'm so sorry. Tell . . . tell Foy that I . . ." Again, his voice got too quiet to be audible.

"Tell her what?" I said, but I had a pretty good idea of what he was going to say.

"Tell her I . . . love her."

I stayed there, in the doorway, just watching his shoulders rise and fall with his laboured breathing. In those moments I wished I could find a way to help him, but it would've meant putting my crew in danger. Gus had made his choices—he had inflicted pain on others, including those I cared about. Now it was time for him to die. To suffer his own cruelty.

Still, I watched on till the final light left his eyes. As I turned to leave, the droid just about scared the skin off me. It spoke.

"Captain?"

I gawked at the little thing. "Uh, yeah?"

"It's me, Milky!"

"Oh, right," I said, stooping down and looking at the tinted lens, which I guessed Milky to be looking out of. "Er, how in the hell did you manage to get this thing all set up to come and save me?"

"I'm controlling it through the remote. They never took it off me. I can see everything the droid does. I had the droid hack into the central systems and I came across the electro circuit room—that's where I heard they were planning on taking you. From there on it was pretty easy, just guiding the droid around the ventilation ducts and to your rescue."

Now wasn't the time to tell Milky he'd just killed someone —even if it had been by proxy, it still counted. It was something I could only burden him with when he was older, old enough to understand what it really meant. I kept the emotion out of my voice. "Yeah, that's great kid, I really appreciate you saving my life and everything, but what am I supposed to do now that I'm on the loose in this hostile, enemy mother ship?"

"That's easy," he said, as the droid hummed out ahead of me. "Just follow me through and I'll show you where they're holding us."

"And you're sure that blaster's not about to jam up on us?"

"Sure as I can be, sir. Hasn't let you down yet, has it?"

"No, I suppose not."

The droid headed off on its way, following an invisible track set down by Milky. I was not much more than a passenger on this mad quest, jogging to keep up. I had to ask Milky to slow things down a bit. Not all of us are athletes. When we reached a corner section of the ship—with an electronics panel—the droid rolled to a stop and seemed to consider. Then, out of nowhere, its cannon whirred to life and shot off a beam at the panel. It burst open in a shower of blue sparks. As the panel peeled back on its hinge I examined the stencilled name written there, the ship's name: *Fonch Express*. Well, I guess Radley hadn't done a half-arsed job on keeping the identity of her fleet a secret—she'd really gone the whole hog with his cover up job, not that it would be necessary for much longer. Still, as a captain, it seemed a mite disrespectful to give the ship such a generic, corporate name.

A mechanical arm shot out from within the droid and slithered into the electronics. Milky kept me informed as the droid did its work. "Now I'm accessing the main security network, seeing if I can't jam all the locking mechanisms, send them haywire. If this does work you should expect a great deal of security officers running this way and that, looking panicked. I'm going to tell them that they're under attack. You'd probably do well to keep out of the way as far as possible."

"Thanks for the heads up—"

Alarms bawled out above me, near enough shattering my eardrums. Just as Milky had declared, boots stomped all around me, appearing to arrive from all directions. The droid wasn't waiting around, and I just about caught sight of it as it ploughed on around the corner. I trotted onward, ducking and diving security officers, indeed, looking wound up and not a little intimidating with those blasters clutches to their chests. Me and the droid reached the familiar white zone once more, where I'd been held captive, and where it appeared the others were being held captive too. We bucked onward till the droid came to a stop outside a seemingly random door. As if the door sensed our presence, it swooped back to reveal Milky standing right there, grinning ear to ear. Smug bastard.

I couldn't help myself throwing my arms around him and hugging him to my gut. In my rush of affection he almost downright dropped the remote. Once I'd got over myself, thanked him again and again for saving him and 'for having smarts,' he informed me that he had little idea of where they others were being held. He told me that Foy had demanded that she at least be kept together with her cousins, so we could fairly assume— her being stubborn and convincing, especially toward guards of the male persuasion—that they would be all squeezed in together somewhere. Unfortunately, during the droid's virtual adventures through the mother ship hard drives, it'd been unable to uncover any sort of data indicating where they might be held. And so we were resolved to checking out the entire white zone of the ship, going door to door, in our search.

I guess it took us ten minutes or so to get all the doors open, generally having the droid blast them into oblivion, without any luck whatsoever. When we reached a dead-end, a wall at the end of the corridor, we decided that it might just be time to move onto other things. I knew that we had to locate Michaels and the stone. If we uncovered Foy and the kids while we did that, or the droid managed to get some info on their whereabouts, then so much the better. One thing was for certain following our droid's nosing through the ship's systems, and that was that this place was flat out enormous.

What the droid did uncover, however, was the location of something ominously marked 'laboratory' so I decided that might well be a good place to get looking right off the bat. We twirled our way down yet more corridors of flashing lights and whining sirens, passed more and more fraught security officers—

glad that none of them thought to stop us and ask questions. At the entrance to the laboratory we found our first real obstacle. A stubborn door. No matter how much our droid flirted and schmoozed the ship's computers it was not budging an inch on opening up this door. And so, as had proven effective thus far, we resorted to old reliable, that rather fine laser cannon. And, what do you know, it did the trick.

Granted it did take several hails of laser fire to get through the various layers of reinforced steel but we made it through in the end. The droid turned out to have yet more tricks up its sleeve as it bucked up onto a series of jets which propelled it up and over the wreckage of the door. Me and Milky just followed on behind, trusting that it would take care of any hostiles on the other side of the threshold.

As it was, though, nothing much stood in our way. In fact, this laboratory could just about have been anywhere at all, any corporation in the universe—and not some place stowed away in the depths of a villain's lair. There were all sorts of machines churning away to either side of us—some which reminded me of washing machines, twirling away on never-ending cycles, sloshing clothes into a clean, odour-free state. As you've probably guessed by now, I've got my suspicions about cleanliness, and especially agents dedicated to its task. We pushed onward, deeper into the lab till we came across a booth in the centre of it all, a yellow light illuminating the whole thing—an area apparently unaffected by the craziness taking over the rest of the *Fonch Express*. I was sure, right then, that we'd found what we were looking for. Well, *one* of the things we were looking for, if you counted that we were searching for Foy and the boys too.

I gestured for Milky and the droid to hold back. Milky opened his mouth to protest, no doubt worried about my safety —bless him—but unaware that scientists, even ones dealing with life and death, universe-wide-implication levels of science, more often than not eschewed all types of weapons, even scientists dabbling with the dark arts.

And so I crept closer, ready to take this guy on alone. I rounded the frame of the cubicle to find the scientist sitting there, at the desk with his eye glued to a rather serious looking microscope.

"Hey!" I said.

———

I've got more than a few regrets littered throughout my smuggling career and I'd probably have to count this little incident among them. You know I said that I trusted, assumed, that pretty much all scientists will go out of their way to avoid laying their hands on weapons? Yeah, well, I guess I learnt a pretty valuable lesson that day—notably that all people are different, and this scientist no less so than the rest of us.

At the sound of my gleeful greeting, he just about toppled right off his chair, only problem was, as he lay there on the floor, he had time to slip the blaster out of his shoulder holster and fire off a shot at me.

The beam caught the fleshy part of my cheek. If I hadn't had the good sense to dodge that bright light at the last moment he would've had no trouble in making the headshot. Needless to say, Milky arrived on the scene pretty *pronto*, the droid returning fire and catching this rogue scientist right on the gun hand. The blaster clattered to the floor and I found that I could allow myself to breathe again.

The scientist grasped his hand and gritted his teeth in pain.

"Michaels, I presume?" I said, wincing as I applied pressure to my cheek with my fingers.

He panted a couple of times and then nodded.

I took a second look at the table where he had been working and fully absorbed the scene. It wasn't a microscope perched there. The device was box-shaped and had several cables snaking out of it. I saw the Stone of the Angels jammed into a compartment at the centre. I guessed this was no less than the energy centre of the whole operation. I approached the desk, stooped to snatch up Michaels's blaster—pocketed it—and then examined the device further. "How do I shut it down?" I said.

Michaels snivelled to himself, something between hysterical laughter and snorts of pain. "You . . . can't . . . it's too late now."

A shudder ran up my spine. "What do you mean, 'too late?'"

"The process, it's all happening, everything's in motion. We're headed for the centre of Fritten—for Garton-1."

Garton-1's the centre of the universe, as far as all things administrative in the Fritten System are concerned, and while I'm far from being a fan of those politicians and bureaucrats that inhabit it—if you backed me into a corner, maybe after buying me a few moisers in *The Bitch's* you might be able to get me to loathingly admit how important it is in terms of keeping the universe from slipping into all-out anarchy and destruction. Even a smuggler would struggle to operate in complete anarchy. Without rules, there's nothing to smuggle *per se*.

I looked over the device again, the stone sat there snug in the contraption. It didn't appear that there was much at all happening. "Uh, and what about if I just pull the plug on that thing?"

"Go on," he said, eyes flashing. "I dare you. Try it."

Something in the tone of his voice convinced me that it really *wouldn't* be a good idea to pull the plug on this thing. "What'll happen if I do?"

"Oh, I should say that it would set off the bomb I've had wired up. It'd destroy everything around us, all the systems we pass through. The blast wave might even be enough to destroy Garton-1 by itself. There would be no need for any standoff. The whole universe would be blown to smithereens."

"Is that so?"

"Please, feel free to test my honesty."

Again, I wasn't much in the mood for that. Thinking fast, I looked back to Milky. "You reckon you can wire up the droid to this, have it see if there's any way around the mechanism?"

Milky's eyes looked bulbous and unbelieving. "I guess I could try."

"You'd do so at your peril," Michaels said. "Any attempt to bypass the system would trigger the bomb. Really, you'd be better off just letting me get my hands back on the device, that way you might be permitted to live a few hours more."

As I stood there, trying to work out a win-win outcome of this, and having a real hard time over it, I heard the sound of footsteps entering the lab. Before I got the chance to instruct Milky to investigate with the droid, I watched Radley's unmistakable, angular face appear around the corner of the cubicle.

She held a blaster in her hand. "Captain Wright. I hear that you've had something of an eventful few minutes. Please," she said, wagging the blaster, "step away from the stone. I wouldn't like to shoot you. There's still so much I think you can tell me."

I kept hold of the blaster in my own hands—the one Michaels had fired off at me.

"Toss it," she said.

I hesitated, wondering whether I might be able to outdraw her, and then, realising that, seeing as I had ten thumbs, I probably couldn't. I dropped the blaster.

"Good boy," she said, crouching to retrieve it before tucking it away into the back of the waistband of her skirt.

I sidled up alongside Milky, both of us with our hands raised.

Michaels stumbled to his feet, still holding the afflicted part of his hand.

When Radley spoke her words were short and sharp—like she was running low on time. "Will you still be able to operate the systems, be able to do what's required?"

Michaels returned to his position at the device with the stone all hooked up. He clutched his bloodied hand to his lab coat, now covered in bloodstains. "Yes," he said.

Radley turned her focus back to us. "Good, because I'd like some time alone with Captain Wright here before we get to Garton. It turns out that it was a false alarm—no idea how it got set off." She glanced over me and Milky then turned back to Michaels. "Once I've coordinated the security teams, got all of them back from their little fit of nerves, I'll have some assigned here. Although, considering how they reacted to that alarm, that might be putting the mission in more danger than safety." She nodded to us. "Come on, then, don't slouch."

For just a second I was sure that Milky was going to take the opportunity to snap the droid into action. I knew that he still had the remote on him, stuffed deep in his pocket somewhere. If only he could reach for it, set it to attack Radley, blow that gun out her—

A laser beam flashed, illuminating the whole room. It struck the hapless droid and blew it into a thousand pieces. Smoke coiled up from the snout of Radley's blaster. "I *hate* droids," she said.

"Yes," I said, stepped out of the cubicle, leaving Michaels to his work, "I think I can see that."

———

Milky went all quiet as Radley led us at gunpoint through the mother ship. I guessed that Milky had put a lot of love into that little droid and to see it all go to waste in the flash of a laser beam and a puff of smoke must've been heart breaking for him. As for me, well, I can understand why people get attached to objects sometimes—catch me on a bad day and I might admit that the *Nava's* merely 'an object'—but affection for a droid? From what I've seen over the years that can be a slippery slope. People who obsessively build droids seem to be compensating for something, trying to manufacture something they can't find in humans—striving to create perfection that they've given up looking for. I'm one to talk, though, I've got my own fetish in the form of the *Nava's* security systems. Hell, I guess we're all just as fucked up as one another really.

Radley led us past some security guards all looking more-than-a-little panicked. I guess that she'd left out the important parts of the plan but they probably knew enough to realise that this was a high risk mission, one which could see every last one of them getting killed. We emerged on what could only be the bridge. An enormous vidscreen displayed the area out in front of the *Fonch Express*, revealing what I made out to be the familiar run up to Garton-1—the greenish light of the Vun System, the asteroid belt just off to our right and, of course, the giveaway lack of space debris. I mean nothing at all. It's no exaggeration to say that politicians are great fans of keeping their own front doorsteps mighty tidy. Shame their doorsteps don't extend to the rest of the universe.

At some time along our trip Radley had seen fit to put her blaster away. That was probably more down to the fact that we were so hopelessly outgunned, what with the dozens and dozens of armed security officers scattered about the bridge, than the prospect that she'd decided to trust us not to do anything else disruptive. To be honest, I really saw nothing we could do at all to put a spanner in the works—to somehow thwart her plans. One of the biggest problems was that I really had no idea what her plans were.

Radley led us off to a section of sofas which sat on the bridge. This was most likely where she would hang out when the heat wasn't on—and she probably led us there to, on the face of it anyway, put us at ease. She indicated for us to sit and then took her own seat opposite. She laid her hands on the table and clutched them together, just like I remembered she'd done back at her headquarters. "Captain Wright," she said. "There's one very simple thing I want to hear from you."

I pressed my lips together, thinking that I wasn't in much of a position to refuse anything she might ask. Other than something to do with the *Navaplastas*. A man has his limits.

She continued, "All this business with the Stone of the Angels, I'm sure you've heard the story—that you're familiar with it—and I'd like to know what you think about the prospect of aliens."

My heart rapped against my chest, just at the thought of those aliens meeting up with us after we'd destroyed Dromodis. It seemed like something that just wasn't open for debate. I felt guilty over it, even though, in a roundabout way, I'd done exactly what they'd wanted from me, namely delivering the stone to Alis Radley-Hadton. I decided it was best to keep my cards close to my chest. "I really don't know that much about it."

A faint smile perked up her lips. "Don't lie, I can see it there, sketched out on your face. You saw them, didn't you? Yes, you did. That's the reason that you keep cropping up all over the place. They've got a plan for you."

"Uh, I don't know what you're talking about."

"Captain Wright, you're an important person, an *extremely* important person, but you're really not all that sharp are you? Not much blessed in the brain department?"

"You could put it like that."

"Then let me enlighten you."

21: RADLEY'S STORY

W HEN I WAS AROUND eighteen years old, still growing up on the planet of Tetrahedron-2, I was just getting around to finishing my studies and in the middle of signing up to do my service with the FSA. Don't look surprised, it may surprise you but I haven't always been a massive crook. Anyway, I'd just got myself out of school, flying through the exam period, if I might say so, and everything about my future looked very bright indeed. I planned on moving into robotics—droid programming and management—somewhere in the higher end, though, nothing of this programming droids for mainte-nance or for security, I wanted to push the boundaries. In fact, my interests lay in micro design. I wanted to make droids that could be used by surgeons to correct medical problems with a high degree of accuracy previously unknown. But that's a story for another day, because what I'm about to tell you about now is the moment of my life where everything changed—when a great big line was scratched right through it.

On my planet, a fairly small settlement on the outer edges of the Frak System, I lived a pretty simple life. Oh, I suppose it was quite like all these colonists who would set out with their families for a new world—which is to say that it's kind of a return to rural life. I turned out to be among the second generation on Tetrahedron, in their previous lives my parents had both been financial advisors, back on Garton-1—of all places—so they must've been quite successful. Although we never did talk about their careers much. Out there on Tetrahedron they got the idea to build the Fonch business—I suppose they must've used the money they saved up from quitting their jobs. It all started out with just a single building, a few dozen machines cranking out the bars. And it all just exploded from there.

My childhood was spent pretty much going between milking the cows, snatching up the chicken eggs and then heading off to market in the afternoon. Rather like the life of one your crewmembers, Foy, we'll see what we can do for her once I've relayed what I've got to tell.

In the evenings leading up to my final examinations I would attend a study group—just four or five of us, all students at the same age, studying together, pressing one another to remember more, pushing for more accurate answers. Looking back on it now it was some sort of heaven. Or purgatory. I was waiting for that one moment that would truly define my life, although I hadn't yet any idea.

One of those aforementioned evenings I was heading back

home, going along the dirt road which led to my house, when what did I see but a strange light in the sky. Now I was pretty unaccustomed to seeing lights in the sky. Out where we lived we got one shipment a month from Central and no one on the planet could afford a ship since the economy was just about getting itself going. So naturally I got suspicious. In the absence of any other form of entertainment in the dark evenings—electric lights being a bit of a luxury and we wanted to save as much of our energy ration as we could for the machines in the Fonch factory—we would sit around and tell stories. It was my dad who would relay the stories about aliens, back on Earth, when people had lived on Earth. The way I remember it, I felt like we were similar to those farmers he would describe in the stories. They would start out the same, with someone called John or Paul or Mark ploughing his fields on a sticky summer evening, with the sun lighting up the sky in a pinkish-orange glow, and then the protagonist would spot something strange up in the sky, and the ship would swoop down and abduct them. Dear Daddy would alter the story which happened at the centre of the tale, but, for the most part, the formula remained the same.

Anyway, this particular evening, as I headed home with my interface, with all the information I needed to pass the coming exams, I noted this light in the sky. And I just stopped and stared. Maybe I could've kept on walking, perhaps then things would've turned out differently, but I chose to stand my ground, to stare up at them. That might have been what convinced them.

The light got brighter and brighter, and it occurred to me that it was a space ship drifting closer and closer. A mixture of excitement and anxiety hit me. As I'd never travelled in space at that point, only seen the spaceships with supplies landing once or twice at the terminal, there was something exotic and exciting about it. I looked around, in a half-hope of being able to share this unexpected phenomenon with *someone*, but, as is always the case with truly remarkable events, there was no one there. At that moment I had the urge to run. But I didn't.

The ship floated down and landed in the field, not more than a few steps from me. I recall the feeling of the breeze in my hair, blowing strands of hair over my face, tickling my nostrils and mouth. On Tetrahedron there wasn't much in the way of wind, and that was the first time I'd felt that sensation. I'll remember it forever, just as I'll remember exactly what followed.

The ship sank down into the field and the noise of its engines subsided. I watched on, I'm sure with my mouth hanging open, as a pair of aliens descended from the ship. That pink-purple complexion, the skin sort of like fish scales. Well, just as you know, I was raised up to be told that aliens were nothing but a myth, told back on Earth to gullible people—back in the times when we were afraid of space. But this was really happening. These were actual, *live* aliens.

They approached me as if they had all the time in the world, like they had no idea what this sort of encounter could mean to me—as if this were some sort of everyday occurrence. They're just better than us, aren't they? Of a higher plain. A superior plain. But, Captain Wright, I'm sure you will have noticed that in your own meeting. I digress.

As they drew closer I could've sworn that I watched the

skies darken, and those alien skins glow. But who's to be sure? It's only my account of events. The aliens stopped when they got within a few inches and both of their eyes flickered over my entire body—I remember that, it felt as if they were, I don't know, scanning me or something. Just drinking me in with their analytical glares. I just stood there, of course, rooted to the spot, for all intents and purposes paralysed.

At first they told me right out that I was a special person and that I was to carefully follow a set of instructions that they themselves set out for me. It was all very detailed. Everything was exact and to the point. I had no trouble remembering what they told me. They informed me that the Fonch business would grow to become nothing less than an empire, and that through it I was to buy up the universe, to get myself involved in all sorts of enterprise. Well, they never told me straight out that I was to get involved in the darker side of the universe, the drug running, the prostitution, all those unsavoury enterprises, just to name a couple, but that was the general gist of it. And, I don't know, but I've always felt that those two aliens have always accompanied me, been whispering little pieces of advice into my ear all these years. This is their empire really, I suppose. Or at least that's what it feels like.

It really was a chore to get the universe hanging by a string, but things just seemed to fall in place for me. For a start my parents were both killed in a bizarre industrial accident—late one night in the factory—both of them mangled by a pair of crazed droids. That was my only doubt, when I felt that if I'd done something, gone off to university like I'd wanted, that I somehow could've programmed them better—at least looked over the work done by the lower-level employees. At first my ire turned on the programmer herself, but I knew she wasn't anymore to blame than the system, that horrid dependence we've built up, leaving ourselves at the mercy of *mere* machines, and I've hated droids every since. They destroyed my family.

Anyway, Mummy and Daddy did leave behind a rampant and successful business. A substantial inheritance at a time when most young adults on Tetrahedron were either upping sticks and heading off to other, more affluent planets, or robbing produce from neighbours' fields to avoid starving to death. In the end, I bought up the whole of Tetrahedron, employed those that didn't wish to leave. If I'd had enough human resources I would've put them to work in the factory, but, as things were, I had to make do with just taking on fairly dumb, low-level machines, and to make sparing use of human operators. That was a reasonable compromise, I suppose. I like to feel that the *Fonch Express* is something more of a success story. I had managed to keep it reasonably droid free till that unfortunate entrance of your little ally a little while ago.

Things just kept growing, out of control really. There was no way to stop it, though. It had to keep expanding. And I waited for those aliens to revisit me, to let me in on the next stage of their plan. But they never did return. Until one night, a few years back.

They informed me that I was to transform the basement of my Fonch factories into arms manufacturers, and then I was to distribute the arms throughout the universe to my closest allies, so that I might build up an army. Well, that took me by surprise, I don't need to tell you. I mean, it's one thing to dominate the universe through an assortment of organised crime and legitimate business, but quite another to have an all-out physical war. It sounded crazy. But they assured me I was doing the right thing. Actually, well, there was one point where I wavered, which is to say that I just couldn't see a way forward for the plan, a few weeks out, and I decided to shut down production. Those aliens visited me that very night and one of them did something to me, made me . . . this is so difficult to explain . . . but they made me observe my parents' death, that *droid* crushing them, the blood sweating out of their bodies, the *crack* of bone. After that I never did ask any questions. I was, and am, their instrument, for better or worse. I can never experience what I experienced then. It was too much to take.

And then they brought Michaels to me, a scientist they claimed could change everything, all that was left up to me was to get a hold of an item known as the Stone of the Angels, which was kept in a museum back on Garton-1. Michaels revealed the power of the stone to me, how he had spent his entire young life studying it, working on new theories, and he was sure that he'd found a breakthrough. But he had no intention of sharing the information with the FSA or, indeed, anyone involved with the Fritten System. He had had his own run-ins with the authorities —he believed the state had conspired to have his parents killed, and from what he revealed to me it seemed like more than mere conjecture. There was nothing he wanted more than revenge. After a brief surveillance operation I determined that it would be impossible to steal the stone from the museum, even exerting my influence over the politicians I kept, still keep, in my pocket. This was something that was deemed to be untouchable for any price. That rarest of things. And then, as chance would have it, one of my senior directors at Fonch—Susie—turned out to have a deadbeat brother-in-law who worked security at the museum. Turned out what he had always wanted was his own space, somewhere miles out of range of everything. And so I decided to part with an exceptionally unremarkable moon—even throwing in a bubble for good measure, so that he wouldn't choke to death from lack of oxygen. He sprung the stone and got in touch with me. We arranged the meet-up with him at *The Bitch's Leap*— God, what an awful name—and then, getting a little anxious, I sent a bunch of men to the moon to snatch the stone ahead of time. They killed him, much to my disappointment, but they failed to find the stone. As it turned out, he had a better nose than I'd given him credit for and he'd palmed the thing off to you—a smuggler—for safekeeping. Surely worried that I might take his moon away. Some of my men have especially itchy trigger fingers. It can be a real logistical problem sometimes. Or maybe there was more to it. Who's to say these aliens hadn't visited them too?

The last words they extracted from his lips were 'Arkle Wright' and a quick word in the right circles showed you up for who you were, a smuggler. It seemed a minor inconvenience, nothing more. In fact, as it turned out, it seemed the perfect excuse—you were a scapegoat, a means to divert attention away from what I was trying to achieve. Who wouldn't believe there was a smuggler out there looking to turn a profit by selling on a valuable piece of the universe's history? And then I had the men intercept you on Hortenine-6. What went on then I'm still not totally sure. Needless to say, shots were fired, yet again, and once more there was nothing to show for it. And . . . well . . . a lot's happen since then, to both of us, I suppose, but the upshot is that now I have the stone and I'm going to make happen what I promised all those years ago. I am going to declare way on the Fritten System and take control. Victory shall be ours.

22: ON THE BRIDGE OF THE FONCH EXPRESS

"**H**ANG ON A SEC," I said. "What do you mean by 'us?'"

Radley smiled, showing off a perfect horseshoe of teeth. "The aliens, they are readying to take control, don't you see? They shall take things over from us and no longer will we have to worry."

"Worry about what?"

"All of it!"

I eyed Radley out of the corner of my eye, as only you can eye someone you're convinced is totally *loco*. Sure I'd seen those aliens, had them press the stone back into the palm of my hand, but that didn't mean that I was looking any further than I could definitely see—which at that point was just about beyond the tip of my nose. "What makes you think," I said, "that if you do go through with this plan, declare way on Fritten, that the aliens will have *any* place for humans in whatever it is, this new world order you've got yourself so wrapped up in?"

"Can't you see, Captain? We just need to trust them. Surely you of all people can see that? You've been in their company, you've met with them, don't you realise that they're the ones, they've always been the ones."

Now this was getting weird beyond words, if this had been a fairground ride I'd have been waving my arms and screaming at the top of my lungs at the operator to let me off. Wasn't a fairground ride, though. "Still, I'm not sure you've got things totally worked out."

Her cheeks reddened slightly—I think probably the first time I'd seen her display any sort of anger. "Of course I have! What else could it possibly mean? They're our saviours, and we, you and me, are their disciples. They chose us, Captain Wright, and we must serve them."

"I ain't nobody's servant, I'll tell you that for nothing."

This just seemed to infuriate her further. "Captain, you really have no idea what you're talking about. You're seeing only the gloss, you have no concept of the content."

"Well, actually, I think I have it down pretty well—in a purely no-nonsense way, that is. Way I see it you're planning on flying this fleet out to go and blow a bunch of people to hell, all because a bunch of aliens told you to? Are you for real?"

"That's enough! Stop! They believe in us. They *love* us. You must know it's true."

"Look, I don't doubt that these guys have been meddling pretty whole-heartedly in our affairs for a while now. That stuff with those three stars, yeah maybe that was them—seems to me they probably forged the Stone of the Angels. But that doesn't mean that we should just go about doing whatever they say just because they *seem* more powerful than us. Listen, I'll tell you something for nothing. You've been going around all your life blaming droids for the death of your parents. Haven't you stopped to think, even for a second that it might, *might*, have been your beloved aliens that did that?"

"No," she said, eyes glaring. "No, it's not true. Why would they do that? It was an accident."

"Certainly looked that way. They found themselves a pretty convenient scapegoat—just like you thought you'd done when I got the blame for snatching the stone. They drove you into this, made you what you are, and they had you kill all those people—Susie, Milky here's daddy, and the massacre of Trivus-3—"

She held up her hand. "Wait, Captain. Please. Did you say that Susie's dead?"

"'Course she is, and you killed her."

Her whole face turned completely white and her hand shot to her mouth. "Oh, God," she said. "Oh, God."

"Listen, you can save all this for the inquiry, all that matters to me is that you turn this damn fleet around and forget all this. What a damn mess, start to finish."

"No, Captain, you've got it all wrong. I had nothing to do with any of those—the only person that was killed under my command was Lionel Fox, and regrettably at that. You have to believe me, I never want to kill anyone. It's the most hideous thing I can think of, destroying another human being."

I opened my mouth and then decided that this might warrant something thinking before I sprouted some nonsense or other. As I retraced my mind, thought back over all those situations, I recalled that I'd never seen the killers. Closest I'd ever got was hearing the sounds of them leaving Susie's house. Now I was entering a pretty sketchy area. I was starting to believe Radley's story.

But then I thought of Gus, what he'd said as he'd died—that he was sorry. That the *aliens* had made him do it. With or without Radley's say-so I got the impression that Gus did those people in. Whether or not he was really led on by the aliens is another matter entirely.

"Please, Captain, I was acting on good faith. The aliens, they told me to do it."

As I stared across the table at Radley I saw a trapped little girl, frightened, someone who'd been pushed around, this way and that, just completely confused and terrified by the power which had been passed down to her. I thought back to my own brush with the aliens, when they'd made me see that tragedy, the crashing of the ship. Made me relive that trauma all over again. How could I not feel some shred of sympathy, empathise in some way with what it was that Radley had gone through. Perhaps Gus too, was that how they'd got to him? And then that was that. Before I knew it I was empathising. There was just no other way. I'm human after all.

"Ma'am?" I said, glancing across the table.

A single tear rolled down her cheek and then dripped off her chin.

"Know what you've got to do now?"

She shook her head solemnly.

"Turn this ship around and go on home."

———

Things got much easier following our little heart to heart. For starters Radley wasted no time in delegating power to me. I thanked her kindly, knowing that turning over a ship to another captain is never an easy thing to do.

Now, turning a fleet around is a bit tougher than it sounds. In theory it should just be a case of getting on the global communicator, getting through to all the pilots at once and letting them know just what's up. Problem was, considering that their previous commanding officer had been recently deposed, I had a tough time convincing them that I was really in charge. I got around thirty or forty private communications where I had to go through with each of them, outlining the change of plan, most of the times having to put Radley on so that they'd understand that I hadn't tied her up and shut her off somewhere.

Once I had got all the pilots onside, we went through the task of getting everyone pointing in the right direction. As I did so I was glad to see Foy and the kids enter onto the bridge, looking a little bemused as the armed security officer led them over to the table where Radley continued to sit—still white-faced and looking somewhat stunned. No way in hell was I leaving Foy off the weapons systems, or Milky off the electronics board for that matter. So I called them over. Foy had her cousins checking over her shoulder, learning from her—if they had the same shooting genes I had no doubt that they'd make fine cannon operators. All this had more to do with me stamping my authority on the ship than making any practical provisions. If there's one daunting prospect a newly appointed captain always faces, it's brewing mutiny. And with a ship carrying that sort of payload it was imperative that I took full control, 'no half measures'—as I say to the service droid in *The Bitch's*.

A while later we'd achieved what I'd thought to be impossible only an hour or so go. We had the whole fleet flying directly *away* from Garton-1, and back en route for Tetrahedron-2. Already I found my mind slipping into practicalities, how one would go about disposing of the unwanted weapons. I thought it would be pretty much a case of digging a great big hole in the ground and stuffing them in it. Tetrahedron-2 was a bit of a dump, what with that factory just about covering its entire surface, so I had no real fears for the environmental health of the place. And then, out of the corner of my eye, I noted the Communications Officer waving his hand at me.

My heart plunged right through my stomach as I granted him permission to speak.

"Captain? I'm picking up a large fleet on the navigational system, they're closing fast. Look to be of large number. I'm getting the identifications through now." He paused, read, then said, "It's the FSA."

My heart beat faster. This was what I'd feared, getting drawn into some sort of a showdown. I thought quickly, wanting to get a message through as swiftly as possible. "Officer, put me in touch with the mother ship."

The officer nodded and returned to his console. He scrabbled away at the controls, sweat glistening on his brow.

I watched on the large vidscreen as the fleet closed in on us, realising with each passing second that they weren't slowing down. They were assuming an attack formation.

The officer rose from his console once more. "Captain? They're blocking our requests. They've got a synthesised message claiming that we've committed an act of war by breaking the territory carrying the weapons we have. There's no way to reach them."

I pondered this for as long as I had. Within a minute to ships would be all over us. And I thought about the stone. Whose hands would it slip into next? There was one thing I'd established throughout the course of my adventures and that was that, against all odds, I might well be the best person to take on the burden. Everyone else who got close to the stone seemed to crack into a thousand pieces, become a veritable psychological wreck. But there was no way of getting in touch with them. As far as the FSA was concerned, this was Radley's fleet. I had no option. "All right, stick the shields up."

Even as I delivered the command I regretted having to take the action. I knew fully well that it would be interpreted as an admission of circumstance, that we were prepared for war. But if I left the shields down that first strike—the one it took them to realise that we weren't firing back—it might well leave people dead. If only I could get through to the mother ship.

I looked over to the officer. "Look, son, no offence, but do you mind letting my kid have a go at that over there?"

The officer looked far too frightened to take anything so complex as offence and he gladly backed away from the communications console and allowed Milky to take up his seat. Milky immediately went to work on the communications. I hoped that he'd learnt well from Wodd—picked up some of those nimble tricks. If he had learnt how to charm the electronics panel as well as he'd learnt to charm the droids then I was sure he would do just fine.

The fleet closed in on us, fighters spreading out and manning their laser blasters.

"Remember," I said, speaking to all of the ships under my command, "do *not* return fire. Repeat, your orders are to stand down from any confrontation. Attempt to communicate by all means, but do *not* fire in retaliation."

My hands shook as I watched the fights dive bomb the *Fonch Express*. Their lasers rapped against the shields, bouncing off in some cases, being absorbed in others. I estimated that the *Fonch* would take quite a bit of damage, but if they decided to target one of the small or medium-sized ships then there would be every chance they'd take it down—shields or no.

As the first wave of fighters left the vidscreen, swarmed out behind the fleet and readied for another strike, Milky gave me notice that one of the fighters was attempting to communicate. This was our one chance. If they came at us again we'd have to fight back, or we'd start losing men ourselves.

"Yes, fighter," I said, jabbing at my inner ear with my index finger. "This is the captain of the *Fonch Express* here, mother ship. We surrender. Repeat, we surrender."

The vidscreen ebbed in and out as it tried to get a visual on the pilot. It's always much easier to conduct negotiations face to face, makes it more personal. You learn a lot more about your negotiating partner that way. Not that I'd ever bargained for something as high stakes as this current situation we found ourselves embroiled in.

The vidscreen got clear for a moment then slipped back into

static. The voice came through clean as a bell, though. "Copy, Captain. You should've thought about that before you led a strike on Fritten, before you decided to attempt to destroy Garton-1. That massacre on the Corfus System will never be forgotten. Now you've crossed the line and we've got permission to blow you damn mobsters right out of space. You took my planet too, but instead of putting us out of our misery, you decided to corrupt us—strangle us to death slowly."

I had to maintain some sort of dialogue with this irate pilot. "Look we can talk about the Corfus System, later, okay? I believe it was something of a misunderstanding, but you've got to give us a chance to explain."

"Not a chance. You'd only stab us in the back."

Clutching at straws, I decided to make a direct play. "And which is your planet, pilot?"

And then, in that instant, the vidscreen came clear. We achieved two-way visual contact. Inside I praised Milky to the heavens, man I'd really stumbled upon a boy wonder. And as I absorbed that image, the face on screen, even obscured by the visor of the helmet, I would've known him anywhere at all.

"My planet's Hortenine-6," Wodd said, sending a burst of laser beams right at our energy core.

23: THE FONCH TAKES A HAMMERING

A S WODD SHOT OFF what seemed to be his entire payload of lasers, rockets and bombs, I could only scream out. But it was too late. The communication stream cut out before I got a chance. I wondered if he'd seen me, recognised my voice. I guessed that he hadn't, that he'd been so swept up in his rage, so satisfied to finally have the infamous Radley in his sights that he'd forgotten everyone and everything he knew.

The *Fonch* lurched from side to side as the shields balked at the load of fire. The damage meters flew off the charts. All around me officers jabbered away, demanding that we return fire. But I told them all to hold themselves back. Fighting them head on would only make things worse. So we sucked up the laser beams, waiting for another chance.

Milky continued to scrabble away at the communications panel, trying to patch us through to the *FSA-01061*, where I hoped to find Reynolds still in command. But pretty soon after the first few waves, we simply lost all power in the communications unit. Our stabilisers, too, were suffering, the *Fonch* felt like a ship caught in the high seas, at the mercy of the rolling waves below it. There was nothing else to do. I had to declare an emergency. Officers bounded by me, heading for their posts, ready for the loss of control, for the *Fonch* to slip into a flat spin, sending us in who knew which direction. And then, right as I stood ready to abandon my own post, a message came in. The *FSA-0106I* wanted to get in touch. I allowed it through, of course.

Reynolds popped up on the vidscreen. His uniform looked especially well-pressed, the brass buttons very shiny. If thunder did faces . . . "Captain Wright? What the *hell* are you doing on that ship?"

Feeling the entire bridge sliding from beneath my feet, I said, "Well, Captain, if you'd thought to do a thorough search you might've found the *Navaplastas* down below—in the cargo hold. They took us prisoner. Long story short, we worked things out. We're turning the fleet around." A thunderous vibration ripped through the floor, almost knocking me down. But I held on. Just. "Now call off your men. They'll slaughter us at this rate!"

Despite my measured words, Reynolds took a moment to consult with someone off screen. He did a whole lot of nodding and then he turned his attention back to me. "All right, Captain, I'll call off my men. But I'll have to take you into custody, do you understand that? Until we get all this sorted out you're officially captain of the *Fonch Express*, which up until a few moments ago had been determined to blow Garton-1 out of space."

"I know it looks bad," I said. "But I promise you a top-notch explanation. Top-notch!"

———————

And so the *FSA-01061* crew boarded us, took over the running of the *Fonch*. As promised, Reynolds delivered a pair of guards, too of his bulkiest and brightest, to cuff me and escort me off the *Fonch*. It seemed like I'd been led halfway around the universe in handcuffs.

I got a final look at Radley, cowering over on that rather comfortable sofa, rocking back and forth gently. I guessed that I was going to have a hard time explaining that she was the master planner behind all this—and that I'd not, somehow, seen my way to subverting Captain Reynolds, and the FSA, twice over.

My crew watched on glumly as I went, Foy's eyes looking a touch moist—or maybe it was just my imagination, she's a tough girl, after all—and Milky giving it a bit more welly, crying out that they'd got the wrong person, and that I wasn't to be taken away. I was getting to like that kid more and more.

The officers led me along the walkway, out of the *Fonch* and back into the familiar confines of the *FSA-01061*. And, what do you know, I found myself right back where I'd been taken on my first visit—namely the jail cell. Not having much else to do, I just slouched down on the floor and stared at the wall, wondering why I'd agreed to take on that job to smuggle the Stone of the Angels in the first place—agreed to take it from Kools to *The Bitch's Leap*—but, then again, I was coming around to the idea that I might not have had much choice in the matter at all.

For all the honesty and mutual respect that had previously flowed between us, Reynolds took his sweet time in coming to see me. I guessed that he was clearing matters with the higher-ups, getting their opinions on the chain of events. He had a lot of protocol to see to before he could afford to show some good manners. When Reynolds did arrive he was flanked by the same two guards who had escorted me onto the *FSA-01061*. I got a bit of a chill around the collar of my shirt—those goons reminding me a bit of Radley's hoods. And I'd had enough of electro circuits to last me a lifetime, however long mine that turned out to be.

Reynolds kept his aspect professional, hands clasped behind his back and lips pressed firmly together. If his flies hadn't been half open he would've looked like a real hard arse. "Captain Wright? It is my duty to inform you that the council of Garton-1, which is to say the headquarters of the Fritten System Authorities, sees fit to call you before them in a court of law to advise them on your course of action during your time in charge of the *Fonch Express*. Will you require any form of legal representation or shall you be representing yourself in court?"

For this level of stupidity I needed to be fully vertical so I shoved off the ground and stumbled onto my feet. "Whoa there, good Captain. Would you mind running that by me just another time?"

He did so. Deadpan.

"Here, you see, you've got it all wrong. You've got to listen to my end of things. It's not at all what it seems, okay? I just—"

Reynolds cocked his head to one side. "Listen here, *Captain* Wright. Do you think this is the first time a common thief has had the nerve to try and fool an FSA officer, to get so close to them, to pull the wool down over their eyes while they take what they want?"

"What're you talking abou—?"

"I should've snagged you when I got the chance—you had the stone all along, but I was weak, too easily convinced by that carefree façade, the one that you're putting up right now. And then, just when I thought I could trust you, you seemed to hand the stone over to me, only to—*somehow*—sneak it back off this ship without my knowledge. Now, if you have anything to say to that then I'd be glad to hear it."

I needed to make this good, but there wasn't much leeway for dropping in any mention of the aliens—that would get me committed as a psychopath rather than tried as a war criminal. "It's just a misunderstanding, you see, I was way out in the Quail System where I picked up this job, see? And this . . . this client, he handed it over to me in this brown paper package. I had no idea what it was, let alone how he got it off you. I promise."

Reynolds flashed his eyes. "Yes, well, I can't say that your promises are worth all that much. How can you promise me anything when I don't know your real name?"

"Arkle," I said. "Arkle Wright. That's me, always has been, give or take a job or two."

"Really? I think your name is Radley, and that you've been running this whole racket for years now, using that poor woman as your decoy, palming her off as the linchpin. You built this fleet up and had us all fooled—had us all looking into *Fonch Confectionaries*, for goodness' sake. And then, right at the last, you got cold feet. Why you did, I really have not the foggiest clue."

"Well that's just it, ain't it? Can't you see that Radley—and she *is* that woman back on that ship, I can assure you of that—took us hostage, stole the stone from us, and had her scientist hook the damn thing up in the *Fonch*?"

"No, I'm afraid I can't see that at all, and, to be honest, it's rather beyond my remit to do so. You'll have your day in court, don't you worry about that. And, until then, you might like to think your story through. Chances are that they'll reconsider imposing the death penalty if you tell the truth right from the start—perhaps then the council will look favourably upon you."

My mouth dried up. "'Death penalty?'"

Reynolds shot me a steely glare, glanced at his escorts and then beat a hasty exit, their bootfalls echoing off down the corridor, leaving me very alone, and in a very sticky situation.

———

As I sat there with my knees crunched up to my folds of flab, feeling sorry for myself—funny how that doesn't get boring, even after several hours—I thought out how exactly I was going to extradite myself from this position. It seemed pretty hopeless. If Reynolds didn't believe me then I had nothing. If he'd believed me, just a little bit, then I might've been onto something—but he had basically just flat out called me a liar. How was I supposed to recover from that?

And seeing as I spent most of my life trying to put as much distance between myself and the council of Garton-1, I had no great urge to go there and plead my case before them. I knew just what they were like—I'd got a sniff when I'd been in the FSA. I remember hearing all my superior officers bitching and moaning about them, how they were just out to line their own pockets, not at all interested in actually putting an effective strategy in place for the FSA—to have an efficient fleet of space ships. Probably another reason I saw my future elsewhere than the FSA.

I flexed my mind around to seeing Wodd up there on the vidscreen, and I wondered whether he really bought that *I* was Radley. What with Reynolds telling him so much, making me out to be some horrible conman, I thought it would've been pretty irresistible. How well did we actually know each other, anyway? He had leapt on board *my* ship without having any real information on me, other than I was a bit of a deviant. How did he know I *hadn't* been lying to him all along? I wished I could get him in that cell with me right then, to beat some sense into him. After about five minutes we'd see who he believed. Okay, maybe more like ten, considering that I hadn't been putting in the morning crunches recently. If all else failed I reasoned that I'd be able to smother him to death with my mighty flab.

Then I thought about Foy and the kids, Milky. Would they all get themselves tarred with the same brush, seen as in on my act? Seeing as Reynolds really did believe his hypothesis about me being this great, big terrible mobster, then it would follow that they'd be in some pretty big trouble too. They'd aided me.

My mind dulled after all this dealing in *ifs, buts, and what ifs.* As I think I've said before I'm nothing if not a man of action —I like to get my hands dirty, not sit mooching about feeling sorry for myself. Not that there was all that much I could do.

There was a single window out there, just beyond the laser bars of my cell. I looked out it, into the empty space stretching out forever and ever. I yearned to be free, to get myself right out there into the thick of it. If they patched me up in a spacesuit right then and there, gave me a push and sent me off floating I thought I'd die happy. But that wasn't quite what fate had in store for me.

Out there, in that seemingly solitary space, I eyed an approaching object. At first I thought it to be a patrol ship, one of those quick ones the politicians on Garton-1 use to get around fast—maybe it's just me but I'm sure that they hold out on the latest technology, not letting whatever it is they propel themselves with out onto the public market till they're sure they've developed a superior upgrade for themselves—however, as I took a closer peek, I saw that old familiar, cigar-shaped ship. And it was headed right for us.

24: IN CUSTODY ON THE FSA-01061

I SAT THERE transfixed by the approaching ship. It came closer and closer, no lights visible on board, just that silhouette blocking out the stars behind. I was expecting lasers to fire at any second, for the *FSA-01061* to turn sharply and assume an attack pattern. But the ship, apparently, went unnoticed except for by me.

Soon it filled the entire window and I couldn't comprehend how the *FSA-01061* hadn't spotted this approaching ship. This might well be my way out of this mess. I could actually resort to telling the truth with these aliens arriving on the scene. Or, at the very least, some aspect of my story would have weight—because I still had a lot of explaining to do in relation to how the stone managed to get itself off the *FSA-01061*, after I'd, to the best of my knowledge, handed it over to Reynolds.

Still there was no reaction from the *FSA-01061*. That ship was just bobbing around, right outside my window now. I could make out all the hatches on its sides, the knobbly parts of its design. It seemed strangely unaerodynamic—not that it had to be in space. The ship just hovered by the window. I wondered what was going to happen next, whether these aliens might request permission to board from Reynolds. Whatever game it was that they were playing, it would be exposed now. I could easily pass it on to the FSA to sort out. Alien invasions were well beyond my sphere of activity.

The air all around me crackled. Vibrations passed through my gut, up through my body. I got a whiff of cinnamon and then, standing all around me, there were ten or so aliens. Not quite sure how. There *just were*.

Looking back on it, teleportation would've been a pretty good bet. In fact I'm sure that's how they did it, not that that really brings me any closer to understanding how they managed it. All I know is that they stood all around me, surrounding me, when only a matter of seconds before they'd all been out in their ship.

"Captain?" one of the aliens said.

I thought I recognised him as the shorter one from my encounter back on the *Nava*. Really couldn't be all that sure, though, they all looked pretty similar. And, thinking about it, there were a few shorter-looking ones. The main point was that I was speaking with an alien. Again.

Seeing that I wouldn't be permitted to put this conversation off, I replied. "Well, hello there. Fancy seeing you here, on this FSA ship. What can I do for you kind folks this beautiful evening."

Either the alien side-stepped my kindly greeting or it had a better capacity for understanding sarcasm than I'd bargained for. Either way it got right down to brass tacks. "Captain, you failed on your mission."

"Did I now? I wasn't aware that I had one."

"But we are prepared to grant you a second chance."

"Well, lucky me."

I felt their collective alien glare on me. It freaked me out quite a bit, because who hasn't heard all of them stories about anal probes?

The alien continued, "You were supposed to destroy Garton-1 and thus trigger and all-out interplanetary, universe-wide war. This would have led to the destruction of the human race or a much depleted, more manageable population."

"Say what now?"

"The humans. They are too much to manage."

"What makes you think that we need 'managing?'"

The alien glowered at me, again not much emotion there, but the silence told a thousand stories. "We do not 'think' or 'believe,' we *know* what is for the best of all of you."

"And why's that exactly?"

"Because we created you."

Me and my big mouth.

———

I got this really funny, itching feeling and it just spread out over my entire body. I thought I might go crazy from it. Those memories flooded in through my mind again. All those screams, the scratch of branches on impact and the blood seeping its way along the floor of the ship. I was back in that jungle. And it wasn't like any kind of memory. I was *back*.

Only then I was back in the cell again, being stared at by those aliens again. The leader alien, or at least the talkative one —sometimes there's a thin line between the two—looked rather satisfied with himself. "We can control your subconscious, bring memories to the surface, make life a living hell for you."

I really didn't doubt that.

"We made you all, after all, and now you're out of control, like a virus, spreading out through the galaxy without any sign of stopping. And now there are only us left. We are the last of our species."

"I'd say that's pretty ironic."

"Yes," the alien replied, "you might say it's *ironic*."

"So you've been involved with this all along, trying to get us to destroy one another?"

"It started a long time ago, with that stone, the one you've decided to call the 'Stone of the Angels.' I suppose, in a way, that is true. What you construe as being an angel might well be a representation of ourselves. That was the work of our final bout of strength, the last outpouring of our race, the last hope to somehow have you destroy yourselves—so as to give us a hope of living."

"Sorry, man, maybe you should've picked out some scientist for all this info, yeah? In fact, just over there"—I gestured in the direction I believed the *Fonch* to be in—"I think you'll find a pretty bright one. He managed to work out how to fix the stone, put it to some use. Think you might be better off with him."

"No," the alien said, "the only reason that he knows the secret is because of our intervention."

"That's convenient."

The alien continued without pause, apparently just getting swept up in a raconteureal tide. "Our people have been dying for so long now. It was with our much greater numbers that we decided to cause those three stars to collide, to forge this 'Stone of the Angels,' our intention that the human race should discover it—and thus destroy themselves."

"Whoa, wait a second, eh? If you're dying yourselves then what possible reason have you got to take care of us while you're at it?"

"We wish to take responsibility for what we have done to this world. Humanity is a scar on the face of the universe, is it to be our legacy?"

"Well, at least you'd *have* a legacy."

"No," the alien said, "the whole reason for this stone was the basis that we would have you discover it and that you might turn its power on yourselves, and so invest the power in us, return energy to our withered, diseased bodies, to make us well again. But, even then, it was too late. We could not be saved. This disease shall claim us all. But not before we leave the world in the pristine state that we found it."

"Right," I said," and what's my role in all of this exactly."

"You shall bring about the fall of the human race."

"Doesn't sound like such a great deal for me. They'll call me something like Arkle the Bastard when they write history books about it."

"There will be no history books because there will be no humans to write them."

"Yeah, I got that, it's what I like to call a joke. Don't know if you noticed, but all this talk of apocalypse is mighty gloomy—just thought I'd lighten things up a bit."

"There will be no *light*. There will be no *nothing*. Just space. The hollow echo of absence. Nothingness."

"Gotcha, really don't feel like you have to layer on the poetry or anything, that sort of stuff's pretty much lost on me."

The alien took stock of me, took a long while to gather his thoughts—or whatever it was that he was gathering—and then said, "Arkle Wright. You must aid us. We shall release you now. And you must take control of the ship, use the power of the stone and fire on Garton-1. It must be obliterated so the end of mankind may begin."

"Look, if you've all got such a high opinion of yourselves, why don't you go and do it for yourselves?"

"We are too weak. Before we could mould whole planets, grow life from the tips of our fingers. But our power is almost lost now. All that remains is the control we can take over the human subconscious. We can make you feel pain inside, bend you to our whim, but we can hardly impose ourselves on your world. Soon the disease shall take us completely and we shall disappear from existence."

"So, what you're saying is that you *want* me to go and blow up Garton-1, but you don't actually have any way of making me do so?"

"Would you like to live through that crash again, hear those screams, smell that blood?"

A shudder passed right through my body. It felt like my spine might jiggle right out of my back. Good thing that I had lots of fat padding that general area, keeping all the vital bits inside. Those memories seeped back into my mind and I felt myself slipping away once more, that overwhelming sorrow sweeping over me, consuming me totally. And then, right at the fringe of my hearing, I heard the alien speak.

"Arkle Wright. Will you do as we ask?"

Tears leaked down my cheeks and my brain felt like it might implode on itself. I tried to swallow, to scream out, to bring the FSA officers to the lockup area, so they might see that I was innocent after all. But all I could manage was a stifled *moan*. And then I did find a word. "Yes!" I said.

"Good, we shall be watching you, Arkle Wright. If you fail us we shall take your mind."

25: ESCAPING THE FSA-01061

THE ALIENS SWARMED AROUND ME, extending their arms into the air, that eerie hum emanating from them, sending vibrations tearing through me. I closed my eyes, almost unable to support the sensation and then, through a cracked open eye, I made out the laser bars dissolving, leaving their places. And then, all of a sudden, they were completely gone. Just like that.

I took a tentative step out of the cell, unsure whether or not I should trust my eyes—that the laser bars had actually dissolved. But it worked. I arrived outside the cell. Free, or at least not behind bars any longer.

The aliens formed around me, their shapes blurring into one, so that it could've been a crowd of a hundred, before they separated again and took up a guard, all around me, shepherding me toward the window, to where their ship waited. And, next thing I knew, I was standing inside their ship. It was dark and moist, the surfaces more like earth than anything manufactured. I guessed, if I was going to take their word for them having created us, then I could stretch myself to accept that they had somehow 'grown' this ship too. There really wasn't much time for reflection on being on board an alien ship, as I felt the motion whisk us at full power, whipping us through space at speeds I'd never known.

Before I'd got a grasp on my bearings, the aliens were doing that half-smothering, half-circling thing and—*hey presto!*—I was standing in the cargo bay of the *Fonch*. I knew it was the cargo bay because, right there before me, I saw the *Navaplastas*. Man she looked beat up, and I mean *really* beat up. Her whole outer shell looked like it had suffered a hundred monkeys with sledge-hammers. Cracks sprouted out of every window. I realise it sounds a little crazy that at such a crucial period in the development of mankind I decided to take a good, solid look at my ship, but if you're a captain, then I'm sure you'll understand. I make no apologies for being honest.

Those aliens, they kept up their guard, leading me right on through the ship till I got to the bridge. That was when things started to get somewhat tricky. See, the problem there was that Reynolds had posted quite a few of his men to keep an eye on things—to ensure that Radley, who continued to cower over on her captain's sofa wouldn't try and pull a fast one, snatch hold of the ship and shoot off a bunch of lasers pumped up by the stone. That was at least something—that Reynolds wasn't completely sold on his own theory, or perhaps he was just being conservative, as FSA captains are wont to be.

They escorted me through the vacant-looking FSA officers

and back over to the control panels, where I'd taken my brief position as captain of the *Fonch Express*. I took control then, feeling back on familiar ground. Those aliens formed a ring around me, keeping any officers at bay—any that came close were soon reduced to screeching at the top of their lungs, gripping their skulls in their hands, reliving all their worst memories. Soon I saw that the aliens' range extended to more than just the immediate, trouble-making officers, because they got every officer on the bridge and—I bet—the entire ship, screaming for their lives.

While this scene played out, the leader alien leant into me and said, through the blaring racket, "We shall finish these ones and then we must return to our ship, to recharge. This is more than we have managed for a long time. Your mission is now clear."

"What do you mean by 'finish' them?"

The alien made no response, but, within seconds, I had my answer.

The best I can describe it is as some sort of invisible wave. I remember once going to a beach, seeing the sea. Not on Arkle-4, of course, we never really had seas—just great big bodies of water, what we needed for drinking. I forget which planet it was, but I just have this ever-so-clear image of the tide lapping at the sands, lightly dragging stones into it, turning them up and down before tossing them onto the shore. And that was what happened on the bridge of the *Fonch Express*. Just this great, big invisible wave crushed them all. And I watched on as they breathed their final breaths, their chests sighing shut for the last time. I remember staring at those reposed bodies for the longest time. Only when I snapped to my senses did I realise that the aliens had just floated away—slipped off into the mist, or whatever. Out ahead, I saw their ship, I felt their presence. And, I just can't describe it at all, but I knew that they'd do exactly the same to me if I didn't do what they wanted.

———

I got on the communications system and patched through to the lab. It was a long wait. I expected the carnage down there, I thought about all those FSA officers who had no doubt boarded, surely scientists among them, looking for some way of disarming the stone. They were all dead now. And I just needed to speak with Michaels.

Michaels did come to the communicator, breathless. "What the hell was that? What just happened?"

"You think you can hook the stone up to the weapons systems?"

"*You!*"

"That's right, now are you going to do as I say or did I have to come down there and shout it into your face?"

There was a long pause, a rummaging sound in the background and then he said, "No, I can do it. Are we . . . I mean, are we really going there? Are we going to do this?"

"Looks that way, don't it, sunshine?"

Considering the magnitude of the task ahead, I surprised myself with my pragmatic thinking. I steered the *Fonch* right onward, well away from the FSA fleet before they twigged what was going on. I got a few communications requests through from the *FSA-0106I* and denied them all. This was all or nothing now. I had no choice.

I felt Radley's presence at my side. I turned back to look at her.

She craned her neck, taking in the destruction all around. "They did this, didn't they?"

"Yes, ma'am."

"And they told you why you have to do it?"

"Yes, ma'am."

"I'm glad you came around, saw sense in the end."

At that point I was more interested in those FSA fighters sneaking up our behind than our final destination. Without Foy or Milky about—both of them having been taken aboard the *FSA-0106I*—I had to make do with the *Fonch Express* home range. They weren't that bad of a lot, all told. By that I mean that they could shoot straight, knew just where to point those crosshairs. Thanks to Michaels, we had the stone firing up our thrusters, sending us dancing on our merry way, leaving the FSA fleet in our dust.

———

We poked into the space surrounding Garton-1. This was the moment of truth. I knew what I had to do. What was the difference between the destruction of the whole universe and my own destruction? If I refused now, those aliens would do me in and move onto the next person on board the *Fonch* who would be willing to blow up Garton-1. Michaels would've been a sure bet, I suppose. But if he had refused them they would've got to someone eventually. So I might as well have taken the responsibility. Goodness knows it would've been the first time in my life.

I had the rest of the fleet—now powered up by the osmosis effect of the stone—circle around the *Fonch Express*, have them form a protective barrier to guard against any defensive thrusts from Garton-1. The idea was to channel all of our blast power together, to suck up all the energy we could muster from the stone and fire it all at once at the doomed, little planet.

Officers muttered in my ear, asking for their orders, the confirmations of the final parts of the process. I answered them monotonously, telling them just what they wanted to hear, telling them that they were doing just fine. Deep down I'm sure I realised that no one on board the *Fonch Express* felt the least bit good about what we were about to do. But there was nothing to do. We had set out our stall and it was time to stand our ground and do our duty.

I always thought that the Vun System was somewhat ugly— what with that nuclear green glow to it. Always made me feel queasy. And Garton-1 itself, that orphaned little planet, orbiting the Vun star. Okay, so all stars are nuclear reactors, but the Vun, well its colour just makes that a bit easier to understand.

Our ships formed up around Garton-1, making a ring around the place. I watched on as a few fighters swarmed up out of the atmosphere to engage our own. And I got to experience— for the first time—the real firepower vested in the lasers, as they sapped the stone.

Those fighters—FSA marked, of course—buzzed around our fleet. There was nothing to do but give the order. It was a matter of our men or theirs and I reasoned that considering the fact that, after the destruction of Garton-1, humanity would soon descend into out-and-out war those poor sods, those fighter pilots, would be better off dying in a comparative paradise. That's what I tell myself, though I'd wager that their screams are added to those I hear in my dreams, when I dream up those memories of my downed ship when I served back in the FSA.

All those unquiet souls.

The beams flew from the cannons, scorching those ships instantly. It was like watching a matchstick head vanish into flame. They were simply gone. No trace. Our fighters circled back and joined the fleet, triumphant. After that, Garton-1 offered no resistance. I guess they were waiting on Reynolds's fleet, expecting them to turn up at any moment to save them. But we had time. A long time before Reynolds could catch up with us. Time enough to reduce Garton-1 to no more than whatever had become of those fighters.

I prepped the big guns, got us all focussed on Garton-1, aiming at the core of the planet—although I wagered that our weapons would destroy everything in their path, that there'd be no need for any accurate aiming. All the officers waited on my orders. A hush fell over the entire bridge, maybe the entire ship. They knew that we were going to make history. No one had actually destroyed a planet before. Sure there had been thermo nukes blowing the surface to bits, making life impossible, but no human had ever blown a planet completely out of existence. But, I guess if human history teaches you anything it's that there's a first time for everything.

My throat dried as I thought over the order, how I would simply give a nod and Garton-1 would be no more. And then, out of the corner of my eye, up on the vidscreen, almost impossible to see in the lime glare of Vun, was the alien ship. They were there, hovering on the periphery of everything. Our loving overloads, or something like that. They wanted to witness this up close, see to the beginning of the end of mankind—*their* babies, if you believe of a word of what they say.

There have only been a few times when I'd claim that something of a moral compass has ever kicked in with me. And right then, staring at that alien ship, that was one of those times. I knew what I had to do. What was right. It was weird, almost like floating, pure inspiration. I knew that there was a single path opening up to me—one thing I could do.

I held up my hands, told my underlings to abort the strike on Garton-1, and to swing our aim around, to bring it onto that alien ship. There were a few mumblings of dissent. And, I was sure, Michaels was watching the transmission on the bridge—doing his nut that we hadn't already fired on Garton. But everyone did as they were told, brought that alien ship into our crosshairs. I hesitated for the longest time, sure that they would simply vanish, or that their ship would zip toward us, and they would board, send me back down into that spiral of memory and pain. I don't know why they didn't. Perhaps, like they said, they were weak, that they simply had no strength left. Or maybe they knew that even they had seen the error of their ways—that the solution to what they saw as the problem of Man wasn't outright destruction, obliteration of what we've all achieved. Or it might be that they were just *tired*. And they knew their time had come. That, in fact, it was their own destruction the universe craved. Whatever it was, they didn't move out of those crosshairs. And when I gave the order, oh how those cannons fired—every inch as effective as they'd been against those fighters sent up from Garton to engage us. That ship, well, it just fried up, slipped off the face of the world.

And that, gentlemen, as they say, is that.

Any questions?

26: GARTON-1 COUNCIL

A S I RETURN to my seat, my account of events fully rendered, I catch sight of Foy and Milky, sitting up there in the gallery. I give them a brief wave, the flicker of a smile. This has been one *long* day, I can assure you of that. One which I hope has worked out. I've left everything I have out here at this council, but they've still got every right to ask me questions—to grill me for clarification on any issue that just hasn't sat right with them. All I've got now is honesty. Nothing better than that to offer. Whatever fate they choose for me I'll have no choice but to accept.

Rick Strut, head of the Honourable Council of Garton-1, slouches in his chair, several metres above me. He tilts his head to one side as he taps away at his recorder, no doubt replaying certain moments of my testimony, giving them further scrutiny. Before my trial I garnered from my cellmate—a former member of Radley's crew—that Strut has access to lie detection technology, that any suspect piece of my testimony will be flagged up by the system as unreliable. One too many flags and I'll be guilty by default.

As I take in the rest of the court, I see Radley there too, awaiting her turn in front of the Council. Things have stayed pretty much as Reynolds reported them—what with the Council deciding not to try her as being in charge of the ship. But she was found to have a case to answer in terms of her criminal empire. Now that it's out in the open there's not much her bought political friends can do to keep her immune. Not that she has much reason to worry since a subsequent psychological assessment, taken before this session, declared her to be of a fragile mental state—unable to answer the charges. She's just here to give evidence, a means of closing this extremely bizarre report.

Strut straightens up from recorder, eyeballs me and says, "Arkle Wright, following the recounting of your testimony it is of my opinion, and that of the truth-telling systems relied upon by this court, to drop all criminal charges in relation to your attempts to lead a fleet to attack, with intention to destroy this planet, Garton-1 of the Vun System. While there are some rather large gaps in your statement"—he squints at me—"not least these reports of *aliens*, I can find nothing in your testimony which would indict you any further in this matter. All I may ask of you now is that you cooperate fully with a full-scale inquiry—led by our lead scientific expert—in which the various technicalities of this case may be put to rest.

"Thank you, Mr Arkle—"

"That's *Captain* Arkle," I say.

"Yes, Captain, you may leave the court."

Well, right about now all my cheeks are flooding with blood and my brain feels like it might just float right out my skull. I guess when you've just been given a reprieve while facing up to the death penalty your body has its own habits of celebrating.

I get up, have the nearest guard undo my handcuffs and I bound down the aisle, past the assembled crowds—surely two or three hundred of them—and out through the nice, *swooshing* metal doors, which pretty much remind me of the *Fonch Express*. As I trot down the marble steps of the court, I think over how much power I had in my hands, back then on the ship, and how I didn't really get a chance to enjoy it—having those aliens breathing over my shoulder somewhat spoiled it, I guess.

Just as I get down to the final step, seeing Milky and Foy, kids in tow, making their own way down out of the gallery, I hear a familiar voice behind me. I pivot around and glance over my shoulder to see Reynolds marching toward me, door to the court swinging madly on its hinges behind him. He puffs out his cheeks as he jogs down to where I stand and then faces up to me.

I flash my eyebrows at him. "Strut says I'm free to go."

"Yes," Reynolds says, "I know."

"Then are you content to give up on all this conspiracy, all this guff you somehow cooked up about me?"

A slight smile pulls at the corner of his lips. "Listen, Arkle, I have no idea what went on up there, how you managed to slip out of my jail cell and find yourself back at the controls of the *Fonch*. What I do know, though, is that I made some pretty wild allegations. I guess you could call it pressure. And, just maybe, I gave you a little too much credit in running a whole crime empire. I mean, just think about it, *you*, Arkle Wright, running something like that?"

"Hey!" I say. "I thought this was supposed to be an apology session—"

"Point is," he says, "Radley's empire's extinguished now, we've seized all her assets. The stone's to be kept under lock and key—twenty-four hour surveillance, until our scientific minds, perhaps Michaels might be of some use, work out how to dispose of it. No more threat to the good people of the Fritten System, so I think we can draw a line under all this."

"What? No medals for saving the entirety of mankind?"

"Like Strut said, we'll have to wait on the outcome of the investigation."

I grin. "That's okay, even if you offered me one I wouldn't accept it. No way I'd take any sort of charity from anyone in the Fritten. I'm through with that. I've made my choices."

Reynolds's lips part, as if he's got something else to say, then he closes them up and extends his hand. "Fair enough, Arkle, stay safe, won't you?"

"Wait," I say. "What were you about to ask me? You were about to offer me another in with the FSA, weren't you?"

"If I was then would it have been anything more than a waste of time and breath?"

Again, I grin. "Nope, I don't suppose it would have."

Reynolds smiles for what I believe is the first time in the course of our fledgling relationship.

I accept his handshake. "Take care, Captain. Keep fighting

the good fight—give it an especially good go for my sake too, won't you?"

Reynolds nods and then breaks off the handshake. "I'll do my service, nothing less, nothing more. That's all that the FSA ask of me."

"Why," I say, glancing at him from the corner of my eye, "I bet your superiors just love you. Their own little gimp, their go-to guy. Turns my stomach."

"That's one way of putting it," he says, his smile not giving an inch.

I give Reynolds a final, attaboy slap on the shoulder and then go off to join Milky, Foy and her cousins. This is going to be one hell of a celebration party. Staring death right in his pitted eyes has a habit of sending a rankling thirst straight through a man.

———

And where else would a proper celebration party take place apart from *The Bitch's*? Well, I guess if you're anything other than a smuggler then your answer would be just about anywhere else. But, as the case is, I *am* a smuggler, and a mighty proud one at that. That's why I sit here, propping up the bar, bothering the service droid once every ten minutes for another moiser, while Foy and the kids play with this ancient gaming machine over in the corner, Milky watching on behind them. I've got my worries for him, but I can put them to one side, at least for one night. I know that it's up to me to bring him up right—give him as good a life as I can as a surrogate father. And sure, maybe there are better people than me, better father figures, to bring up a kid like Milky, but I kinda like the prospect and impending responsibility of bringing up the kid, teaching him all I know. I guess 'brainwashing' is a pretty strong word, but why not make a carbon copy of myself while I'm at it? Just kidding, bet he'll be way too smart for any of that sort of nonsense, at least I'd be disappointed if he wasn't. I've no reason to worry about Foy, or the cousins in her care for that matter. She'll pull her weight on the *Navaplastas* with those gunning skills and bring up those kids just right, with all those terrific morals and values she learnt back on Trivus.

If getting off the criminal charges wasn't enough, and getting my fifth moiser of the evening down my flabby neck, when I got to the spaceport back on Garton-1, I saw that the *Nava* was not only waiting there for me—released from evidence—but all spruced up, not so much as a scratch left on her following her recent adventures. Actually, if I'm honest, I have to say that the level of cleanliness inside my girl was pretty disconcerting. I'd come to thinking of some of those dust balls as no less than family. And now everything's all set for many adventures to come. Hopefully without any nasty aliens cropping up at any point, but I'm not counting my chickens just yet.

Just as I'm on the point of ordering my sixth moiser, I hear that old familiar *screech* of the door to *The Bitch's*. I turn my head, one hand on the blaster at my thigh—just as *Bitch's* etiquette dictates—when who do I see but Mr Clive Wodd himself, fully-fledged officer of the FSA. Now, if there's one thing I ain't never seen in *The Bitch's* it's an FSA officer striding in like he owns the place. Over in the corner someone swears under their breath. My grip tightens on my blaster.

Once I get over my shock, akin to seeing a monk hoverboarding ...habit hitched up to reveal fishnet stockings beneath, I turn away, not having much time for traitors in this, my moment of glory.

Wodd, however, doesn't seem to get my hint and he takes up the stool beside me, even going so far as to order a moiser for himself.

We sit there, neither of us chomping at the bit to break the silence, each of us sipping away at our own.

There's a *chirrup* of glee from the corner of *The Bitch's* and Foy bounds over to the bar, arms outstretched, grinning like an idiot. She embraces Wodd, engages him in conversation. I notice Milky, too, strut up to Wodd and give him a hefty handshake. He has the courtesy to flash me a glance to check that this was all right. I give him the response this deserves and turn to stare right into my moiser, already thinking about my seventh.

Wodd holds forth for a while, telling them his perspective on things—his adventures so far in the FSA, how he took on *our* fleet of ships before we just upped and disappeared. He goes on to say how he thought I'd been tricking them all along, and that when the truth all came out back on Garton-1—with the Council—he just about beat himself up about everything.

After he gets into the details, all the great things about the FSA—the *benefits*, the *career prospects*—I decide I have to draw a line under all of this. So I spin on my stool and glare him right in the eye. "You'd best be getting along now, boy. Guess they'll be wanting you back on board pretty soon." I nod at his glass of moiser. "And if I remember right they don't take too kindly to officers supping that stuff while on duty."

"Well, actually, I got granted leave."

"Still, doesn't mean that you can go hanging about in our places. You people have got your own hangouts. Why don't you see sense and leave a smuggler and his crew in peace?"

Wodd exchanges glances with Foy and Milky. "Actually," he says, allowing the word to linger out before us, like a Goddamned ellipsis, "I was wondering if you'd take me back on the *Nava*."

Well, my eyes just about roll right out of their sockets. "What you say?"

"I'd like to come back onto the crew, if you'll have me?"

I spit my mouthful of moiser back into the glass. "I'm still waiting on that apology you owe me? You know, that one for when you went full out trying to blow me up?"

He averts my gaze. "Look, I'm sorry. But it was circumstance. That was what Reynolds told us, and the more I thought about it, the more it seemed to be true. I know now that he was wrong, that—"

I swig the moiser around the base of the glass. "That I'm far too stupid to be able to run anything like that?"

His eyes bulge. "No, no, that's not—"

I shoot him a smarmy grin. "Kid, I'm joking, okay? I'd be the first to admit that I don't have much in the way of the brain department. It's just"—I shake my head at my moiser—"sometime I wish people would *trust* more."

"You *are* a smuggler."

"All right, all right! And who's trying to get a job on a smuggling ship here?"

Wodd buttons his lip.

I go all pensive again, getting all interested in the slop of moiser remaining. "Listen, kid, what do you want to do with a loser like me? I mean, out there, in the FSA, I'm sure you could make something of yourself, you know? Just because I couldn't make it work for me doesn't mean that you'd not be a good fit for a life of discipline and servitude." I finish off the moiser and order another. As I watch the service droid fulfil my request, I say, "You're a Goddamn genius, boy, you can do much better than me. Hell, you should take Milky here with you back to the FSA, sure they'd make him a junior cadet. It's a sure thing that both of you have got better career paths with them—not indulging some bottom-feeding smuggler."

At the mention of his name, Milky perks up. I guess I regret saying that right out loud because, I can see it in his eyes, that this kid looks up to me, wants me to show him the way.

After taking a sip of my fresh moiser, I say, "All I'm saying to you—*all* of you—is that there are no contracts, there are no promises, there are no commitments on the *Nava*. Just doesn't work that way. *But* if you do want to come along with me, see some of the universe without someone barking in your ear, telling you to mop faster or grease more, then I *can* promise you'll see some great stuff and some rotten stuff, too. And what's more, you'll be like my family." My throat gets all constrictive all of a sudden. "Or close enough."

I feel their collective glare on me. Well, I've fed them just about a decade's worth of bullshit. Chances of another emotional outpouring along the lines of this one? Nil.

And then, over in the corner of *The Bitch's*, I hear a cough. A wooden stool *screeches* against the floor. Someone says, "Bloody FSA. Get out of our fucking bar."

I reach for my blaster, withdraw it from its holster. I look to Wodd, and to the others. "Well, are you with me or not?"

Foy grasps the blaster down at her ankle, and comes up just as quick.

Milky produces a blaster from the waistband of his trousers. How he ever got hold of it, I'll never know—although I guess he fitted those droids with laser cannons easily enough.

And then my glance falls onto Wodd, who feels for his own service blaster, which he keeps tucked inside his uniform jacket.

"All right, then," I say, rising from my barstool, gun held straight in my grip. "Just who the *fuck* said that?"

THE END

AUTHOR'S NOTE

Thank you for taking the time to read one of my books. If you would like to hear about my latest releases you can sign up for my newsletter here: www.raymondsflex.com

Thanks for reading!

Raymond S Flex

Stone Of The Angels
The First Arkle Wright Novel

www.ingramcontent.com/pod-product-compliance
Lightning Source LLC
Chambersburg PA
CBHW020942260626
47169CB00006B/1778